A HERO'S *Love*

JAN SPRINGER

ELLORA'S CAVE
ROMANTICA PUBLISHING

What the critics are saying...

An Ellora's Cave Romantica Publication

www.ellorascave.com

A Hero's Love

ISBN 9781419955396
ALL RIGHTS RESERVED.
A Hero Escapes Copyright © 2003 Jan Springer
A Hero Needed Copyright © 2005 Jan Springer
Edited by Raelene Gorlinsky, Mary Moran.
Cover art by Syneca.

This book printed in the U.S.A. by Jasmine–Jade Enterprises, LLC.

Trade paperback Publication July 2009

A HERO'S LOVE

ഔ

A HERO ESCAPES
~11~

A HERO NEEDED
~169~

A HERO ESCAPES

&

Chapter One

On the planet Paradise…

೧

Frustration screamed through Queen Jacey's naked body, making her yank hard at the velvet bonds securing her up-stretched arms and spread-eagled legs.

Nothing budged.

She might as well relax. No use in wasting her energy. She'd need all of it when the time came to endure whatever form of sexual torture her enemies, The Breeders, had planned for her.

A whisper of uneasiness tingled up her spine at the sound of footsteps.

Two sets of footsteps.

Okay, two against one. She could handle it. She was a Queen after all, trained to resist torture.

Swallowing the lump of fear clogging her throat, she braced herself against her restraints and kept her eyes glued to the door of the tiny stall they'd brought her to.

Suddenly the door swung open and a male was quickly shoved inside.

Not just any male, but a tall, golden-brown-haired male.

And he was totally naked!

Stormy blue eyes ringed with thick black lashes snapped with desire the instant he saw her. His delicious-looking lips curved upward into an appreciative smile making Jacey's breath back up in her lungs. He had an exquisite masculine face with a straight nose, strong jut to his jawline, and a square chin.

He possessed a sensual neck, broad shoulders and a muscular chest with a generous spattering of curly golden-brown hair that arrowed down over his taut belly and…

Every nerve ending in her body sparked to life as her gaze drew straight to the rock-hard looking balls and the massive eight-inch cock stabbing out at her from between his powerful legs.

Goddess of Freedom!

The male looked so tasty she couldn't wait to wrap her mouth around his thick pulsing rod or kiss his tan nipples.

She blinked in shock.

What in the world was she thinking?

She couldn't allow herself to be fucked by a male.

She had to speak with The Breeders about this. Needed to remind them that Queens did not mate with males.

It was unheard of. Scandalous. Illegal.

Absolutely delicious.

Her enemies were about to give her something she'd dreamed about for as long as she could remember.

Why deny herself a taste of her deepest fantasies? Her darkest desires?

"Go fuck her, Slave!" A female guard cackled from the open doorway.

The sharp sound of a whip cracked against his flesh and the male winced with pain.

Jacey didn't miss the ugly red whip welts peeking over his massive shoulders and a sliver of sympathy shot through her at the thought of what he must have endured at the hands of The Breeders, who were famous for beating their slaves into submission.

Behind him, the door slammed shut with such a fierce bang, Jacey jumped against her silky restraints.

Her movement snapped him out of his trance.

Muscles rippled everywhere on his well-formed body as he took a step toward her.

She shivered with both want and fear as her gaze was once again magically drawn to his shaft.

It was the thickest, longest, most impressive looking cock she'd ever seen in her life.

And it was pierced!

How interesting.

She'd never seen a pierced shaft before.

A gold ring adorned the opening at the tip of his heavily veined cock. He'd also been favored with an impressive barbell-shaped piece of heavy metal, pierced horizontally through the thick purpled head.

The jewelry fascinated Jacey and she couldn't wait to run her hands up and down his remarkable length and to touch those rock-hard balls that swayed proudly as he walked.

When he stopped at the foot of her bed and looked down at her, she was surprised to see he wasn't staring between her legs anymore, but at her face.

And directly into her eyes.

He possessed the brightest, bluest eyes she'd ever seen and he studied her as if she were some sort of wonderful prize he'd won.

Excitement roared through her like wildfire.

She wondered what he was thinking.

Did he like what he saw? Did he like the fact her breasts were larger than most women's? Did he like the way her two clit rings were arranged to visually arouse? Did he notice how wet she was getting for him?

The way his gaze devoured her body made her grow so hot for him, she couldn't believe a male could make her feel so horny just by him looking at her.

And there was something different in this male's heated gaze. He didn't look at her as other slaves did.

He didn't appear submissive, frightened, or shy.

This one seemed bold.

Layers of emotions swirled in those stormy blue depths.

Anger. Hatred. Confusion.

Desire.

The tips of his full mouth tilted even higher into an amazing grin that made sexual energy crackle deep inside her. If she wasn't mistaken, his seductive smile was assuring her that his large cock would give her all the pleasures she'd ever craved.

But she must be wrong.

Males couldn't communicate. They were uneducated brutes. Good for only a handful of things.

Including what he was about to do to her.

A fluttery feeling she rather liked floated through her belly at the thought she was about to be fucked by a magnificent male.

She'd always wondered how it would be like to lie with one. Always wondered why she'd been stupid enough to accept Queen status, thus allowing her to have sex only with women.

Impatience urged her to whisper, "Come closer, slave."

Although males weren't educated, she was sure he'd been taught the basics of slave language and the meaning of 'come closer'.

She wasn't mistaken.

When he stepped forward and leaned his knees onto the mattress to peer at her now drenched cunt, her heart crashed against her chest like a battering ram.

Sweet sunshine!

His lust-filled eyes devoured her as if she were a feast to be dined on! And his spicy masculine scent washed through her lungs in powerful waves.

She loved the smell of him.

Raw. Powerful. Dangerous. Intoxicating.

She wondered where they'd found this male. Wondered if there were more like him.

He leaned forward and his hot male fingers seductively brushed the outer slopes of her breasts. Heated fingers slid into her nipple rings, pulling her nipples until they were aching tips of need. Hot hands kneaded her tender breasts, quickly bringing sensual pleasures crackling to life within her body.

Then he stopped.

She twisted wildly against her restraints as masculine hands shimmered up the insides of her thighs leaving a scorching trail of need. A moment later a calloused thumb stroked her tender pleasure nub, making the blood pound through her veins and searing pleasure slam into her cunt.

The hot thumb attacked her tender clitoris harshly. Sliding erotically against the sensitive bundle of nerves until her breath grew raspy and a wild pleasure she'd never known mounted with lightning speed deep inside.

The beautiful sensations snowballed and she couldn't stop the moans of arousal from escaping her mouth. Before she could climax, his invading thumb stopped.

Jacey's eyes popped open with frustration.

The male grinned wickedly at her. His heated gaze shone dark with a savage desire and sexual promise. His eyes dropped to her mouth and she could almost feel his seductive gaze caress her lips.

She bolted when one and then two hot thick fingers slid inside her tormented vagina. Sucking sounds rose from her cunt as his long fingers dipped in and out of her in a sensual motion.

Within seconds an inferno claimed her, forcing Jacey to close her eyes and moan shamelessly as the intense pleasure between her legs screamed for satisfaction.

She wanted to plead with him. Beg him to satisfy the burning lust he so magically created. A lust that was fast becoming so powerful she feared she just might lose her mind in the obscene pleasure.

But she couldn't say anything. Couldn't give The Breeders the satisfaction that their slave was reducing her to a torrid bundle of need.

Oh Goddess of Freedom! She shouldn't be feeling this way. Shouldn't be whimpering like a helpless sex slave beneath his wonderful touch. Shouldn't be craving this male to thrust his thick rod deep inside her. But wasn't that why she'd left the security of her own village in the first place?

Without warning, the male's fingers and thumb stilled. Through heavy-lidded eyes she found the slave once again gazing down at her quivering cunt.

Hesitation brewed in those blue depths.

At this point she'd do anything to keep him touching her with those magical hands.

"I'm not afraid of you, slave," she taunted.

Something flashed in his eyes, something similar to puzzlement. She wasn't sure. And she really didn't care anymore. She just wanted satisfaction from his sweet sexual torture.

"Fuck me, slave," she found herself begging, not caring about the consequences of having this male's thick flesh penetrate her and bury itself deep into her very core.

"Please, fuck me."

His eyes darkened deliciously at her words.

With stunned fascination she watched him lower his aroused body between her widespread legs.

She could feel the heated length of his heavy rod drape against her cunt opening. To her disappointment he didn't enter her. His rock hard chest crushed her swollen breasts. The impact of the rest of his male flesh upon her body made flames of arousal lick every inch of wherever he touched.

His warm breath caressed her face with feather-like touches and within a second his hot lips clamped hard over her mouth.

He wasted no time with pleasantries as he roughly bit the bottom curve of her mouth until she opened to him. His tongue shot through the opening quickly, clashing with hers in such a brutal violence, her body erupted in searing vibrations that threatened to consume her.

Through the haze of sensations assaulting her, Jacey bucked as his heavy swollen member stabbed at the entrance of her wet cunt.

Fear of the unknown brewed in her mind. His warm mouth grew more demanding, drawing her attention away from those growing fears, back to the tidal wave of want screaming throughout her body.

This was the first time in her entire life she'd felt so alive. So excited. So aroused.

Hot hands settled upon her hips and he held her tightly in place.

She gasped as his pulsing member slowly bore into her slick channel like a heated piece of metal. His thickness stretched her vaginal muscles to unbelievable proportions and his hard flesh scraped wonderfully against her clit rings.

Metal hardware rubbed erotically against the inside of her vagina, scraping against sensitive places that had always craved for further attention after her female lovers were finished fucking her. Places that had never been satisfied with a double-ended dildo.

His strong hands held her hips firmly. Preventing her from moving. Preventing her from thrusting her hips upward in an effort to accept his massive length all at once.

He penetrated two inches, perhaps three and instead of plunging himself into her as she craved he would do, the male slowly withdrew his thick rod and grinned wickedly down at her.

What was he doing? Why was he stopping?

Didn't he know she wanted him? Didn't he know she wanted him so badly she was prepared to beg yet again?

"By all means, please do continue." Jacey whispered.

Chapter Two

℘

It was all the encouragement the male needed.

Jacey cried out with triumph as his thick rod eased back into her aching cunt. One inch. Two inches.

The jewelry adorning his shaft scratched delightfully against her insides as he continued to fill her. The smooth metal rubbed her aches and made her yearn for more of his length.

He kissed the column of her neck as he slid deeper. Teased the edges of her mouth with his eager lips as his thickness filled her like she'd never been filled before.

"Faster, slave. Faster," she hissed with desperation, wanting his heated passion deep within.

He didn't listen. His neglect to obey her orders irritated her. Made her attempt to raise her hips against his steely grip.

But she couldn't move. Couldn't attain immediate satisfaction.

She was helpless beneath him as he slid deeper into her very core. Helpless and totally under his control.

A shiver of fear scooted up her spine at the idea she was at his mercy. It quickly vanished as his warm lips once again clamped over her mouth.

Flames of lust devoured her body as his lips fused with hers. She tasted heat, desire, and aroused male. His thick rod continued to gouge deep into her womb. He was so big inside her that pain and pleasure intermingled in his wake. Fear and joy fought with each other.

Within seconds her vaginal muscles stretched to accommodate his width and length. His monstrous penis crashed into her woman's core. She threw her head back crying into his moist mouth as an orgasm like no other she'd ever experienced came out of nowhere, searing every inch of her flesh, splintering her mind and ripping her body apart with sheering bolts of fire.

His tongue slid into her mouth, unleashing a powerful urge for more of this wondrous magic.

The heated scent of their mating sliced into her lungs, making her dizzy with desire, making her heart beat wildly in her chest.

Her entire body convulsed as her cunt muscles spasmed violently around his thick rod.

From somewhere far away she heard him growl. The sound of it so beautiful to her ears, it only added to her ecstasy.

She became lost in a tornado of bliss. Craved nothing but the male. Wanted nothing but his hot hands holding her hips captive. Desired nothing but his lips devouring her mouth as if she were a prized possession.

Perspiration and heat flushed her body as his deep pounding strokes stoked yet another orgasm. It jolted through her with such violence it pushed her dangerously close to the edge of erotic madness.

His hands flew from her hips, freeing her pelvis. She thrust upward allowing his male flesh to ravage her. The silken bonds holding her arms hostage suddenly were gone and her hands were free. Free to grip his massive shoulders.

Her nails dug into the hard muscles, drawing his male flesh closer to her craving body.

Squeezing her eyes tighter, she opened her mouth wider, greedily pressing her lips against his marvelous moistness. More growls stirred deep in his chest.

The erotic sounds drove Jacey to urgently cling to his shoulders as the blazing passion reigned.

Their naked bodies slammed into each other as he pumped furiously and she met his every violent thrust.

Never had she experienced this bursting lust with her female mate. Never had she experienced this pure carnal joy with a dildo. This slave was the answer to her dreams. The one fantastic sex toy she'd been waiting for all her life. Yet he was the only thing denied to her for eternity.

The last thought made her frantic. Made her anxious this would be the first and last time with this male.

Suddenly he quickened the pace of his fucking. His rod thickened inside her and another deep wrenching orgasm hit her like a tidal wave. The unbearable pleasure swallowed her senses and stole her breath clean out of her lungs.

Ripping her mouth free from his, Jacey gasped as his thrusts spurred the shocking waves of ecstasy to greater heights.

It felt so good, it hurt.

She found herself sobbing at the beauty of the spasms engulfing her. Found herself whimpering as he showed her no mercy, thrusting into her like a wild beast in heat.

Stars exploded behind her eyes, her insides splintered, and her senses went into freefall.

Soon she began to calm. Her body finally satiated, her mind weary.

She became aware of his continued thrusts as he drove toward his own ecstasy. Within seconds, he growled violently and gloriously filled her insides with his hot sperm.

* * * * *

United States astronaut Ben Hero lay on his stomach and pretended to be asleep as feminine fingers trailed a scorching line along one of the painful welts crossing his left ass cheek.

Cripes! Didn't this woman ever get enough? Heck, didn't he? Damned if her sexy touch wasn't arousing him all over again.

Perhaps he shouldn't have untied her restraints while he was fucking her senseless. It would have been easier to keep his mind on figuring out a way to escape.

Unfortunately as long as he wore the golden bracelet wrapped around his ankle, he was stuck here. When they'd snapped it on his ankle, he'd heard the guards say it would track his movements and kill him the instant he left the building. Although they had no idea he understood what was being said, he figured it was best to heed their words.

A tingle of anticipation shot up his anal canal and zipped along his shaft when the woman's fingers lazily dipped between his butt cheeks and sunk an inch or so into his asshole.

He forced himself not to wiggle against the onslaught of pleasant sensations. But it was hard not to take her into his arms again.

Oh man, why was he reacting so strongly to this particular woman?

The instant he'd seen the startling beauty all laid out on the bed, her arms tied over her head, breasts heaving, legs spread eagle, her cunt decorated with clit rings and all wet and waiting for him, his shaft had thickened like a growing snake.

Maybe he was reacting so violently because he'd been in space and without a woman for many months? But he'd been without for long periods of time before.

This woman however, was different.

No woman on Earth had given him this much of a hard-on just by looking at her. She was so damn cute he couldn't help but stare at her every chance he got.

She was tall. Gorgeous. Curvy.

A brunette with curly shoulder-length silky hair. Hair his fingers itched to touch. A voluptuous mouth curved just right for kissing. And her warm welcome cunt…

Ben shivered with desire as the erotic memories washed over him. He'd been scared shitless when he'd sunk into her juicy cunt. She'd been so tight, he had feared ripping her apart.

The fit, however, had been damned perfect.

"You know, if they knew how much I was enjoying you, they would never have brought you in here," she said.

Ben kept himself from answering. From telling her he was having a damn good time too.

Men weren't supposed to know how to talk on this planet. He'd learned that fact a few days ago when he'd been cooling himself off in a river and he'd heard voices in the distance. Swimming to the shore, he'd parted some reeds and blinked in surprise at seeing a women-inhabited village.

Shock had coursed through him to see clothed females leading silent naked men around the dusty streets by penis leashes.

His curiosity piqued, he'd followed one particularly sexy looking gal who'd led a man around like he was a docile dog. The scene had aroused Ben's curiosity. Pushing caution aside, he'd gotten closer. Close enough to get a birds-eye view of the female instructing the male to lie down on the ground. She'd caressed his small penis with careful strokes until the man's flesh had lifted.

Ben's mouth had dropped open when, a moment later, the woman removed her clothing and sat upon his erection, grinding her hips into his shaft. The scene had left him with one hell of a hard-on.

He hadn't even heard the women come up behind him, until several strong feminine hands had grabbed him.

Now here he was getting another hard-on because this gorgeous chick couldn't keep her curious hands off him.

Cripes!

Wait till they found out back on Earth about the women running their own planet.

And that one of them was fucking his brains out.

Well, he wouldn't tell them that last part. It was a direct contrast to his orders. Orders instructing him and his two brothers to study this planet and the inhabitants without letting themselves be seen until a diplomatic message could be sent to introduce Earthlings to them.

Unfortunately he couldn't tell Earth anything until he could figure out a way to escape and get back to his spaceship and his brothers.

Shoot, they were probably worried shitless. Most likely frantically searching for him. He knew they wouldn't stop looking until they found him. Unfortunately, he couldn't wait much longer for a rescue.

A few more whippings followed by women's arousing touches like what had happened before they'd led him into this room might cause him and parts down south some serious damage.

Ben winced as the woman's velvety fingers made their way from his ass crack up along another fiery welt on his lower back.

"They are fools for whipping you so hard," she whispered softly. "You should be whipped to arouse, not hurt."

She rolled away from him and got out of bed.

He didn't dare lift his head and open his eyes to look at her curvy body. If he did, he wouldn't be able to keep his hands off her.

He listened to her bare feet pad to the other side of the small room.

His eyes popped open as she rattled the bars on the window. "Hey! Where's the service around here? Hello! I'm getting hungry!"

A sob hitched her voice.

Oh boy, he hoped she wasn't going to get all emotional and everything.

He'd had some women get that way on him after a good servicing. Some smoked. Some cried. But none had made him feel so alive like this gal.

He wondered what her name was. Wondered how long she'd paid to be in here with him.

From her perch near the window she sighed heavily.

The sound grabbed at his heart and encouraged Ben to turn his head toward her. What he saw in front of him made him suck in one hell of a deep breath.

She stood with her back to him. Her hands gripped the bars as she looked out.

She had beautiful shoulders. A long torso. Small waist. Nice hips, wide and generously rounded. A curvy butt with a gorgeous crack. And damn great looking long legs.

"Hey, out there! C'mon let's move it with the chow!" she shouted.

Silence.

She swore very unladylike, pressed her face against the bars and sighed in defeat. It was a harsh sound. A sound he didn't like.

Suddenly she pushed away from the bars and began pacing, totally oblivious that he was watching her. His gaze immediately snapped to her large breasts that bounced wildly with her stride.

"Y'know when I get out of here, the first thing I'm going to do is get my clan together and raid this place."

Her clan? Raid this place? What the hell was she talking about?

She stopped and noticed him watching her. "Ah, I see you're awake. The first thing I'm going to do is break you out of here and find a cozy spot for you in a brothel."

A brothel? What the hell? Wasn't he already in one?

"Why am I talking to you, anyway? You barely understand a word."

Ben couldn't help but smile as she began to pace again. Her curvy ass jiggled seductively as she walked. Oh yes, she had a very nice ass, indeed.

He moved off the bed. What he wanted was a good stretch. His legs were getting a little stiff lying around.

He had to pace, too. Maybe pace off a bit of the anger growing inside him at being cooped up in this little room with a gorgeous woman he couldn't seem to keep his eyes off, not to mention his hands off.

"Don't tell me you want to go at it again? Not that I wouldn't like to..." She'd stopped pacing. Her hands were now perched on her bare hips.

A cute dreamy look slid across her face, and a shiver of ripe excitement roared through him when he found her gazing at his penis.

She moved closer, staring at him with gorgeous green eyes. Eyes he just couldn't seem to get enough of looking into. A man could do just about anything for her when she had that dreamy expression.

Or maybe she could do something for him?

That thought socked him a good one in the gut. Could he trust her enough to tell her he needed her help?

First though, he should come up with a plan.

Without warning her warm arms curled around his neck and her luscious lips melted against his. The seductive feel of her mouth sliding over his made his entire body go rigid with want. Lust fired his veins.

Her sexy scent sent his thoughts reeling. He shouldn't cave in to her. Shouldn't be so easily seduced. But damn, the sharp want consuming his hard cock couldn't be denied.

To hell with the plan of escape. He could work on it later. He had better things to do with his time.

Chapter Three

When Jacey awoke snuggled in the slave's powerful arms, she fought back a sudden rush of sadness as curious thoughts invaded her mind.

Why did males have to be so stupid? Why couldn't they be smart like women? Why couldn't they work their cute butts off and contribute to society like women did?

Why did they come out of the Breeding Prisons illiterate and the females full of knowledge? If males were given the same education as the females, wouldn't they be smart too?

Jacey rolled her eyes with disgust.

Wishful thinking. That's all it was. The males were segregated from the females because the females were smart. They thought with their brains. Males thought with their sex organs.

It was as simple as that.

She sighed and ran her fingers along another raw whip welt on the male's strong back. These injuries must have burned as her fingers had dug into his injured flesh while they'd fucked. Yet he hadn't so much as winced.

Perhaps he'd concentrated on the pleasure in order to forget why they were here?

He'd fucked her quite nicely indeed, but now it was time for her to get out of here. Time to figure out a way to escape. Then she would have to figure out why The Breeders would break the laws by having a male impregnate a Queen.

Jacey stiffened when she heard footsteps approach the cell. At the barred window, a female guard appeared.

"Prime male, isn't he? When he's through with you, there's a waiting list of prison females ready for him to entertain them too."

Anger burned inside Jacey at the idea of this male slave being forced to fuck strange women. She held a sharp retort in check.

The guard slid a tin cup onto the windowsill.

"Pee in that. We'll get the results shortly. If you're lucky...perhaps I should rephrase that...if you're unlucky, you can leave."

"What if I refuse to pee? Maybe I'll just go on the floor. Let the dirt suck up the evidence."

The guard chuckled. "He's that good, is he? Looking for an excuse to stay?"

"Bitch!" Jacey whispered.

"You pee in the cup, do you hear me?"

"I'll pee, if you bring me some ointment for his whip wounds."

The guard looked shocked. Jacey couldn't blame her. A Queen showing sympathy for a sex slave was unheard of. Then again, today seemed to be the day for many scandalous affairs, wasn't it?

"I'll get the ointment," the guard mumbled.

When the sound of the guard's footsteps disappeared down the hall, Jacey got up and did what she'd been instructed to do.

She knew exactly what they were looking for. They wanted to examine the contents of the tin to find out if his seed had taken.

She had to admit it was an ingenious plan. Impregnate the Queen of the rival tribe and she'd be stripped of her powers, allowing The Breeders to move in and claim her territory.

Could all of this be because of revenge? Because she hadn't sold them the well-hung male her second-in-charge, Cath, had wounded and captured a few days ago?

Word about him had spread like wildfire through surrounding regions. All the hubs had wanted to possess him simply because of his large cock. She'd had many offers for him and turned them all down flat.

Now she wished she had sold him to the highest bidder, The Breeders. Her hub would have been rich, she'd still have her slave doctor—who'd inconveniently run off with the male—and The Breeders wouldn't have had an excuse to exact revenge. On the other hand, when they'd found out he was a talking male, they would have been required by law to put him down or at the very least cut out his tongue to prevent him from communicating.

Lucky for her though, this male was even bigger than the other one.

It made her question if perhaps this male and the other male had come from the same place?

Her heart picked up a frantic speed at that thought and she hurried with her business of filling up the cup.

After doing her duty, she placed the now-warm tin cup back on the windowsill, crossed her arms beneath her heavy breasts, and examined the male on the bed.

He was still asleep, his massive shaft lying limp and satisfied on his abdomen.

Did he know the talking male? Or was it just a coincidence that two well-endowed specimens had shown up at virtually the same time?

It had to be a coincidence. This male hadn't so much as spoken a word. He'd only shown interest in pleasuring her like a properly trained sex slave was supposed to do.

And he'd done his job well.

She turned and called through the bars of the window.

"C'mon, let's get a move on!"

She listened for the guard's reply, but heard nothing.

Sighing wearily, she muttered heatedly under her breath, "All of this because of a stupid talking male."

A sound from behind Jacey startled her and she cried out when a pair of strong hands curled tightly over her shoulders swinging her around.

She came face to face with the sex slave.

Dangerous fury danced in those blue depths and it frightened her.

Before she could even think to back away from him, his thick sinewy arms came up on both sides of her shoulders, effectively boxing her in against the wall. He looked down at her as his massive chest heaved with angry breaths. An angry muscle twitched wildly in his left jaw.

Sweet sunshine, had he snapped? Gone insane?

"What talking man?" he asked in a thick voice that did crazy things to her body.

Jacey blinked in stunned disbelief.

His lips had moved! Coherent words had tumbled out.

He'd spoken, just like that other talking male who'd been brought to her village days ago.

Suddenly her legs wobbled with weakness. Dizziness swept over her in a tidal wave and Jacey felt lightheaded.

His big hands came off the wall and slid around her naked waist, keeping her from slumping to the ground.

"Shock. That's all it is," she muttered to herself. "Shock from too much fucking and lack of food. Lack of fresh air."

"Easy, I've got you. Just breathe slowly. Focus your eyes on me." The sound of his warm voice didn't stop her decline into shock.

Her ears began to ring. She bit her lips in an effort to keep herself from screaming.

"This can't be happening," she whispered. "Not again. Not another talking male. I thought it was a fluke last time. I'd hoped he was a freak of nature. Goddess of Freedom! He was mighty handsome. And so well-endowed. Just like you are. Well, maybe you're bigger than he was—"

His hot searing lips clamped down over Jacey's trembling mouth cutting her off.

Goddess, he tasted so yummy.

Explosions rattled her cunt as his hard cock stabbed at her entrance.

Okay. So maybe this was a scorching dream. A fantasy of fucking a talking male. She could handle that. And he wanted to do it standing up this time, a totally forbidden position, but certainly a delicious one.

All thoughts of him talking and their illegal position disintegrated as he pushed her body against the cool wall and slid his massive erection into her.

The metal on his thick rod scraped her insides sensually and she moaned from the wonderful impact.

A moment later he was pumping. Long, easy, torturous strokes that made her whimper beneath his onslaught.

If he hadn't secured her waist with his large hands, she would have sunk down to the floor. On the other hand, the hard rod buried deep inside her would have done the job of holding her up.

From somewhere behind her she heard the guard cackle, "At it again, are you?"

At this point, she didn't care if the guard was watching them.

Hot fever seared through her veins. And then without warning brilliant explosions ripped her cunt apart sending her body into convulsions of pleasure.

Oh sweet sunshine!

The orgasms kept coming. And coming.

His solid hips bucked violently. His hot seed spilled inside her womb, filling her with warmth and giving her mind and body such a beautiful high she thought she'd never come down.

After the guard left, the slave stayed inside her, impaling her to the wall. Their harsh labored gasps screamed through the air as they held tight to each other.

When Jacey finally opened her eyes, she found his blue lust-filled gaze studying her. He was searching for something. If she had to take a guess, she'd say he was searching for trust.

Her trust.

Suddenly she felt nervous. Self conscious. Exposed.

Her heart pounded violently in her ears at the thought she had just been fucked by a talking male.

"You okay?" Concern etched his voice.

Jacey nodded, then shook her head and attempted a reassuring smile at the same time. It was a weak and wobbly smile. But it was there nonetheless.

"Was it as good for you, as it was for me?" he whispered.

She blinked with wonder at his bold question and found herself nodding.

"I heard the guard coming back," he explained. "It was the only way I could think of to shut you up."

Anytime, slave. Anytime.

Jacey noticed how his eyes looked slumberous. Tired. As if he hadn't slept in a few days. Stubble darkened the solid curve of his jaw, giving him an air of danger she found rather appealing. Her lips and cheeks burned because of the rough way his mouth had seduced hers. Even now as she stared at him, she found herself wanting his hot lips branding her flesh again.

As he watched her watching him she could feel his rod growing and pulsing deep inside her and the exquisite throbbing made the flames of want soar yet again.

"Um...I've never really spoken with a male before. I mean, I've spoken *to* one briefly but I'm not used to actually conversing *with* one. This is a bit overwhelming."

"I can imagine, but I don't really have time to be sensitive about this. You said something about a talking man. Was he like me? Talked like me? Did he say his name?"

"He was very angry."

"What did he call himself?"

"Toe, I think."

"Joe?"

"That's it. That's what Annie called him."

"Annie?"

"She helped him escape. She ran off with him."

He smiled warmly and her heart did a funny little flip that she rather liked.

"My brother always was rather impulsive. Takes what he likes. Doesn't give it a second thought. Did he mention where he was going?"

"The Outer Limits is where I saw them last."

"Outer Limits?"

"A largely unexplored part of our region. There isn't much there. It borders along Freedom Sea."

"The ocean?"

Jacey nodded. She still couldn't understand why she was allowing him to leave his hot, solid cock buried inside her as if it naturally belonged there. Or why she was even talking to this male. He was a lowly slave, of no importance.

Yet, she was answering his questions and hanging onto his every word, as if she were smitten with him. Jacey shook her head at those disturbing thoughts.

"I don't know why I'm reacting this way to you," she whispered.

Impulsively she reached up and ran a finger along the area of his left jaw where she'd seen the twitching muscle earlier when he'd been so angry.

He cursed softly at her touch. His eyes seemed to glaze over with pleasure, and his grip tightened around her waist. His rod swelled greatly inside her. Her vaginal muscles, hyper sensitive, rose to the occasion, clamping around his thick intrusion.

"I seem to be having the same reaction," he breathed. "Tell you the truth, this hasn't happened to me so much in one day."

"Me either." Actually never, but he didn't have to know he was her first male, did he?

"What...what do they call you?" he asked.

"Jacey."

"Jacey." He said and smiled. "That's a nice name. My name's Ben Hero."

"Ben Hero," she repeated.

His sexy grin widened and her heart did that funny little flip again that she liked. It made her realize this male was in serious danger.

"We have to get you out of here. We have to do it fast. If they find out you can speak, you will be put to death. Although since you're so well-endowed, they'd most likely keep your education a secret and cut into your brain, taking away your speech, or perhaps cut out your tongue to keep you—."

Without warning his head dipped into the crook of her neck and his hot lips touched her there. It was a tiny butterfly touch that made her breath back up into her lungs.

He nibbled seductively on her ear and her knees melted.

Sweet sunshine! Was this male for real?

"Why the sudden hurry to get me out of here?"

"No hurry," she whispered and tilted her hips, allowing him to penetrate deeper.

Once again he was as hard as a steel rod deep inside her. So hard and so deliciously hot that her cunt felt as if it were engulfed in a wildfire.

"I guess we can work on a plan later?" she breathed as she curled her arms over his solid shoulders. Her hands feathered through his silky hair to cup the back of his head.

He nodded in agreement and his eyes darkened with steamy need.

His powerful hips began to thrust into her and his moist mouth seared over her lips, capturing her moans of pleasure.

* * * * *

Ben awoke to Jacey's soft fingertips smoothing something cool and inviting over his fiery welts. For one endless moment he found himself wishing he could spend the rest of his life with her. Wake up next to her every morning. But the idea was fleeting and quickly vanished as reality caved in around him.

He'd been captured and held against his will for several days now. He should be figuring a way out of here, not lying here like some king enjoying this woman's silky touch or her hot body.

And what a hot body she had. He'd made love to her up against the wall for quite a long time. He couldn't seem to get enough of this brown-haired goddess. His cock had throbbed with a ferocious hunger of its own as she'd clutched him tightly against her needy body. He'd thrust into her succulent womanhood, pressing his lips to her curvy mouth, capturing every one of her sweet whimpers.

After they'd both climaxed, they'd climbed onto the narrow cot and he'd fallen into a deep slumber.

He'd slept hard. Too hard. Anything could have happened. Jacey could have left and he probably would never have seen her again.

At that thought a horrible knot wrenched his gut and he groaned aloud.

"I'm sorry," she whispered and her warm fingers stopped massaging the cool ointment into his hot flesh.

"It's not you. You're doing great. It's helping."

"Are you hungry? They brought us food while you slept."

"The food they have here is nothing compared to mom's home cooking, but it'll do in a pinch."

"Mom? Is he another talking man?"

Ben smiled into the pillow. "No, mom's a female. She took care of me and all my brothers and sisters when we were little. She did a damn fine job of it too."

A desperate need to see his mom suddenly gnawed at his insides. He wondered what she'd think of Jacey. Would she like her? Would they get along?

Cripes, he shouldn't have left her. He should have stayed on Earth with her and dad. Stayed close to them in their old age years. But his two brothers, Joe and Buck, had recruited him for NASA's top secret mission to this planet.

Ben blinked back the sudden tears of emotion burning his eyes as he wondered if he'd ever see his parents and siblings again.

What in the heck was wrong with him? He hadn't so much as groaned when they'd taken the whip to his back. Hadn't spoken a word to any of these sex-crazed ladies and yet just thinking about his mom...

"We really should try and figure out a way to escape," Jacey said softly.

Her fingers drew away from his sore back. Then she fiddled with the gold ankle bracelet they'd slapped on him shortly after his capture.

"I heard the guards talk to each other, saying something about never being able to escape as long as that was on my ankle. Said something about the drones not letting me get very far."

"You were wise to stay put, Ben Hero. The drones are deadly."

"I've tried to unlock the anklet," Ben said. "But it's a tough piece of work."

Despite his words, her warm hands remained at his ankle. Ben twisted his upper body and looked over his shoulder to see what she was doing. Her perfectly shaped mouth was set firm with determination and her large breasts jiggled seductively as she poked some of the ointment into the keyhole of the bracelet.

"What are you doing?" he asked.

"Breaking you out. I don't know why I didn't think of this earlier."

"I just told you, I've—"

The bracelet suddenly popped open. She lifted it from his ankle and held it up for him to see.

"You were saying?" she asked.

"How the heck?"

"An inventor with our hub designed this model. I know its weakness," she explained. "The women are always losing their keys to their slaves' bracelets, so the inventor designed it to open with some salve in case of a severe emergency. And I think this is a severe emergency."

Her eyes squinted as she examined the piece of metal. Suddenly her face brightened. "I think I might have an idea of how we can escape."

"How?"

"Clobber the guard over her head, slap this on her ankle and run like hell."

"Sounds fascinating. But how do we get the guard in here?"

"I can tell you that while you eat."

She pointed to the tray of food sitting just inside the door on the floor. Suddenly Ben Hero was starving.

* * * * *

"Are you sure you don't want any food?"

"Not hungry." Jacey shook her head as she sat beside him on the bed.

"Won't you be in big trouble if we clobber the guard over the head and I make my escape?" Ben asked as he bit into a juicy apple for dessert.

"You mean when *we* make our escape?"

Ben blinked in surprise.

Jacey frowned. "I'm just as much a prisoner here as you are, Ben Hero."

"I don't understand. I thought you were paying to have me..."

Jacey shook her head and Ben's stomach dropped as if he were on a runaway elevator. The sweetness of the apple he'd been chewing suddenly turned sour in his mouth.

"No, I've been brought here to be impregnated."

"Impregnated!" Please tell him this was a nightmare!

"Yes."

A sudden wave of light-headedness swept over him. Whoa, this was not good. He wasn't ready to be a daddy.

"Why do they want you pregnant?" he squeaked. Wasn't that the most logical next question?

"To discredit me, of course."

"Why?" Another logical question?

"Because I'm a Queen and if you were from around here, you'd know why," she said smugly.

Shoot! He was blowing it big time.

"Queen? You're a Queen?" he babbled.

"Surely you know why you were fucking me? How a woman gets pregnant?"

He could feel the blood literally draining from his face.

"Did I say something wrong?"

"I just assumed you wanted to be here," he said. Suddenly he felt rather desperate and found himself hoping she was simply teasing him and that he hadn't just taken a woman against her will. More than once.

Jacey smiled. It was a pretty smile but of little comfort.

"I enjoyed the sex, Ben Hero. I wouldn't have traded it for anything in the world, but now's not the time to discuss this. We should be planning our escape. I don't want to wait until I'm pregnant before they let me out of here."

"Um, I hate to tell this, but you might already be pregnant."

"I'm sure I'm not."

"That makes two of us." Ben slumped onto the bed and shoved his hands through his hair in frustration. "If I'd known you were being forced...I would never have touched you."

"Did I look like I was being forced? I ordered you to fuck me, remember? I must say I don't believe I'll ever go back to women."

Back to women?

Footsteps echoed in the hallway and he let her comment slide.

"Hit me," Jacey whispered.

"What?"

"Hit me and then I'll scream. It'll get the guard's attention."

"I've never hit a woman in my life," Ben hissed.

"Do it."

"No."

The stinging blow on his right cheek came out of nowhere. It took him a full second to discover she'd slapped him.

He blinked in shock.

She slapped his face again. Really hard.

Ben grabbed at her wrist and to his surprise, Jacey screamed.

Ben flew into action. Yanking Jacey against his chest, he pushed her backwards.

She flopped onto the bed. Her breasts heaved as she landed on the mattress, her legs spread-eagle, her shaved cunt shining up at him in an eager invitation.

Ah man! Any other time and he'd be slamming himself into her again. Now was not that time.

"He's trying to kill me!" Jacey shouted and winked at him.

Silently he cursed himself for what he was about to do.

He leaned over and wrapped his hands around her long slender throat.

"Too loose. Tighter," she whispered.

He had to make it look good, didn't he? His hands tightened.

He could hear a key jingle in the door lock.

"Help me!" Jacey gurgled.

Damn, she was good. Almost had him believing he was killing her.

He heard the guard's quick footsteps as she entered the room.

"Now," Jacey whispered.

Ben let go of her. Whirling around, he found the female guard who had taken so much pleasure in whipping him this morning, standing not more than two feet away, whip in hand, poised to strike.

"I do hope you don't intend on using that on me again, because if you are, you'd better be prepared for the consequences."

The guard's mouth dropped open in shock. She didn't so much as move a muscle as Ben reached out and retrieved the whip from the guard's paralyzed fingers. Jacey quickly clamped the gold bracelet around the guard's ankle.

And then they both ran. He followed her down the long hallway and out a back door.

Fresh night air slammed into Ben's face as he picked up speed, heading across the open stretch of meadow. Jacey ran beside him, having no trouble keeping up.

Halfway across the meadow, they heard the guard's hysterical screech from the open doorway they'd just escaped through. The guard took one step out of the building and a spectacular lime-green flash arrowed out of the dark sky. It zeroed in on her.

Ben watched helplessly as the green light encircled her. She stiffened for a couple of seconds and then disintegrated into a puff of lime-green smoke.

"The drone!" Jacey gasped.

"Shit!" Ben mumbled with shock, not quite believing what he'd just witnessed. Grabbing Jacey's hand, he yanked her into the seclusion of the nearby forest.

Chapter Four

&

Fear gripped Jacey as Ben pulled her through the darkness. She wasn't sure why she was frightened. She'd been in much worse situations than this. Situations more dangerous than witnessing a drone disintegrate someone or merely running naked through the woods from her enemies.

Being a Queen for five years and enduring grueling training for two years prior had taught her the importance of keeping a cool head when chaos reigned.

For years she'd lived by that one rule. But tonight, shards of emotions ripped through her like sharp edges of glass.

Perhaps it was because of the male. Perhaps it was because he held her hand so firmly. So tightly that it seemed he wanted to keep her with him forever.

Strangely enough she didn't want him to let her go. Didn't want him to simply disappear into the darkness and leave her life forever.

The mere thought of losing him stoked an unreasonable fear inside her mind. Somehow within the past few hours the male slave had gotten to her and Jacey didn't like the feeling. She didn't like it one bit.

Behind her, she could hear The Breeders crashing through the brush, their voices shrill with anger. She ducked at the sound of a rifle crack and quite literally heard a bullet slam into a nearby tree.

Ben only held her hand tighter, guiding her through the blackness as if he could see in the dark.

Despite his night vision, branches whipped painfully against tender areas of her body and beat mercilessly about her shoulders, breasts, and legs.

By the time Ben slowed their killer pace, her lungs burned and perspiration cooled her tortured body. Relief zipped along her nerve endings as she realized the rifle shots were much farther away. Soon they disappeared altogether, as did the trees.

They were in the open now, their bare feet pounding against rough rocks instead of soft mossy ground.

A niggle of warning ripped through her mind a split second before the brilliant flash of white lightning lit up the entire sky overhead.

Suddenly she knew why The Breeders had stopped chasing them.

They had crossed into The Acid Zone.

* * * * *

The flash of white lightning was unlike anything Ben had seen in his life. In its wake it left a bitter scent flooding the air. A metallic scent oddly like battery acid.

He wasn't at all surprised when Jacey tugged at him to stop.

"What was it?" He puffed as he surveyed the now black sky.

"Acid lightning. We have to find cover until it's daylight. When it starts to rain, the acid will burn right through our skin. We'll be dead within minutes."

Ben shivered at the cold tone of her voice.

"Perhaps we should go back?" he suggested.

"No, they might be camping there, might come after us in daylight when it doesn't rain. Just wait for another acid flash and maybe I can get my bearings."

"You've been here before?"

"I've trained in the area. Acid Lake is pretty close to the north border of The Acid Zone. I'm sure—" She was cut off as another flash sizzled through the night air. This time it was so low Ben could swear if he reached up he could have touched the white light.

"Over there." She pointed slightly to their left into the now complete darkness. Ben couldn't see a goddamn thing.

But she was already tugging on his hand, pulling him with a great urgency in the direction she'd just indicated.

"If we make a run for it we can make the caves before the rain starts."

And they almost did make it.

At first, Ben thought fiery insects were biting him, until he realized rain spit down on him. The drops peppered into his skin like little needle pricks.

More flashes of white lightning streaked around them. The air filled with an acrid smell and Ben found himself feeling a tad panicky as the burning sensations intensified.

He was just about to ask Jacey where the hell the shelter was when she dragged him into the mouth of a cool cave. The burning spots on his flesh instantly stopped, and so did Jacey.

"Stay right here and don't say a word," she commanded.

She let go of his hand and the urgency in her voice, not to mention that the memory of the guard getting disintegrated right before his very eyes was still fresh in his mind, made him stand right where she left him.

He cocked his head in an effort to hear where she was heading, but she was already gone.

Silence swooped in around him and Ben found himself wondering if she'd taken off. Had she left him here in this godforsaken place to find his own way out?

Damned if he was going back out the way they'd just come in. And damned if he was ever heading back to the area where he'd stuffed his clothing and gear before taking that swim. There was no way he would chance getting caught again.

He looked out the mouth of the cave and saw the white flashes of lightning dance wildly around the rocky outcrops. In the brief moments of light, he noticed the terrain was bare of any vegetation.

A shiver of uneasiness ripped up his spine as he remembered where Jacey said they were.

The Acid Zone.

And if he remembered correctly didn't one have to flush acid-exposed skin with water in order to avoid severe burns?

Shit! He gritted his teeth against the pain beginning to sink throughout various points of his tender flesh. Places where the acid rain had struck. He willed himself not to rub the areas. It would only get onto his fingers and burn them too.

"Come! This way!" From somewhere up ahead, Jacey's soft voice echoed like a lifeline through the darkness of the damp cave. It took him only moments to reach her and he felt her warm hand shift against his palm.

Relief whispered through him. She hadn't deserted him like he'd feared.

"We got lucky," she whispered as she led him through the darkness. "I found the right cave."

"How the heck can you tell? I can't see a thing."

Her amused giggle soothed some of his frustration and a moment later they emerged from total darkness into a rocky room about ten feet by ten feet.

Obviously she'd lit some torches, because several of them flickered where they'd been placed in cracks in the nearby rock walls. The buttery light cast a welcome glow over the dark glass-like surface of a small pond.

"It's best we get into the water immediately to soothe our burns."

"I sure hope this isn't the Acid Lake you were mentioning earlier?"

He thought about dipping his toe into the water to see how warm it might be, but opted to wait for her answer, in case his toe decided to disintegrate.

"The water is pure and drinkable."

Before he could ask if she was absolutely sure the water was safe, she dove in with an ear-splitting splash.

He had just enough torchlight to make out her bare silhouette as she swam. Long silky legs paddled seductively. Arms waved confidently. And the sexy curves of those luscious wide hips made him respond violently.

His shaft hardened like an iron bar and Ben groaned inwardly, suddenly feeling shy and vulnerable at his reaction to her.

After the harrowing escape they'd just been through he had no right to think about satisfying the lust ripping through his every fiber as she swam innocently in the pool.

Hoping she wouldn't notice his arousal, he dived in quickly. The cool water soothed the acid burns and eased the heated arousal zipping along his nerve endings.

When he broke the surface, he found Jacey swimming toward him. That dreamy look brightened her face again and he knew she'd seen his arousal.

"Exactly how do we get out of here?" he asked and tried desperately to keep his mind and eyes off those heavy breasts that broke the surface.

"It'll be safe to travel during daylight through The Acid Zone. It only rains at night."

He noted the red dots on her silky skin. Dots compliments of the acid. They looked oddly similar to a light case of the red measles. He noticed the same on his skin.

"Don't worry, they won't scar. In a few days they'll be gone," she reassured.

"Scars are the least of my worries," he found himself muttering, as his gaze seemed to magically caress her glorious breasts.

Shimmering ringlets floated on the water away from her body as she moved closer to him. Her intoxicating scent simmered into his nostrils, arousing him to greater heights.

"Um, I was wondering exactly why The Breeders want you pregnant?" he asked, hoping that the realization of having sex with her yet again and getting her pregnant might douse the fire raging between them.

It didn't have the desired effect. Actually the opposite was true. That she might be pregnant by him only increased the urge to bond with her on more than a physical level.

As she drew closer, emotions he'd never experienced in his entire life came out of nowhere and bombarded him. A strange kind of happiness that this woman might actually be carrying his child flooded his senses. That idea swamped him with a feeling of protectiveness. If she was pregnant, he had to do the right thing by her. He had to keep her safe and she sure as hell wasn't safe in a place named The Acid Zone.

But for now all that could wait. For now he just wanted to be near her. To swim in the happiness that perhaps he might have found a woman he could settle down with.

In the past, such a thought would frighten him and send his shaft into sleep mode, but not this time. Not with this woman.

Her arms went around his neck and she pressed her wonderfully naked wet body against him.

The softness and warmth of her silky flesh cradled Ben. Made him bury his face into her wet hair and inhale the beauty of her sweet essence. His arms came up to wrap around her waist and pull her softness tightly against him.

She gazed up at him with those dreamy eyes and his brain fogged to any semblance of common sense. Her curvy red lips were slightly parted, ready to be taken. Her breath escaped her luscious mouth in aroused gasps.

"What have you done to me, Jace?" he found himself muttering. "Why can't I keep my hands off you? My mind off you? It's insane. I've only known you for such a short time and yet I feel as if I've known you all my life. Wanted you forever."

"Could be the sex drugs in the food," she said breathlessly.

"Damned good sex drugs." Although he was pretty sure these intense emotions were real. They had to be.

"The Breeders are well known for putting drugs in their slaves' food. Keeps them aroused and ready to perform at all times."

"But you didn't eat any food, Jacey. What's your excuse?"

A wicked smile tilted her red lips.

"I haven't been with a male before."

Shock zipped up his spine. She was kidding, right?

She nodded and his thoughts spiraled with a mixture of emotions. The idea he'd taken her virginity should have made him feel honored.

It didn't. She'd been tied to a bed, not of her own free will. Although she'd encouraged him to have sex with her, it still didn't sit right that her first time wasn't with a man of her own choosing.

The desire in her gaze intensified. Her warm fingers slid around his aching shaft and he sucked in an aroused breath.

Her erotic touch electrified him, sending sharp sensations straight up his cock, through his sensitized balls and right into his belly.

"And until I return to my people, I'm going to satisfy myself to my heart's content."

With her warm hands clamped tightly around his shaft, she guided him into her sweet satin hole.

She was already wet for him and her velvety vaginal muscles clenched around him immediately, making him groan from the erotic tightness.

Her mouth clamped over his in a sensual kiss that was so greedy and intoxicating it sent his senses reeling with passion.

There was no mistaking it. He wanted this woman in his life.

Screw protocol. Screw NASA. And damn whoever told him there was no such thing as love at first sight.

His hands slid down the velvety contours of her waist to cup her soft ass cheeks. Lifting her against him, he shoved his cock straight into her very core. A wild purr erupted from somewhere deep in her chest. It was a beautiful noise. A seductive sound he wanted to hear again.

He thrust his hips forward, stabbing deeper into her warmth. Stopping only when she gasped into his mouth.

He took the opportunity to plunge his tongue between her lips and teeth and thrust himself against her silky tongue. He felt her thighs quiver. Felt her velvety cunt muscles clamp even tighter around his rod.

Heated blood ripped through his veins and he began to thrust his shaft into her. Waves of pleasure cascaded over him like a roaring waterfall.

From somewhere far away he could hear her musical moans as he fucked her. He could feel her body tense. Knew she was going to climax and he speared harder and deeper into her tight hole, filling her completely.

Her body bucked violently against him, her vaginal muscles contracting, drawing him deeper into her hot cunt as the climax wrenched her apart. Splashing sounds of water filled the air as his frantic thrusts found their way home. With long hard strokes he made love to her, capturing her moans and whimpers with his mouth.

He felt her legs come up and twine around his hips, tightening her cunt muscles harder around his throbbing rod and lodging him deep inside her.

He groaned into her mouth as the agonizing spasms of pleasure ripped his body apart.

He came so hard light fragments erupted behind his eyes. He found himself inhaling sharply at the intensity of her cunt clenching at his shaft as it sucked up his hot release.

Her cunt muscles were quivering lightly long after their orgasm had subsided when, still buried deep inside her, her long legs still clasped around his hips and her arms wrapped around his neck, Ben carried her out of the water and padded barefoot to the far side of the pool. Here he found a nest of dry pine needles that was big enough to accommodate two comfortably.

Jacey's eyes fluttered sleepily as he slid out of her pussy and placed her on the soft makeshift bed.

"It just gets better and better every time," she whispered and held her arms out to him, a seductive smile on her lips.

Ben lay down beside her and allowed her to cradle him in her arms. Her breasts pushed provocatively against his flesh and to his surprise he felt the stirrings of another arousal. Before he could allow himself the pleasure of taking her yet again, he discovered her eyes were now shut, her breathing shallow and steady with sleep. He buried his face into her wet hair and it wasn't long before Ben joined her in slumber.

Chapter Five

ဢ

The next day Jacey awoke to discover him missing. "Ben Hero!" she called, suddenly frantic to think he'd left her alone. Forever.

From somewhere in the direction of the cave entrance, she heard his reply.

Sighing with relief, she stretched languidly, finding certain parts of her body very sore, especially the area between her legs. But it was a wonderful soreness and she couldn't wait to have Ben inside her again.

Jacey bit her bottom lip at that thought. How in the world could she ever go back to being a Queen? There were special laws Queens had to abide by. And not fornicating with a male slave was one of them.

She even had witnesses for goddess sake. The Breeders certainly had heard her cries of joy and a guard had actually watched as Ben had taken her standing up against the wall.

Jacey shivered with delight at the memory of his thick shaft stabbing deep into her woman's core, making her cry out from the pleasure. Ben Hero certainly did know how to please a woman.

Her stomach growled angrily, prompting her to follow the mouth-watering aroma that drifted through the cave.

While she'd slept Ben Hero had been busy. A string of torches hung at various points along the tunnel and Jacey followed them until she emerged from the cave.

Holding up her hand to shield her eyes from the blinding sun overhead, she discovered Ben right outside the entrance.

His luscious body glistened with a sheen of perspiration as he squatted in front of a small smokeless fire.

The delicious aroma sifted through the humid air and to her delight she noticed what appeared to be a rather plump-looking skinned rabbit speared to a horizontal pole roasting over the cheerful flames.

"Good afternoon! I hope you like rabbit," he grinned.

The sight of his beautiful mouth made the flames of arousal flash deep inside her lower abdomen.

"My favorite meat, actually. It smells absolutely delicious."

She licked her lips with anticipation and hunched near the fire beside him.

"I found some wild onions growing between a couple of rocks. I guess the acid rain hadn't been able to get to them."

His voice lowered, capturing her attention. "I saw something else while I was scouting around."

"What?"

"A group of women skirting along the edge of the tree line about a mile from us."

A knot grabbed at Jacey's stomach. He pointed to a nearby outcrop of rocks.

"I hiked up to the top. Got a pretty good view of the landscape. Can see for miles. Six women, heading away from here."

Jacey sighed with relief. "Thank the Goddess of Freedom."

"I don't think they were The Breeders. These ladies were carrying bows and arrows and were shapely blondes."

Jacey's gut clenched up again. "The Yellow Hairs."

"Yellow Hairs?"

Obviously he wasn't from around here if he had to ask that question.

"They're cannibals."

The look of shock on his face made her laugh. Her stomach growled harshly at the same time. "How long before the rabbit is done?"

"Cannibals? Blonde cannibals?" He prodded.

"I'm hungry," she complained, trying hard not to grin at the panic etching his face.

Reaching out she tried to pry a piece of meat off the roasting rabbit, but jerked away from the heat.

"Careful, it's hot," Ben said as he quickly maneuvered in between her and the rabbit. Lifting the carcass off the makeshift spit, he expertly ripped away the hind leg she'd been planning to grab and laid it on a smooth section of rock.

"Give it a minute to cool off," he said and ripped off the other hind leg and laid it beside the first one. Then his worried gaze snapped to her again.

"These cannibals? They're cannibals like in eating people?"

"Don't you know that word? I would think you would know it, if you were from around here. You are from around here, aren't you?"

She held her breath as she awaited his answer.

"Close by."

And yet he didn't know about The Yellow Hairs. He was lying to her and that knowledge hurt.

Jacey frowned. Why she should care if he was lying? It shouldn't matter to her, but strangely enough, it did. It mattered too much.

Did it have something to do with the sex with him? She'd had sex with females before. Wild, frantic sex. It had been merely a physical release, nothing emotional.

Having sex with Ben Hero seemed different somehow. She'd never experienced such physical and emotional turmoil as when he touched her or looked at her. And never in her life had she given up total control to anyone. And now suddenly she'd given control to a male, allowing him to lead the escape.

After escaping, she should have simply sent him on his way, but she'd stayed with him. Had found sanctuary for him and she'd fucked him again in the cave pool. Clung to him with a burning need as he'd slammed his wicked delight into her with all his might. Her body had burned with lust as she'd writhed beneath his assault, her mind oblivious to anything but him and his magical touch.

Even now the flames of arousal throbbed through her body. The thought of feeling his thick shaft slicing deep into her core as he intimately covered her heated flesh with his, almost made her cry out.

As he moved to pick up the rabbit legs he'd laid on the rocks, Jacey couldn't help but notice his semi-erect penis sway proudly between his legs.

Her heart thudded at the wonderful sight. This male was always aroused. Always ready to fuck and so was she, it seemed.

She remembered curling her fingers over his thick arousal last night while they'd stood in the water. The heavy weight of his throbbing cock cradled in her hands had made desire vibrate through her senses. He'd been so big. The skin of his arousal was so velvety smooth; yet beneath it, immense power had pulsed in his veined shaft. Power that she wanted inside her. Power that she'd guided toward the opening of her very soul.

Jacey's cunt moistened at the delicious memory.

"Jacey?"

She blinked in surprise when she found Ben waving the rabbit leg in front of her face.

"You said you were hungry."

She was hungry all right, but not for a silly rabbit.

"Famished," she whispered and accepted the meat.

His eyes snapped with lust as their gazes clashed. Despite his apparent arousal, he frowned and broke eye contact, turning sideways in front of the fire, hiding his delicious penis from her view. Muscles rippled in those powerful thighs as he huddled and returned the remains of the rabbit to over the fire. He cleared his throat nervously. "So, tell me about this Acid Zone. How big is it?"

"It's one of the smaller ones. Ten miles by ten miles. We are at the northernmost tip."

"How did it form?"

"Holes in the protective layers around the planet were formed hundreds of years ago due to pollution from the way the ancestors lived. That's why any type of modern technology has been outlawed for the general public. It is used only by Queens, High Fives, and certain other people like doctors. The decreased use has stopped other acid zones from forming, but the old ones are still there. We don't know if these zones will repair themselves eventually. In The Acid Zones it rains during the night, and during the day the heat is intense."

"I'll say it's hot. Can't wait until I can get under the shade of a tree or take another dip in the ocean."

She noted how he carefully avoided mentioning the cave pool. Did he not want to bring up the memories of their coupling in the cool waters last night? Had she not pleased him?

Doubt was immediately replaced by an exquisite jolt of killing pleasure as Ben Hero shifted his body, giving her a quick peek of his now rigid, swollen and very erect shaft.

He caught her staring at him and once again shifted away, hiding his magnificent cock from her view.

Why was the male suddenly shy? She'd noted the same reaction last night only moments before he'd joined her in the pool. He'd been aroused by watching her swim, and yet he'd tried to hide his erection from her by plunging quickly into the cool water.

Did his sudden shyness have something to do with his shocked reaction when he'd discovered she was a captive too? She'd seen guilt flash in his eyes when she'd told him that he'd been her first male. She'd noticed other emotions as well but hadn't been able to put a name to them.

Did the male actually feel guilty for fucking her? Guilty for pleasuring her?

"How far to this Freedom Sea you were talking about?" he asked, breaking her from her thoughts.

"Is that where you come from?" she asked.

His frown deepened and he said nothing as he studied the crackling fire.

"The reason I ask is because that's where the other talking man was heading. You two come from the same place?"

"We do. He's my half-brother."

"Half-brother?"

"We have the same mom."

Jacey nodded. "The female who raised you. We don't do it that way here. Only females who have broken the laws are sentenced to producing babies."

Ben's mouth dropped open in shock and Jacey continued, "We never know the name of the female who carried us or the male who provided sperm. We are raised by a group of females called Nurturers."

Ben took a bite of his rabbit and nodded. "We know the females who carried us and the males who impregnate them. We all live together as a family in the same house. Both the male and female are our nurturers."

Interesting concept. She'd learned through science class that one planet in particular did things that way.

"And so you must be from…Earth?"

He choked on the piece of rabbit he'd been chewing.

"Earth?" he managed to croak.

"That is where the other talking man is from."

"He told you this?"

"Not in so many words, but he didn't deny it when I asked."

"How do you know about this Earth?"

"I'm a Queen. I have access to information the general public doesn't. I know that other planets exist and that Earth is the closest with life to us. It seems logical you came from there. Did you?"

"It's best you don't ask any questions about that particular subject, Jacey."

Curiosity dug into her. "Why not?"

"You're a Queen. You give orders, right?"

She nodded, not quite understanding where he was going with his question.

"I've been given orders. And one of them is not to reveal where I come from unless I absolutely have to. It's best that way."

Jacey accepted his answer. For now.

"Where were you captured?"

"I was captured just outside the village where we…met."

Jacey laughed. "Only a fool would venture into The Breeder's territory."

"Consider me a big fool then." He grinned. Her heart flipped over wildly and her tummy suddenly protested at the lack of nourishment.

"Eat your rabbit, will you? That stomach of yours is growling up a storm." Ben instructed.

She took a bite out of the rabbit leg and couldn't help but moan as a fantastic flavor burst against her taste buds.

"From the sound you're making, I gather you like?"

"Fabulous. How did you make it so delicious?"

"The wild onions, not to mention basting it with some salt crystals I found hanging in one of the caves in there."

Jacey stopped chewing as a sinking feeling hit her stomach. "You explored alone? It's very dangerous in there. You mustn't wander alone again."

"You care if I get lost?"

"Why should I care about a male slave?" Jacey's heart pounded wildly as she tore off another piece of the tasty rabbit and stuffed it into her mouth. She hoped he didn't notice the way her face was heating up with embarassment for actually making him think she cared about his safety.

"Ouch. Looks like I hit a bit of a nerve?"

"You hit nothing, Ben Hero," she said between chews. "I simply do not want you to get captured or it'll be both our heads."

"Wouldn't want my head to get chopped off, now would we? Might make for some boring evenings?"

She didn't like the amused grin he sported or the laughter in his voice.

"Obviously I've misunderstood something. Please, enlighten me. Why would evenings be boring if you were dead? I'm sure if something happened to you, I wouldn't even notice." That was a big fat lie, but he didn't have to know that.

His amused grin widened into one of knowing satisfaction and it just made her angrier.

"Fine, go and explore. Fall into one of the many mile-deep pot holes or get eaten by a bat."

"Oh, I'd rather get eaten by you," he whispered.

The soft way he'd spoken those words shot a fresh rush of arousal coursing through her bloodstream, chasing away all her anger.

"Or better yet, eat you?" he taunted. She didn't miss the smoldering look in his eyes or the sound of his harsh breathing.

Sweet sunshine! And she'd thought he was shy?

The intimate idea of actually having his male organ inside her mouth, sucking his throbbing head, tasting his cum, or better yet having his own mouth graze upon her clit, sucking her labia lips, his tongue plunging deep inside her, suddenly made her feel shy and vulnerable and aroused.

As much as she wanted him physically, there was a rush of emotions that made her realize if she had sex with him again, she just might not be able to let him go.

Was that why he was hiding his arousal from her? Did he want to protect his heart too? The idea frightened her into changing the subject.

"Freedom Sea is in The Outer Limits. Only Queens have permission to go there."

"Okay, I'll bite. Why only Queens?" The hungry look in his eyes faded into a curious glint.

"It is where the Goddess of Freedom resides."

"Who's she?"

"If you came from this area, Ben Hero, you would know. Nonetheless, she is the woman who is responsible for the freedom of our females."

"Is she the woman in charge around here? Is there any way my brothers and I can meet her?"

More of them? Jacey swallowed against the sudden uneasiness his words created. "There are more than two of you?"

"Actually there are three of us. More brothers and sisters at home."

"And they all talk and are educated like you?"

Ben nodded and took a bite of his rabbit leg.

"Females and males. All educated. All talk. And there are many people who have many different languages and religions."

"How interesting." She tried to stifle the shiver of excitement ripping through her at the thought that males and females existed happily somewhere.

A faraway look flooded his gaze and his voice softened with warmth.

"Like I said earlier, where I come from, males and females live together and have their own babies. Mom's first husband...well I guess I should use the word male, died. They only had one boy together. He's my oldest brother, Joe. The one you met. After her male died, Mom took another mate and they've been popping out babies ever since."

Jacey gulped at the mention of babies.

"How many babies?"

"Many."

"This mom, why does she endure so many babies placed upon her by this male?"

Suddenly Ben laughed. It was a nice sound, a musical noise that came straight from his chest.

"Endure?" he shook his head. "She doesn't endure babies, she wants them with the man she loves."

"I've heard the word *man* before in our history lessons. The meaning is..." She searched her memory and nodded, " Man means, a dominating force."

Ben winced. "Dominating? Force? Not where I come from. Men and women are equal. They both have the same rights under the laws."

"Fascinating concept," Jacey admitted. Although she couldn't imagine males having any rights on this planet, or having them running around loose.

She blinked with sudden realization. Ben Hero was a male and running loose. He was educating her about his world and his people's laws. And she was sucking it up like a sponge. Perhaps Ben Hero was just innocently interested in her world or perhaps he wasn't. Before she shared information with him about her world, she needed to find out more about this male and where he came from.

"It is said that males invented our language without consulting the females. They dominated the language as well as all other aspects of women's lives. These males from your planet, are they like you? Or are they a dominating force as our ancestors were?"

He hesitated just a little too long before answering. It made Jacey uneasy. Made her wonder if perhaps she'd been wrong to trust herself with him.

"You don't have to worry about that. My brothers and I are harmless."

"You are far from harmless, Ben Hero," she found herself muttering.

"I am?" A cocky grin fluttered across his sensuous lips and Jacey's pulse picked up speed. Instantly she knew her brief suspicions about him were incorrect. He was genuinely interested in her world and her and she needed to change the subject or she would end up fucking this male right here and now, losing her heart to him in the process.

"Freedom Sea is at least two days walk if you go straight through The Acid Zone. Or three and half days if we go around," she said.

"We?" he asked.

Did she detect hope in his voice? Or was it only wishful thinking on her part that he wanted her to go with him?

"You prefer I not tag along?"

"On the contrary, it would be my pleasure to have you with me."

Amusement twinkled in his blue eyes and Jacey couldn't help but wonder how horrible she would feel when the time came to part.

Finishing off her rabbit leg, she helped herself to another piece of meat. All that running around and the other activities she'd indulged in with Ben Hero last night and yesterday had left her famished.

He watched the fire silently as she ate and she wondered what he was thinking. Wondered if perhaps he wanted her to guide him to Freedom Sea simply because he would be pleasured by fucking her.

She tried to ignore the sultry look clouding his hooded eyes as he stared into the fire and the way it made her body heat up yet again. She preferred to believe the burning of her flesh was a direct result of the fierce sun beating down on her nakedness.

"You sure can put the chow away," he said as he watched her lick the rabbit juice from her fingers.

His comment suddenly made her flush with anger.

"I'm simply hungry because I haven't eaten anything in two days. There is nothing more to it," she snapped.

She'd heard that Paradisian women got ravenously hungry when pregnant. Also their hormones changed drastically, leaving some women very emotional and with an intense sexual appetite.

She certainly had an unbelievable sexual appetite since meeting this male slave, not to mention her emotions had gone haywire around him. She couldn't seem to stop herself from watching his every movement or from craving to touch his hard flesh.

"Your skin's starting to get red, Jace. Why don't you go inside? I'll go take another look and see if those blonde cannibals are gone before we head out.

"We can't leave today. It's already too late."

He looked at her oddly, as if he suspected she was stalling their departure so she could satisfy herself again with him tonight.

"It would be best not to return the same way we came, in case The Breeders are still searching for us," she explained. "If we wait until tomorrow morning, it'll give us that much more extra time in The Acid Zone before we re-enter the forest at another angle. Besides, there is a slave training cabin we can stay at tomorrow night before we—." She cut herself off.

"Before we what?" he asked cautiously.

"Before we decide what to do next."

He nodded, accepting her quick response. She'd almost blown it by telling him she was thinking it might be better if they parted tomorrow. Before she lost the rest of her mind to this insanity of wanting to stay with this male or lost her heart to him.

She stood and headed inside. The damp coolness relieved her heated body, but only to a certain degree.

She watched Ben Hero, as with a rabbit leg in hand, he climbed along the rocks of the craggy outcrop.

She had to admit, he was a magnificent specimen. As he climbed, bands of muscles quivered in all the right places in his sweat streaked naked body. His thighs were powerfully built. The muscles in his abdomen were rigid, and the width of his shoulders, startling.

What a shame she would have to part with him.

That thought jolted her from her dreamy state and damped her spirits.

Why in the name of the Goddess of Freedom had she even entertained the idea she could keep the male all for herself? And why was she even considering letting him go?

She didn't have to lose him at all. She could use him to somehow barter a way into keeping her Queen position and then her hub could house him in the brothel town and she could visit him any time she wanted.

Jacey blinked in shock at the way her thoughts had headed. She was a Queen and she should know better. Negotiations about keeping her position, especially after what Ben had done to her—and what she wanted to do with him again—were totally impossible. It was her duty to turn herself into the authorities.

But first, she had to find some way of getting Ben far away from here. If anyone found out about the little illegal tidbit of him being educated, he'd be in big trouble and she right along with him. It would be best if she could keep casualties to a bare minimum and face the music, so to speak, on her own.

A familiar cry from somewhere in the distance split through the humid air.

"What was that?" Ben called down softly from where he stood halfway up the rock.

"The battle cry of The Yellow Hairs. I think we might have been discovered."

Chapter Six

໕ວ

As it turned out, they hadn't been discovered. A few minutes later, Ben and Jacey crouched low behind a rock and watched six blonde and very naked women racing along the plateau about half a mile away. Each wore a quiver of arrows on her back, and each held tight a bow in her hand.

"They're young females on their first male hunt," Jacey whispered. She pointed about a hundred yards in front of the blondes. Across the barren plateau, a dark-haired naked man stumbled away from the women. An arrow was buried in his left shoulder, blood poured from the wound.

"Shit!" Ben swore softly. He made a move to get up but Jacey's firm grip on his elbow stopped him cold.

"Do not help him! He has already been hit by an arrow. It is too late for him."

"The hell it's too late," Ben growled and tried to yank himself free. Jacey refused to let him go.

Instinctively he knew he wouldn't be able to free himself from her death grip unless he hurt her, and he didn't want to do that.

He watched helplessly as the male wavered and finally fell to his knees. The first female to reach him let out another spine tingling cry that made Ben shiver despite the heat boring into his skin from the intense sun overhead.

His heart crashed painfully against his chest as he watched the rest of the blondes surround the man who now writhed on the rocky ground.

"The Yellow Hairs are well known for poisoning their arrows. Poisons that render a male helpless almost instantly or can kill him slowly. We have no way of telling which one was used on him. If I were to venture a guess at the way he is suffering and the females are merely standing around watching, I'd say it is a deadly poison for the male."

A sickening knot clutched his guts as the male suddenly stiffened and then went still.

The females cried out their victory in one unified shout.

"He's dead," Jacey whispered. "We must go. Hurry. They may come here."

Ben cursed quietly as she led him back down to the cave opening.

"We will go deeper into the caves," she said.

"What about the fire? If we put it out, the smoke will definitely attract their attention."

"Leave it, but bring the rabbit," she instructed. "I'll start dousing the torches and meet you inside. Hurry!"

Ben grabbed the two ends of the spit containing the rabbit just as another volley of spine tingling female cries rent the air.

"Poor bastard," he muttered and hurried to join Jacey.

* * * * *

They traveled quickly through the damp cave, Jacey very confident in the way she sidestepped the mile-deep potholes, urging him to stay close to her.

"Obviously you've been in these parts before." Ben kept his voice low enough so only Jacey could hear.

"I trained nearby."

"Trained?"

"For Queen status. Watch your step here," she pointed to a sharp two-inch spear-like rock object sticking straight up from the cave floor like some oversized thumbtack. This certainly would cause some serious damage to a bare foot, and that's the last thing they needed when they were on the run.

"Exactly what do you have to do to train as a Queen?" he asked as he followed closely.

"Many things. We learn how to hunt, fish, build shelters, history of our planet, science, business aspects of running our own hub, different types of technology..." Her words trailed away and she pointed out a nasty-looking projection sticking about a foot out from the cave wall. If she hadn't pointed it out, the sharp rock would have sliced right into the side of his bare hip.

He cursed silently as he skirted the item and hurried to keep up with her.

Holding his torch higher in an effort to see better, his eyes became glued to the sensuous sway of her hips and the gorgeous crack in her ass. What would she do if he came up behind her and reamed himself straight into her ass? Would she struggle? Or would she welcome him?

He felt himself hardening at the thought. Felt the now-familiar heat of lust rip through his blood.

Damn her! Why'd she have to be so beautiful? So perfectly toned. So sensually curvy? Not so much as an ounce of fat on her body.

She was like a perfect ten. Hell, an eleven.

Ben frowned with disgust. Was he so shallow that he was attracted to a woman because of her great looks? He shook his head in denial. He'd gone out with lots of Earth gals with great looking bodies like Jacey's. They'd been nice eye candy but their attitudes had been lacking something. Jacey possessed something different. Something he liked.

He couldn't be sure what. Perhaps it was because of her innocence to sexual experiences with a man? Her vulnerability? Maybe he liked her because of the way she gazed at him with that dreamy look in her eyes? He'd never seen a woman look at him like that before.

Or it could be her unique feminine scent. He'd heard certain scents attracted men and women to each other. Pheromones, wasn't it?

Maybe it was a combination of all the above that attracted him to her? Or maybe it was the other features about her character that made him notice her. Features that he couldn't put a name to.

Or could it be as simple as love at first sight? That's what had happened between his mother and father.

They'd been dancing with different dance partners and passed each other on the dance floor, when their eyes just clashed. His father had admitted he'd instantly been captivated by her scent. He'd cut in on her dance partner and asked his mother to dance with him. She'd said yes.

By the end of the night they'd been engaged. Two weeks later, they'd married. Nine months later, he'd been born.

Ben sighed in frustration. Was that what had happened to him? Had he fallen in love with Jacey the first time he'd seen her all bound and prepared for his taking?

He'd always harbored a secret fetish for bondage. Always wanted to fuck a woman who was tied up and willing, but he'd never indulged. And the wild excitement flashing in her eyes when she'd first seen him enter that Breeder stall, he'd known instinctively she'd wanted to be taken.

If he were a betting man, he'd say she was harboring a deep fantasy that would get her stripped of her Queen status if she ever indulged.

Is that what attracted him to her? Did she have bondage fantasies like he did? If so, he wondered how far she would allow him to go.

* * * * *

Jacey lifted her torch higher in an effort to see a little farther ahead. If she remembered correctly…ah, here it was.

"Watch your step, Ben Hero," she warned as she squeezed her body against the cool rock and skirted around another one of the notorious potholes.

She made the mistake of looking back to see if he was following her instructions when the light from both their torches illuminated his naked body in such a way that she was able to see the ripples of muscles in his abdomen and the thick thatch of golden-brown hair nesting his swaying balls.

To her delight his massive penis stuck straight out at her.

She inhaled sharply at the magnificent sight. Obviously the male was once again very aroused. The urge to grab him by the shoulders and pull his hard body to her yearning flesh was so great, she almost did it, but a screeching scream from far behind them chased the lust straight from her senses.

"Did you hear it?" Ben asked.

"Yes," she whispered.

"What was it?"

"The Yellow Hairs. They must have found the fire."

"It didn't sound like that battle cry of theirs before."

"This was a scream meant to let us know they are here. To frighten us further into the caves."

"Isn't that what we're already doing?"

"They won't come in here. They've already gotten their male. They'll be busy all night with him. Besides, I made all the torches disappear. We, on the other hand, won't be able to go too much further than this without it getting too dangerous."

"As if it isn't dangerous enough," he muttered as they finally cleared the yawning pothole. "What do we have to look forward to when we go deeper?"

"Death, if we're lucky."

"And if we aren't lucky?"

"We'll be captured by the High Five."

"High Five?"

"The five High Queens. They rule the area. They make the laws and teach the Queens. This cave is one of many emergency exits from their residences."

"Why wouldn't you want to get caught by them? They trained you. You're a Queen."

Jacey shifted aside her uneasiness at his innocent questions.

"Because it is illegal for Queens to mate with males. Once The Breeders spread the word I was forced to mate and was penetrated, I will lose my Queen status and —."

The sharp inhalation of his breath made her turn around. In the flickering torchlight, his face was so pale she thought he might pass out.

"Are you sick, Ben Hero?"

"Forced you? I thought you said you wanted me to fuck you?"

"Of course I did. But The Breeders will say otherwise. They don't know I had ventured away from the hub looking for a male. That I wanted to experience what Annie was experiencing. Originally, I had followed your brother and asked him to fuck me."

Ben's eyes widened with shock. "Obviously he turned you down."

Jacey sighed with regret. Although now that she'd experienced this male, she didn't think any other one would do.

"He said he would only fuck Annie."

"One-woman man. That's Joe."

"And you? Are you a one-woman man?"

She didn't know why but her whole body tensed as she awaited his answer.

"What do you think?" His voice was warm and gentle.

71

Jan Springer

Somewhere along the discussion they'd stopped walking and their bodies had aligned themselves quite nicely. Her breasts heaved mere inches from his massive chest and his heated arousal whispered seductively near her lower abdomen.

"I think you've had a few women in your past. Possibly more than a few."

"Oh? And what gives you that idea?" He reached up and flicked a strand of hair out of her eyes.

"For one, you seem to know how to please a woman. As if you've practiced many times."

"And?" He seemed to be holding back a grin.

"Number two reason..." She took the torch from his hand and with hers stuck them into a nearby crevice in the wall.

Turning back to him, her hands reached down and cupped his heavy testicles, feeling the deliciously solid weight in her palms.

He growled seductively.

"Number two reason is you seem to be ready to fuck at a moment's notice," she whispered.

Desire flooded his eyes. "Every time I look at you, Jacey, I want to fuck you. That doesn't happen to me with just any woman."

The truth in his words sunk deep into her heart.

"And I want to fuck you too, Ben Hero," she found herself whispering as she uncupped his testicles and wrapped her hands around the base of his swollen cock.

"Are we safe enough here for a little while?" The meaning of his question was quite clear.

Jacey listened for any odd sounds but heard nothing except the tinkling of water seeping down a nearby wall and the powerful crash of her heart pounding in her eardrums.

"I think we're safe, Ben Hero. As long as we're quiet."

"I know one way to keep you from crying out your pleasure."

His head lowered and his hot mouth clamped over hers, stoking the fire of lust consuming her body. Moisture seeped between her legs. Without hesitation, Jacey guided his thick erection into her cunt, gasping into his mouth at the pleasant intrusion.

His hands curled around her shoulders pushing her roughly against the cave wall. Cool craggy rocks dug painfully into her ass and back, but the pain of it only intensified her pleasure as he rammed his rod straight into her woman's core.

* * * * *

"Did you notice that almost every time we have a conversation, it ends up in us having sex?" Ben asked as he cradled her soft hot body in his arms after they'd finally collapsed onto the cool cave floor.

"I've noticed." She nibbled erotically on his earlobe. The sexy touch made a tingly tension begin to build in his spent cock.

"You don't think there's anything strange about that?"

"Considering I shouldn't even be having sex with a male, yes this is strange for me. Although, if I died right now, I'd die happy and satisfied."

A cold shiver raced up his spine at her words. "Don't say that, Jacey."

"What? That I'm a happy, satisfied woman? It's true. My female companions have never fulfilled me the way you do."

"I still can't get over you being with other women," he said as his finger toyed with a nipple ring.

"Why not?"

"I don't know. I just never figured you to be that type, although I can understand why because of your laws. But why is that law in place? Why can't you mate with a male?"

She inhaled deeply and her plump breast pressed against his fingers, sparking off another wave of desire through his body.

"A Queen dedicates her life to serving and leading females. Women are her equals. Males subservient. It would be beneath a Queen to crave, let alone copulate with, a male slave."

"But I'm not a slave and neither are my brothers. remember, where I come from men and women are equals."

"That's something I don't think I can get used to."

"You seem to be doing a fine enough job, so far."

"How so?" Her mouth left his ear and she cuddled her head on his shoulder.

"You let me cook dinner for you. And you let me make love to you."

Jacey stiffened in his arms.

"Something I said?" he asked.

"The word love. It's a forbidden word."

"What? You're kidding?" Although he didn't think she could kid about something like that.

"Love was an emotion males used to dominate women. A brainwashing word to seduce women into allowing males to fuck them."

Ben shook his head, not believing what he was hearing. "Where I come from love is the most important word between a woman and a man. When a man and women say they love each other, they marry and have children and live together."

"Marry? I don't know that word."

"It's a ceremony. We do it in front of friends and family. We tell everyone we love each other, that we want each other. That we will take care of each other in sickness and in health, for richer or poorer, until death does us part."

She said nothing but he noticed the tiniest wistful smile on Jacey's lips and it brought gentle warmth to his heart.

"How far back does your language go?" he asked.

"Many years. Hundreds. Perhaps a thousand. No one knows for sure, except the High Five. I think they know. They know everything about our history." Her words were starting to slur with sleep. In the soft torchlight, he noticed her eyelids droop. Finally they flickered closed and her breath grew steady and deep.

"May as well sleep here," he mumbled and held her soft velvety body tighter to him.

Their conversation made him wonder again how these women knew the English language and how the meaning of love had gotten so twisted. It was totally unbelievable that two planets so far away from each other possessed the same language. Unless a higher being was floating among the stars, dropping in on planets and teaching the inhabitants the English language?

Ben couldn't help but laugh at that absurd idea and willed himself to listen to Jacey's soft breathing.

Soon he, too, fell asleep.

* * * * *

"Oh, shit," Ben hissed when they cleared the mouth of the cool cave and stepped into the searing morning sunlight. It wasn't the heat zinging into his skin that made him curse with outrage, but the stench of burnt flesh and the remains of the human male the cannibal women had captured yesterday.

His stomach rolled at the sight of the charred ribs and other bones and pieces of cooked flesh lying scattered along the dirt of the small clearing amidst the rocky outcrops. The blondes had even used the same fireplace he'd used to make their rabbit meal yesterday.

"Don't look at it, if it upsets you, Ben Hero." Jacey said as she emerged from the mouth of the cave.

"We have to give the guy a proper burial." He forced himself to say, although he didn't know exactly where they could bury his body parts in this rocky terrain.

"There's no time. The Yellow Hairs have only left to show their trainers the head of the male slave as proof of their victory. They will return before dark to finish their meal, possibly this time with another male."

"Hungry gals, aren't they?" Although he felt far from amused at this poor sap's fate, humor was the only thing that had gotten him through life and it seemed appropriate at this time to keep him from truly getting sick.

"They won't be eating the next male. They'll be fucking him. Yesterday they were initiated officially as hunters. The next step will be to lose their virginities. The next male will die a very satisfied death. Come, let's leave before we are discovered."

Ben nodded and turned his head away from the devastating scene, shaking off his outrage. No use trying to give him that proper burial. The women would probably sniff the guy out anyway no matter where he stashed the remains. And the last thing he wanted was a handful of female virgins coming after him. He already had his hands full keeping Jacey properly satisfied.

He couldn't help but smile at that thought.

"Are you coming, Ben Hero?"

He looked up to find Jacey had already traveled twenty feet.

"Right behind you," he called.

She nodded and began trotting. His eyes darted once again to the seductive swaying of her full hips and to the cute crack in her ass.

Ben's grin widened as he found himself growing hard for her yet again. When they reached that cabin in the woods, he was going to have a few surprises in store for her. Surprises that would hopefully seal the fate of their future sex life as well as bind their emotional relationship.

Chapter Seven

෩

"What is this place?" Ben asked as he surveyed the rustic looking log cabin nestled in the dense forest.

"This is the male slave training place I told you about. We have several of them." Jacey replied.

"Are you sure it's not in use?"

"Currently there are no males to train for our hub." She took a step toward the building. "This is where Annie took the talking male when I granted her our ceremony presents."

Ben scrunched up his face in puzzlement. "Dare I ask what type of ceremony?"

"When a Queen picks her mates there is a ceremony. The mate is given clit rings and nipple rings to signify her commitment to the Queen. She's granted presents by the Queen. Annie wanted to dissolve her old life by spending some time fucking a male. I saw no reason not to grant her request, as it would have been her last time with a male. So he was brought here to be with her."

Ben nodded with understanding and Jacey smiled.

"There is so much you don't know about our world, Ben Hero. So much I could teach you. Unfortunately there isn't time. Tonight we'll sleep here and tomorrow we will head toward Freedom Sea." And then they would part, she added sadly to herself.

She started up the steps, blinking back the sharp tears of regret.

"Come inside. It's best we aren't out in view in case the drones are looking for us."

"Please don't remind me. Although if I had the choice I'd much prefer getting zapped by a drone to getting cut up into tiny pieces by a bunch of blond virgins."

"You best not joke about such a serious matter," she snapped.

An amusing tilt lifted his sensuous lips making all her anger disappear. She hated that he could diffuse her temper so easily by merely smiling at her.

"I thought you didn't care?"

"I don't." Jacey said quickly. Although she was beginning to care so much for him it just might kill her when she set him free.

"Come on, let's check out this cabin." He slid his hand into hers, his hot palm burning her flesh with desire as he lead her up the stairs and into the rustic cabin.

* * * * *

The sun had just dipped below the tree line, casting an eerie blue tinge across the back veranda of the cabin. Ben sat on the top of the stairs where he watched wide-eyed and horny as hell while Jacey washed herself right in front of him.

She stood only inches away. Her bare cunt was just about level with his mouth. All he had to do was lean over and flick his tongue out to get him a taste of her clit and the fine juices concealed within her. But he didn't do what he wanted.

He remained still, sucking in her every seductive move as she ran a bar of sweet-smelling soap along the smooth velvety contours of her wet flesh, preparing herself for their night together. She followed it up by pouring water on her body from a tin cup she used to dip into the water bucket he'd hauled up from a nearby river and placed on a chair, making it easier for her to get at.

Streams of soapy water dribbled down the valley of her tanned breasts and over her dusty rose nipples, caressing her silky belly, disappearing between her legs, eventually dripping down onto her luscious looking toes, to disappear in the cracks of the wood-planked veranda.

She reached for the facecloth at the back of the chair and with the tin cup poured water onto the cloth. Her gold nipple rings glittered and her large breasts jiggled while she scrubbed her face.

The sight did wonders for his hard-on, setting his teeth on edge and a tight ache swelling his shaft.

After washing her face, she sifted her fingers through the wet strands of her silky brown hair, loosening them into a sexy wave of ringlets.

The gesture sent another endless current of desire sweeping over him urging him to reach out and curl her soft tresses around his fingers. Kiss the lovely curves of her neck and feel the heaviness of her damp breasts in his hands. But he held himself in check.

He couldn't go jumping her every time she turned him on. He had to control himself.

Although he knew the woman was going to kill him eventually if he didn't get her out of his system and fuck her soon, waiting would only add to the pleasure.

Setting aside the idea of pleasure, Ben frowned. She was unusually quiet tonight. Something was bothering her and she was doing a pretty good job in keeping her spirits up, trying to keep him from suspecting anything was wrong.

He needed to get some conversation flowing. Had to break down her barriers. Most of all he needed a distraction from the intense longing ripping his shaft apart.

"So, tell me a little about the history of your town…or hub. How is it the males are slaves and the females are in charge?"

The question visibly shook her and he realized he'd hit on a touchy subject.

"I don't want to talk about such things." The cool tone in her voice made Ben bristle with curiosity.

"You mentioned the other day that you know we're from Earth. Yet you never said exactly what you know about Earth."

"I know it's another planet, far away from here, on the other side of a wormhole in space."

She poured another cup of water over the seductive length of her neck and Ben watched, helplessly turned on, as the liquid spilled over her silky skin like curious little fingers. Thankfully the red dots from the acid rain were barely visible on her flesh that was now covered by an exotic looking dark tan she'd acquired as they'd walked through the stifling heat of The Acid Zone.

He didn't know why they both hadn't been burned to a crisp. They'd been out in the sun long enough. Perhaps this sun's rays weren't as strong as Earth's? Or maybe he'd wake up tomorrow morning sore as heck and red as a lobster. All the more reason to make tonight last as long as he could.

Jacey inhaled deeply and her heavy breasts jiggled sensuously. But it was the pretty puzzled frown burrowed between her eyebrows that got most of his attention.

"What's wrong?"

She shrugged her shoulders casually and placed the cloth over the porch chair.

"I was curious. What will you do when you reach Freedom Sea? Go back to where you came from? Or will you stay here for awhile?"

"I don't know. I'll have to talk to my brothers, see what they say. Personally I'm all for a quick exit before the cannibals get us."

It was meant as a joke, but apparently Jacey didn't think it was funny. Her frown deepened. She dropped the tin cup she'd been using into the now-empty wood bucket. He grimaced at the loud clunk, hoping no one was around to hear the noise.

"I don't know if you or your brothers will be able to leave here, Ben Hero."

"Why not?"

She sat down beside him and drew her long silky legs up close to her body, hiding her cunt and breasts from his appreciative view. She hugged her knees and looked at him. Sadness and worry marred her green eyes.

"I don't even know how you were able to land on this planet in the first place. The High Five use sophisticated equipment to search the skies for any type of space craft."

"They've got radar?"

"They harvest the energy for the machines from the core of this planet. There is an endless supply of heat down there. The High Five say we will never lack for energy. Nonetheless, every once in a while the machines break down. I believe they must have been under maintenance when your spacecraft came and that is why you weren't disintegrated. Only two years ago they found and destroyed a craft that was circling our orbit."

A tinge of uneasiness zipped along Ben's nerves, damping his arousal.

"NASA's space probe. That explains what happened to it. Before we lost contact, it sent back pictures of your planet. That's why we came. To explore the terrain, seek out life and see if there is a possibility that diplomatic relations between our planets can be established."

"I don't see any of that happening, Ben Hero. The High Five and the Queens want to protect our way of life. We cannot afford to be dominated by males as our ancestors once were."

And so the question about Paradise's history reared its ugly head yet again. Curiosity urged Ben to re-ask the question, but in a different way.

"What happened to your ancestors?"

"I shouldn't discuss these things with you, but I will. And only because I know you are too curious for your own good. You must promise you'll tell no one of this. Not even your brothers."

"I don't like keeping secrets from them, Jacey."

"It's better that way."

Ben weighed the consequences of not telling his brothers everything he'd learned about the planet. Protocol dictated he share everything he knew. It was in the best interest of the crew and NASA. But damned if he was going to tell NASA about fucking Jacey. Some things a gentleman never divulged about his lady.

"Okay, I won't say anything, unless I feel that keeping the secret will harm them physically."

"I see you are very close to your brothers. Very protective and caring. They are good traits," she said softly.

"I have many other good traits, don't you think?" He leaned over and with his tongue licked a ticklish streak up the length of her damp neck making her giggle.

"Now that we've lightened up the mood, tell me about what you know. Why are the females the dominant gender here?"

She met his gaze head on. "If you must know, Ben Hero, I will tell you a little. During Queen Training we learned our history. One course is called the Forbidden Pictures course."

"Forbidden pictures?"

"Moving pictures."

"Movies? They weren't by any chance in black and white where they?"

"No, in color. Why?"

"Just curious." He didn't think she would understand the classical Laurel and Hardy and other ancient movies he'd seen back on Earth.

"There were many different moving pictures." Jacey continued. "I remember one of them showed naked women, their backs marked with scars from whippings, wearing thick collars of metal as clothed men led them around like slaves. Another I remember is five men fucking one woman who was crying hysterically. Afterwards, they all urinated on her. Then they tied her to a tree and began to torture her with a knife, cutting off her nipples, then her breasts, her labia lips…"

"Okay, I get the picture." Disgust made Ben clench his fists.

"There were so many of these moving pictures. All depicted the severe violence women suffered at the hands of males. By the time the course was complete, I didn't want anything to do with males."

"And yet you went out looking for my brother the night he escaped?"

"Lust overcame me," she said softly. "Besides, I saw how well he treated Annie. How happy she was. How protective she became of him in such a short time. I realized the Earth males are not the same as the males here."

Ben didn't have the heart to tell her that Earth did possess cruel people who did exactly the same things to women as she'd described and that every year the violence against women got worse.

"It became so bad for the women," she continued, "that they couldn't even go outside their homes without getting fucked by a male. Every year the males became more aggressive. The women were forced to stay indoors or out of sight. They became depressed, sick and weak. It grew worse. Males dictated every move of the females. Finally in a weak, twisted effort to protect the women, laws were formed forbidding women to show their bodies. They were forced to wear heavy cloths concealing their sex and thick veils to hide their faces when they ventured outdoors. The defiant ones, the women who tried to liberate the females, were raped and killed.

"One day, the Goddess of Freedom came. No one knows for sure where she came from but it is said she was a saviour who came from the skies and she was so beautiful no man dared touch her. She wore a crown of stone jewels and a beautiful silk robe. She carried a torch of fire and she gathered supporters for her cause to liberate women. She quickly led a revolution against the males. The battles were fierce and bloody. The males fought hard but the females were desperate. The males were either killed or imprisoned. The young males, as young as only a few months old, were taken from their mothers and institutionalized, cared for and trained by the females who had been the most brutalized by men. For many years mating with males was outlawed. During this time the Goddess of Freedom and her followers worked on plans to ensure the safe future for all women. What you see now is the result."

Ben sighed heavily at the story. "The Goddess of Freedom must have been one tough broad to take on such a tough task. But you mentioned you go to the Freedom Sea to visit her. How can she still be alive?"

"She's dead. We visit her shrine."

Of course, why hadn't he thought of that? Earthlings did the same thing. Erected shrines, and statues of their heroes or heroines.

Jacey unclasped her hands from her knees and smiled. "Let's not talk about this anymore, Ben Hero. I want tonight to be special for us. Come, I want to show you something."

She slid her warm hand into his and they got up.

"Let's go back inside."

She led him into the cabin where it was now almost dark. Lighting a few candles, she set them on the table. Taking one of the candles, she led him to a nearby door he hadn't noticed earlier when they'd first arrived.

"Tonight, we will do whatever our hearts and bodies want us to do."

She nodded to the door. "Open it."

"What's in there?"

"Have yourself a look."

The amused grin plastered on her face piqued his curiosity. Ben opened the door and sucked in one hell of a surprised breath.

It was a closet.

Full of every sex toy imaginable.

Arousal coursed through him as he surveyed the arrangement of whips, feathers, pussy pumps, various sizes of dildos, two-headed dildos, hand and leg cuffs, butt plugs, ball gags, penis weights, and much more.

"Oh, of course. The male slave training cabin." He grinned.

Warmth spilled against his bare back as she leaned closer.

"Or the female sex slave training cabin?"

"I hadn't thought of that angle," he teased.

"You hadn't? Women love sex too you know."

"Well that explains it."

"Explains what?"

"Why you want to fuck me all the time."

"I do not!"

"The bright red blush on your face is a dead giveaway. And..." He slipped a hand between her legs. She wiggled sexily as his finger dipped an inch into her hot, tight hole. "You're cunt is always wet and ready for me. Besides, it's a well-known fact. Once a woman makes love with a man, she's hooked on sex. Can't do without it. Wants it all the time."

The puzzled look on her face deepened. She was buying into it. Hook. Line. And sinker.

Reluctantly he slid his finger from her moist warmth and surveyed the contents of the closet.

"They also say a few hot sex sessions a day keep the doctor away."

"Why the doctor?" Her hard nipples scraped the muscles of his back, sparking something hot in his cock.

"Because sex is exercise. Keeps your body limber. And when you have it often enough and with someone you care about your mind is happy and your soul is set free. In short, you live longer."

"Women here live to a certain age."

A frisson of fear cleaved into Ben's spine. He'd never even thought that the biology of women on Paradise was different than Earth women.

"How old?"

"Until menopause."

"And then you just die?"

"We outgrow our usefulness of bearing babies. We are killed."

The shock of her casual answer nearly blew him away and he knew she was telling him the truth. Damn, but the people on this planet sure did hold warped traditions.

"As I said, Ben Hero, there are many aspects to my world you don't know."

"I guess I'm going to have to make it a priority of sticking around long enough to learn your culture."

"Would you even consider staying forever?" she asked shyly.

Ahh. This must be the question that was haunting her. The reason she'd been unusually quiet today. She'd hinted at it earlier, asking what would happen once he reached Freedom Sea. He should have sensed she was being serious. Instead, he'd teased her about leaving as soon as possible so they wouldn't get eaten by the cannibals.

"I have to return to my world sooner or later, Jacey. If we don't go home, they'll come looking for us. And there won't be just one spaceship, they'll come by the dozens."

"It would be unsafe for them to come here, Ben Hero."

"Because of the disintegration machines."

She nodded.

Silence was a barrier between them and Ben closed the closet door. The sex toys would have to wait just a little while longer. There was something important that he needed to attend to—reassuring Jacey she was his number one priority. And he would start by showing her one of Earth's most ancient and romantic traditions. Music.

Chapter Eight

Jacey couldn't believe her ears when she heard Ben Hero start to hum a slow sensual melody. His eyes were bright blue, his lips pursued together with determined effort.

"What are you doing?" she giggled.

No male had ever hummed to her. But then again no male had ever fucked her before.

He stopped humming and flicked a stray strand of hair off his forehead. It was a sexy gesture that made heat shoot through her bloodstream.

"I don't just hum for anyone, Jacey." He said rather seriously as he extended his hand toward her, "Your hand, my lady."

"What are you up to?"

He didn't answer. Instead, he started humming again. The sultry sound from deep in his chest was pleasing to her ears and Jacey couldn't resist doing as he asked.

His hand was warm and calloused and so large compared to hers as she slid her fingers against his palm.

"Put one hand right here," he whispered as he guided her until her fingers curled over his thick muscled shoulder.

"The other hand goes here," he said and placed her other hand on the small of his solid back.

Heat poured off his naked body and sunk seductively into her flesh. She could smell the soap he'd used to wash himself earlier when he'd gone down to the river to fetch water for her and bathed.

The scent intermingled with his unique masculine scent and Jacey's senses began to race.

His large hands settled on the curves of her hips, branding her flesh.

But he didn't pull her any closer, leaving a scorching few inches between their bodies.

"I'll lead. You just follow your feet with where I place mine," he directed in a husky voice.

She looked down and watched his feet move back and forth. She found him hard to follow because her gaze kept straying to his thick erection and his swaying testicles.

He moved his feet slowly until she caught the rhythm that coincided with his humming.

"You're a quick learner," he said.

He moved a little closer and Jacey's pulse hammered as his chest touched the edge of her nipples.

The brushing of his hard muscles against her tips shot sparks of pleasure through her breasts. Her nipples immediately hardened in arousal and her breasts swelled with anticipation.

She loved the sensual way their bodies moved so closely together. She could feel his thumbs drawing small circles on her hips, setting her flesh on fire where he touched.

The musical sound of his deep voice sifted through her senses and she found herself leaning her head on his shoulder, drifting in a sea of sensual bliss.

"What is this called?" she found herself asking.

"Slow dancing. But we usually dance to music."

"We have music. Drums, horns from seashells, some women even use reeds and make small holes in them. They blow while they press their fingers intermittently over the holes. It produces wonderful melodies.

"Sounds like a flute."

"We call them melody makers."

They continued to move around the cabin floor, every once in a while the hard bulging head of his penis rubbed erotically against her clit, encouraging Jacey's cunt to moisten with need and her insides to scream with pleasure. Finally she could take the searing sensations no more and arched against his arousal, making him inhale sharply. His erotic grip on her hips tightened and he stopped humming.

"Are you teasing me, my Queen?"

"No more than what you're teasing me." She giggled and looked down at her rock hard nipples.

His full lips parted as he stared at her breasts. For a moment she thought his head would lower and he would suckle her. The anticipation of him doing such a wondrous thing made her blood boil to a fever pitch.

To her disappointment, he didn't take her nipples into his mouth. To her delight though, his parted lips touched her own, sparking a firestorm of desire through her mouth.

Her tongue slid between his parted lips and she slipped into his delicious cavern, fiercely exploring the warm, seductive contours.

He groaned from somewhere deep in his chest. It was an untamed sound and it sent shivers of excitement ripping through her senses.

He pressed his body closer to hers, his hands now intimately cupping her hot ass cheeks. His hips swayed slightly. His huge erection, trapped like a wild animal between their bodies, throbbed against the opening of her vagina.

Jacey's hands drifted off his wide shoulders and slid up along the corded length of his powerful neck, curling around the back of his head, cradling him there.

His silky, damp hair sifted like feathers through her hungry fingers as she pressed his head closer in an effort to deepen the kiss. His lips felt like rough velvet as he devoured her.

One of his hands slid away from her ass cheek and trailed a brand of pleasure over her hip. Somehow he managed to slip his hand between their tightly fused bodies and a finger pulled gently against one of her clit rings to this side of pain. A calloused thumb parted her nether lips, scraping erotically against her pleasure nub, making her whimper as spirals of fire coursed deep into her woman's core.

The sound of her voice seemed to harden his erection, as it throbbed against her flesh.

The urge was so great to feel his thick arousal deep inside her body that she could actually feel her vaginal muscles contracting in response. Suddenly he was pushing her backward until her ass hit the wooden edge of the table.

He tore his hot mouth from hers.

"On the table," he breathed against her neck.

Without waiting for her to do as he instructed, his hands cupped her ass checks and he hoisted her easily onto where he wanted her. Automatically Jacey lifted her legs until her feet were secure on the tabletop and then widened her legs fully expecting him to plunge into her without hesitation.

To her surprise he crouched down on his knees in front of her and peered at her clit. Hunger seared his dark blue eyes. It was a ravenous look that almost made her climax on the spot.

"You are so beautiful," he said as a hand slid up her inner thigh like a lightning bolt.

She found she couldn't breathe as his finger parted her labia petals and he stared at her sex, wonder and worry shining in his eyes.

"Your clit rings, did they hurt when you got them?"

Jacey shivered as a slice of memory ripped through her. Her legs had been spread wide, much as she was sitting now. The female doctor had worked quickly, piercing her skin efficiently. But Jacey had felt the pain tearing her apart. Had almost cried out from it. However she was a Queen. She was supposed to be tougher than the rest of the women of her hub. No numbing agent had been given, and she'd refused to humiliate herself by shedding tears as the whole hub watched the procedure.

She'd made her people proud as she'd received the clit rings and then the nipple rings without so much as a whimper.

"There was pain," she admitted. "But it faded with a Quick Healing Injection which promotes healing and helps prevent infection. And you? What about your jewelry? Did it hurt when The Breeders inserted them?"

"I had them done long before I came here and yes it hurt. Very much so, but in the long run it was worth it, don't you think?"

"Yes. Very much worth it."

His thick finger explored her clit with seductive caresses, outlining her labia lips, rubbing her pleasure nub, creating sizzling pleasure wherever he touched. Without warning the finger slid into her vagina. She bit her bottom lip as her cunt muscles spasmed, clasping his thick finger, trying to draw him in deeper.

Her hands flew to her swollen breasts and she began massaging her plump nipples in an effort to create friction.

A moment later, he inserted another hot finger into her. Need enveloped Jacey. It spread through her body like a wildfire. When he slid a third finger inside her and started to plunge with deliciously slow, torturous thrusts, Jacey closed her eyes as the strong convulsions exploded through her body.

Panting wildly, her body flushed with heat, she sat paralyzed on the table and welcomed his seductive assault as he finger fucked her into ecstasy. Sharp, painfully pleasant sensations ripped her body apart. Shredded her mind. Made her oblivious to everything except what he was doing to her. Orgasm after orgasm slammed into her as his slick fingers slurped in and out until she thought she could bear it no longer. Until she thought she would go mad from pleasure.

She didn't even remember him removing his fingers but suddenly his powerful hands grabbed her hips, holding her still. She opened her eyes to find him standing between her widespread legs, the thick head of his penis bulging and purple, hovering a mere inch from her wet cunt.

He was ready, so ready that his cock trembled with anticipation.

The delicious sight made the fire within burn with renewed frenzy. Automatically she tipped her hips upward, encouraging him to take her.

And he did.

She gasped as his cock drove into her. Her vaginal muscles stretched wildly to accommodate his hot flesh. He slid in easily enough, her slick interior welcoming him, her cunt muscles wrapping tightly around his pulsing thickness.

He closed his eyes and groaned like a wild animal. His breathing grew harsh as he began to rock against her, his thrusts hard and furious, compared to the slow torturous movements of his earlier finger fucking.

Sheer pleasure speared through her fevered cunt as he slammed into her, his balls slapping against her flesh.

His hands flew to her breasts, cupping her. His fingers pulled at her rings and plumped her nipples until they were again two aching beads of desire.

She moaned as hot sensations zipped through her flesh and headed straight into her vagina where he continued to ram into her. Her mind splintered. Her body tightened as violent tremors tore her body apart.

Suddenly his hips jerked, his body tensed and he came violently. His hot cream flooded her womb like an unleashed firestorm, splashing out of her and down her thighs.

Finally he softened inside her and Jacey leaned back on the table, panting erratically, quite ready to collapse from exhaustion.

He withdrew his limp cock and tenderly swept her into his strong embrace. A moment later the warmth of the soft mattress nested against her back. The bed dipped as he lay down beside her, his hot body spooned against her right side.

Nuzzling her head against his damp shoulder, she drifted off into a beautiful dream world where she found herself dancing with a magnificent blue-eyed male sex slave, a perfect mate.

* * * * *

Ben awoke to the soft sound of the back door closing. The candles on the table flickering wildly. When he noticed Jacey lying fast asleep beside him, he bolted into an upright position, his heart hammering like a rabid woodpecker against his chest.

"Damn," he muttered under his breath.

They'd been found!

Quickly he jostled Jacey's shoulder, urging her to wake up.

Her eyes fluttered open and she smiled sleepily at him. She must have seen the fear on his face because a split second later she tensed with alarm.

"What's wrong?"

"Someone just left."

"What?" She lifted herself to an elbow and peered around the shadowy room, her narrowed eyes searched every nook and cranny.

Ben leaped out of bed, grabbed her hand and tugged on her to get up.

She didn't budge.

"C'mon, we've got to leave."

To his utter surprise, she yanked at him. Pulled so hard that he came crashing down right on top of her sweet softness.

"What the hell are you doing? We have to get out of here," he gasped.

She didn't budge. "Look on the counter. Someone left us a gift."

Ben's gaze swung to the area where she indicated. He blinked at the reed basket overflowing with fruits.

"Someone left us food?" Ben asked as he surveyed the rest of the room to see if any other unexpected presents were left behind.

"It was Virgin," Jacey said softly. She stretched like a lazy, calm cat and acted as if nothing out of the ordinary had just happened.

"Virgin?"

"She was following us all day yesterday."

"What? Why the hell didn't you tell me we were being followed?"

"You didn't ask."

Ben frowned, totally puzzled. "You don't seem concerned. I gather she's not a threat. Who is she?"

"She's a Yellow Hair."

Uneasiness cleaved into his spine. "One of those cannibal women?"

"That's right," she said calmly.

Jacey left the bed and headed for the food basket. Ben followed on her heels.

She reached for a fruit and his hand clamped around her wrist, stopping her cold.

"Don't eat that!" he commanded.

She gave him a startled glance. "Why not? I'm hungry."

"She's trying to fatten us up."

"She's not trying to fatten us up." She giggled.

"She's a cannibal! She eats people! Leave the food and let's get the hell out of here before she decides we *are* dinner." He headed for the door fully expecting her to follow him. She didn't.

"She won't hurt us." Jacey said softly.

"How the hell do you know?" he snapped, suddenly irritated that she would risk her life by hanging around with danger lurking nearby. He sure as heck didn't want them ending up like that poor bastard the blonde virgin cannibals had cut up in The Acid Zone.

"Because I'm the one who helped her escape from prison."

Ben couldn't help but blink with shock.

"Prison? She's an escaped convict?" He shook his head with disbelief. "Great! I'm sure she has a posse on her ass too. All the more reason for us to split right now."

That teasing smile slipped along her lips again and he got the feeling she knew some sort of sweet secret. He'd find out soon enough what it was, but not right now. It was adios time.

He was about to grab Jacey and force her to follow him, even if he had to do it kicking and screaming, when he stopped, realization dawning on him.

"Wait a minute. What are you doing letting a cannibal convict out of prison?"

"May I eat something while I explain? I really am famished."

"Are you sure the food is safe?" Uncertainty ripped at his guts at the idea Jacey might be poisoned.

"Please trust me, Ben Hero and let me eat. I'm hungry."

"Let me taste it first, just to be sure."

Before he could grab the fruit, a wet snapping sound of her biting into the juicy apple made him curse.

"See?" She held up the apple and cocked her head prettily. "Nothing is happening to me. Please, relax and trust me. Everything is fine."

Ben nodded. Relief shot through his system at the confidence oozing from her voice. He should trust her. She'd been living here on this planet a heck of a lot longer than he had.

He walked over to a nearby window, cupped his hands to the glass and peered into the darkness.

Nothing moved except a generous scattering of lightning bugs.

"She's not out there, Ben Hero."

"Are you sure?"

"I'm sure. Most likely she's busy right now rustling up a male or two for dinner."

Ben's head snapped around just in time to catch a cute teasing smile zip along her luscious lips. He resisted the urge to go over and nibble on her mouth.

"Have a banana." She held out a healthy enough looking fruit to him.

"I'm not hungry."

"You have to eat something nutritious. Something to keep up your strength."

"I'm strong enough, thanks."

"You certainly are." She winked.

Ben shook his head and grinned knowingly. He focused his attention out the window again checking for any signs of lurking cannibals.

"She really is gone, Ben Hero. Like I said, she's returning the favor."

He watched her reflection in the window as she picked up another apple and a pear and sat down.

"So? What's this Virgin's story anyway? Why was she in prison?" he asked.

"She's the one who was directly responsible for the Slave Uprising."

"Slave Uprising?"

"She was the Queen of the Yellow Hairs," she explained and took another juicy bite of her apple.

Ben threw his hands up in the air in utter exasperation.

"Great! Just great! The Queen of the Cannibals is a friend of my woman."

"Do you want to hear the story or not? And I'm not your woman," she mumbled as she munched.

He let the comment slide. She was his woman whether she admitted it or not. And by the end of this night, if he did everything according to plan, she'd be screaming out that fact.

"Please, do continue. I'm all ears. At least, for now."

Jacey rolled her eyes at his attempt at humor and took another bite of the apple.

"This is good. You sure you don't want any?"

Ben shook his head. He kept vigil at the window, still nervous that a cannibal convict woman had actually been inside the cabin with them.

"Come away from the window and I'll tell you Virgin's story."

"You sure we're safe here?"

"Ben Hero, I am a Queen. I know when someone is following me." She frowned. "Well, except for when The Breeders jumped me the other day. I still don't understand how it could have happened. I was so careful. If I didn't know any better I'd say they knew I was coming down that particular trail. Come, sit and I'll tell you about Virgin." She patted the chair beside her and he reluctantly joined her.

"Virgin and I attended Queen Training at the same time," she began. "We became close friends, despite being from different hubs and our different reasons for being at the school."

"And what were these different reasons?" Ben asked, his gaze sneaking a quick peek toward the back window again.

"I was there because my hub elected me to be their next Queen. I didn't want to let them down, so I went."

"Despite you not wanting to be a Queen?"

"Oh! I wanted to be one. I just didn't want to be limited to life without experiencing a male or two."

"And now that you have experienced a male…what do you think?"

A pretty pink blush flashed across her cheeks. "That is a very personal question, Ben Hero. I thought you wanted me to continue with the Slave Uprising story?"

Ben chuckled. "You're cute when you blush."

She didn't answer but he didn't miss the tiniest smile touch her lips at his compliment.

"Go ahead with the story," Ben prompted.

She took another bite of the apple before continuing; "Virgin was attaining Queen status in order to gain access to The Order of The High Five. If she succeeded she would be the first Yellow Hair to ever make it that high."

"Ah yes, the infamous top five Queens. Did she make it into the High Five?"

"Yes, but she didn't last long."

Ben leaned forward, curiosity nipping at his insides. "What happened? How'd she end up in prison?"

"Before a Queen can be inducted into the High Five, she must first rule a hub for at least five years. Virgin accomplished that goal. When an opening became available with the High Five, she applied for the position. She was well liked in her own hub and the favored to win from all the other applicants. She won the position easily. She was a High Five for only a few months when the Slave Uprising occurred."

"You mentioned earlier she was responsible for it? How so?" Ben asked.

"She illegally educated a slave on how to communicate. He in turn educated some other male sex slaves. The males realized life could be different for them. They decided they didn't want to be dominated anymore. They wanted to do the dominating. The slaves revolted. They conquered the brothel town and took all the visiting women hostage. They forced themselves on the females, impregnating them."

"How long did this Slave Uprising last?"

"It was over within three days. The males wanted to negotiate a deal. If they couldn't be freed, they wanted to get paid to be sex slaves. They wanted better working conditions. But the High Five ordered the army into the town. Most of the males were slaughtered. The rest escaped. And so now we have a shortage of males."

Ben swore softly at the thought of such upheaval surrounding Jacey.

"What happened to the pregnant women?"

"They had their babies. The children are now in the hands of the Nurturers. The female babies will be turned over to the Educators and the males will be trained to do manual labor and trained as sex slaves. We still have to wait many years before the new males are old enough to do their duties. In the meantime, we've had to rely on The Breeders to supply us with trained sex slaves and pay their disgustingly high prices. Which is why we have no males because I've refused to do business with them, until their prices come down to a reasonable level. When we received the well-endowed male, The Breeders made a substantial offer for him. I refused them, thinking we could train the male ourselves."

"But then he escaped."

"Much to the disappointment of the women."

Ben chuckled.

"So, how did you know this Virgin woman was the one responsible for the Uprising?"

"Because she was the one the slaves asked to negotiate their terms. They trusted her. Finally, she admitted she trained one of the slaves who came to work in the fields near her hub sometimes when the brothels were slow. She trained him on the days she was in charge of overseeing the workers. Said she was working on a theory."

"The theory being?"

"That males, when properly educated, can be beneficial to our society."

How interesting. "And so in admitting what she'd done, she got sentenced to prison."

"She got sentenced to a lifetime of babies. No release. Ever."

"And you let her go?"

"I broke her out with the help of a High Five member."

"Why? Why'd you let her go?"

"Because she didn't mean any harm by educating the slave. Besides, High Five Queens are supposed to be allowed to pursue theories. Unfortunately she didn't seek permission and applied her theory in secret."

"But why did you free her after a year?"

The cute pink blush whipped across her cheeks again and she took another bite of the apple. "Because I spoke with your half-brother. He appeared to be highly educated, relatively harmless and..." Jacey hesitated.

"And?" Ben prompted.

"I saw what was going on between Annie and him."

"What did you see?"

"They seemed very happy together. Protected each other from harm. And I watched them...have sex...in forbidden positions."

"Really?" Ben leaned closer. "What kind of forbidden positions?"

"Any dominant or equal position for the male is totally forbidden. She must always be on top, in control. Anyway, they did it standing, like we did. He took her from behind while she was on all fours. Another time he fucked her when she was on her back and he hoisted her legs up onto his shoulders."

"Didn't know my brother could be so creative. And you so nosy." Ben grinned and lightly flicked the tip of her cute nose with his finger.

Her blush deepened.

"I wasn't nosy...just curious."

"Curious enough to try some more of those positions? Or better yet, something totally different? Something dark and delicious?"

Jacey's breath hitched at his question and Ben knew what he would do next.

Chapter Nine

ஐ

"A blindfold?" Jacey whispered a few minutes later when he tied the soft cloth around her eyes.

"It'll make our evening more interesting."

She could see nothing through the velvety material, but she could hear his breath, shallow and quick as he moved around nearby. A long minute escaped and when she didn't hear anything more, her curiosity rose to new heights.

"Ben Hero, where are you?" she giggled.

"Right here." He tenderly brushed his lips across her cheek and the feathery touch made her shiver with want. "But before we start I want to let you know if there's anything you don't like that I'm doing to you, I want you to use a safe word to tell me to stop."

"I'm sure I'll love everything you do to me," Jacey confessed, suddenly eager and curious as to what he wanted to do to her.

"I'm glad to hear you trust me, but I want you to promise to use the safe word to stop me."

"What's the safe word?"

"I love you." The whispered words drifted softly into her ears. Strangely enough, this time the word love brought a rush of wonderful emotions shooting through her. Now that Ben Hero had explained how he perceived the word, it gave her a new perspective on love.

"Do you feel comfortable with those words?"

"Yes. Although like I said, I doubt I'll need it."

"Come with me then." His fingers intertwined with hers and he led her somewhere to the right.

"I want you to lie belly down on the chair. It's cushioned nicely for you."

She hesitated. Belly down on the chair? How interesting.

"Don't be frightened, my fair Queen. I'll make sure you don't fall. Trust me."

Was he kidding? She'd trusted him with her life for the last couple of days.

One hand snuggled seductively against her lower belly and the other curled around her elbow. Gently he guided her body forward until something soft touched her belly.

A pillow?

He moved her forward until her breasts hung free in the air and her ass was bared to him.

"This will take just a couple of minutes and then the fun can begin."

Fun can begin? As far as she was concerned the fun had already started.

She trembled with delight as his hot hands slid against her inner thighs, spreading her legs, sending lightning shards of heat zipping into flesh wherever he touched.

"Ben Hero, what are you up to?"

"Now that would be telling," he chuckled.

Jacey gasped as his moist finger trailed along the cleft of her ass and suddenly dipped inside. Her muscles automatically clenched around the invasion.

"Ah nice and tight. Like a virgin. But not for long."

Her stomach hollowed out in a fantastic explosion at his words.

She tried hard not to wiggle as the finger tucked in her ass did wonderful things to the insides of her anus. He dipped the finger out and a moment later two lubricated fingers sunk in, a little deeper this time and she couldn't help but squirm at the funny fullness.

"Almost ready," he soothed.

He worked her hole gently, coaxing her to relax.

"This might be uncomfortable for a bit, but I've lubricated it very well with strawberry juice."

It? What was it?

His fingers slid out of her, quickly replaced by something cool and smooth.

A butt plug!

Oh Goddess of Freedom!

"Just relax your muscles, Jacey. It'll go easier."

She nodded and did as he instructed. Her heart hammered wildly as the plug slid deeper inside at a lazy pace. She bit back a moan as the item invaded her, sparking a new type of sexual thrill. Having a butt plug shoved into her ass was something she'd never experienced in her life and yet she'd always wondered how it would feel.

And now it was actually happening!

Another forbidden fantasy brought to life by a male.

Her insides quivered at the incredible fullness as the device continued on its mission. The pleasure was now close to torturous and she gasped at the brutal sensations and the mounting pressure.

Suddenly her anal ring popped around the butt plug and she sighed with a bit of relief.

"How's that?" he asked softly.

"Feels…interesting."

"Good, now let's get you up again." He helped her to her feet and led her across the room.

It felt odd walking around with a blindfold over her eyes, not to mention a butt plug firmly in place. Odd, but strangely arousing too.

"Where are we going?"

She tilted her head downward in hopes of seeing something through the bottom of the blindfold, but she saw only darkness.

"Okay we're here."

"Where?"

"The bed, of course."

Jacey shivered with anticipation.

"Let's get you down on your back."

A moment later she was settled. The sound of his rough uneven breath split the air as he moved around nearby.

Excitement snowballed.

The butt plug buried inside her seemed larger now. Hotter. Made her feel like she wanted his thick cock driving inside her ass instead of the mechanical device.

Something warm and dry dropped on her stomach, making her bolt from her thoughts.

He chuckled, but said nothing.

A familiar flowery scent drifted into her nostrils. It smelled wonderful. More of the feathery items dropped along the length of her legs, caressed her breasts and nipples. The items brushed across her wrists, allowing her to touch the velvety softness. Instantly she recognized the texture and the smell.

"You're sprinkling me with lilacs?"

"Shhhh, I'm giving you flowers."

Jacey couldn't help but grin. The scent was intoxicating and she inhaled deeply, allowing the perfumed air to drift into her lungs.

His warm body heat washed over her abdomen area and the distinct shape of his balls slapped across her right hip.

She reached out to where she thought his silky penis might be, but a strong male hand curled around her wrist before she could accomplish her mission. He led her arm up over her head and to the side. Something soft wrapped around her wrist.

Restraints? He was tying her down?

What a deliciously dangerous idea. He wanted to relive their first time together.

A strange dark thrill poured through her body as he tied down her other hand and then spread-eagled and bound her ankles.

"I noticed how aroused you were the first time I found you all tied up. But this time, it'll be a little more romantic." His voice dripped with lust, making her shiver in anticipation.

Suddenly something hot and moist dipped into her belly button.

His tongue?

The seductive poke made Jacey's stomach quiver with a strange urgency to have his tongue and mouth lapping at all parts of her body.

His velvety rough tongue circled around the edges, then dipped into her belly button again making her shiver with a delicious need.

A moment later, his lips trailed tiny feather touches over her stomach and circled around the bottom curves of her breasts. The hot caresses stopped and Jacey sighed in disappointment. But the disappointment didn't last long.

The mattress between her legs dipped.

His hot breath raked across her clit and Jacey couldn't help shivering with anticipation. She bolted against her restraints as the tip of his hot tongue spread her labia lips apart, sucking them right into his burning mouth.

She moaned at his intimate gesture. At the same time his tongue slid possessively over her swollen pleasure nub. Using skillful strokes he slowly licked and sensually lapped at her tender flesh. Alternately, with his sharp teeth he nipped gently on her labia lips, until a fiery tension built between her legs, the tension turning quickly into a burning need to be fucked.

"Sweet goddess, what are you doing to me?" She hissed between gritted teeth.

His mouth and tongue drew away, leaving her feeling abandoned.

"You like?" he asked in a hoarse voice.

"It's unbelievably beautiful."

The bed dipped and he moved away.

"Don't leave!" she gasped.

"Shh, I'll be right back."

She heard the creak of the nearby closet door opening and her heart hammered with conflicting emotions.

Was he going to use more of those sex toys on her?

It was forbidden!

She was a Queen. The only item she'd been allowed to use in the past was a double-ended dildo, with another woman, for sexual satisfaction.

But her momentary uneasiness quickly washed away.

All the wonderful things she'd done with Ben Hero were against the laws. Whatever else he introduced, she wouldn't be in anymore trouble than she already was, so she may as well enjoy whatever he had planned for her.

She was surprised when a moment later something firm and cool pressed against her lips. The delectable scent of strawberries drifted by and her mouth automatically watered.

"You hungry?" he whispered.

"I'm always hungry...for you," she teased.

She opened her mouth and accepted the succulent fruit. Sweetness exploded against her taste buds. A moment later, another strawberry pressed against her lips and she accepted it greedily.

As she chewed on the delicacy, Jacey couldn't help but notice something else.

Another odor.

The unmistakable scent of male.

Instinctively she parted her lips and the thick mushroom-shaped head of his penis slid into her mouth.

Her heart crashed against her ribs and her taste buds exploded as the hard hot flesh laden with metal jewelry, liberally drenched in squished strawberries, throbbed violently between her lips.

A strawberry-covered penis!

How could anything be more delicious?

"I hope you don't mind, but seeing your luscious lips devouring those strawberries has given me one hell of a hard-on," his hoarse whisper was edged with uncertainty.

She wanted to push away his doubts. Ached to tell him she didn't mind at all. That having a male's penis in her mouth was another one of her dark forbidden fantasies, but her mouth was otherwise occupied.

She wanted more of him and eagerly sucked at his silky, thick erection, letting him know her intentions.

Ben growled roughly at her gesture. Slowly he pushed his cock deeper into her mouth.

Her tongue swirled against his hot bulging head. Lust cascaded through her senses, as she tasted a sliver of spicy salt mixed with the sweetness of strawberry.

What a fantastic combination!

Her lips stretched wider as his erection slid deeper into her mouth. Using her tongue she caressed the underneath skin and delighted in the sounds of his growls.

"I'm so damned hot for you, Jacey, I'm going to come in your mouth. Is that what you want?" he hissed as her lips teasingly tightened and loosened over his silky length.

In answer, she tried to smile around his erection, but couldn't. He was that big.

She nodded instead.

"I don't know what I ever did to deserve such a fine woman."

His breathing grew rough as he cradled her head with his hands. He began to thrust, filling her mouth with his heated rod until he hit the back of her throat. Then he withdrew, expertly slamming back inside again. Her tongue eagerly darted around the edges of his incoming thickness.

She tasted him. Licked the throbbing silk. Stroked the powerful male muscle.

Her lips clamped down around his flesh, giving him a tight fit and she began sucking deeply at his erection. Sucking in hopes of tasting more of that arousing salty flavor of male.

His thrusting grew rougher. Her lips and tongue worked faster to keep up.

His cock jerked violently and harsh groans filled the air as his hot cream spilled down her throat. She continued to suck, devouring his male flesh and drinking his flavor until he was dry.

"Now that that's been taken care of, let's get to the business at hand, shall we?" He withdrew his still semi-erect cock from her mouth.

An instant later something flicked lightly against her left nipple.

Jacey smelled leather.

A whip?

Her body trembled with lust at the thought of Ben Hero whipping her.

The item flicked against her nipple again. This time harder, leaving a bit of delicious pain in its wake.

The next time the whip came down, a cry of pain broke from her mouth. Tears blistered her eyes behind her blindfold.

111

To her surprise a wave of sexual pleasure swamped her cunt allowing her juices to flow, wetting the insides of her thighs.

"Oh sweet goddess, fuck me now, Ben," she managed to gasp between gritted teeth.

He only laughed and she felt a light flick against her other nipple. Then another, this time hard enough to cause the blissful pain.

He continued the flicks of the whip against her nipples until they were hot and aching with desire. Then he moved to whip her breasts until she could feel the fiery sensations burning her skin.

The sweet sexual urge between her legs increased to mind-shattering proportions as the painful sweetness of the whip sliced across her flesh. Automatically her hips gyrated as she tried to bring herself to orgasm. She cried out in frustration when she couldn't satisfy herself by closing her legs, due to the restraints.

Ben gave another teasing laugh.

"Please, Ben," she begged.

"Oh, but you wouldn't want me to ruin the rest of the surprise, now would you?"

"I don't care about the surprise. Fuck me now!" She was desperate. Needed him inside her. Craved release!

Suddenly there was no noise except her aroused whimpering. The silence was deafening. The anticipation was mind-boggling.

Had he left? Had he left her alone with her breasts on fire and her cunt aching for satisfaction?

The butt plug in her anus throbbed with a strange pleasure and his cock's delicious salty residue filled her mouth.

"What are you thinking?" His voice was soft and near her right ear.

"I'm thinking about how much I want you, Ben Hero. What are you doing?"

"Watching you. Watching the way your breasts are reddening from the whipping I gave you. The way your nipples have hardened into large solid pebbles. I'm looking at the way your cunt is drenched with arousal and the way your stomach is quivering with anticipation as you wonder what I'm going to do next."

"And what are you going to do next?" she whispered.

"I'm going to fuck you, Jacey. I'm going to fuck you so hard you're going to scream for me."

His softly spoken words made the breath back up in her lungs.

"You've managed to control your orgasms to a certain extent, Jacey," he whispered. "Tonight I'm going to make you lose control and then I'm going to listen to you scream from the pleasure I create."

Her heart cracked against her chest and lust pulsed through her veins. The mattress between her legs dipped and his body heat swarmed against her flesh. She gasped with need as his iron shaft poked against the tender bundle of nerves in her clit. Her heart rate soared when his hard abdominal muscles flattened against her flesh and yet his chest didn't touch her breasts.

His mouth did!

Jacey jerked violently as his moist lips suckled her burning nipples. He devoured them as if he were enjoying a feast.

His cock entered her moist channel. A very tight channel now that a butt plug was buried inside her anal canal. His engorged rod pierced her so agonizingly slowly she wanted to scream at the brutal intensity.

His mouth continued its delicious assault on her breasts. His teeth pulled her nipple rings and alternately nipped sharply at her nipples until they literally throbbed with an insane combination of pain and arousal.

Her mind became dizzy. Her cunt spasmed violently around his thick shaft as it continued to sink leisurely into her. She whimpered at the wicked pleasure his fullness created.

Suddenly his moist lips covered hers in a perfect hot fit. His mouth slid erotically over hers in a greedy fashion. She found herself sucking wildly on the sensual curve of his lower lip.

He moaned at the assault.

It was a primal sound. An erotic noise that made her blood boil.

She struggled against her bonds. She ached to cup her hands over his hard ass cheeks and pull him closer in an effort to shove his thick arousal faster into her.

Carnal pleasure flashed along the length of her vagina as his swollen cock finally slid into her core.

He withdrew with a sucking sound and dove back into her. It was a slow savage thrust, encouraging the metal ornaments to rub erotically against her sensitive vaginal walls, awakening something wild and unbridled within her body.

Heat built. A storm of pleasure so untamed hit her that she ripped her mouth from Ben's and gasped for air.

"That's it," Ben whispered against her ear as his tongue teased the column of her neck. "Scream for me, Jacey. Scream and be mine."

Involuntarily her hips bucked savagely against his torturous plunges.

She'd enjoyed it when he'd fucked her rough, but these new tender strokes as he slid in and out of her with slow controlled thrusts left her panting for breath. Left a wonderful pressure building in the nerves around her butt plug. Left her body fevered and her mind melting. She could hear his fierce male groans as he kept the intensity of his own blazing desire from cutting loose.

His sensual plunges unleashed an orgasm so quickly, so intensely; Jacey found she couldn't breath as it swept against her like a wild untamed wind.

Tender nerves short-circuited. Flesh burned.

She writhed and shuddered beneath him as the pleasure destroyed her mind and her body.

She became frightened at the intensity. Frightened at the way the shocking peaks of pleasure cascaded over her like a bright waterfall. Slamming into her hot body, one after another. Her vaginal muscles spasmed violently. Yet his thick cock continued to drive into her.

"Scream for me, Jacey," he groaned hoarsely.

His warm lips brushed gently against her chin. His hands slid along the curve of her hips in silky caresses.

The physical joy of his touch was fierce. Her mind splintered with the waves of pleasure. All lingering thoughts of control exploded around her like giant bombs of white sparklers.

It exhilarated her. She'd never experienced such fantastic euphoria. Such sweet freedom.

She found wetness dripping from her closed eyes behind the blindfold. Found herself crying as she neared what she perceived as erotic hysteria.

Then the floating feeling came out of nowhere. It drenched her mind. It draped upon her soul releasing the wonderful screams of joy Ben Hero had been waiting for.

At the sounds of her blissful joy, Ben's thrusts became wild and fierce. Another orgasm cracked against her, pushing carnal paradise over her soul. Her body spun out of control as the white-hot zenith jolted through her, drowning her in exquisite pleasure.

This orgasm was long, wickedly wonderful, and drained her body to the point where she couldn't do anything but accept Ben's aggressive thrusts. They grew fiercer as he neared his climax. He showed no mercy as he violently slammed his hips between her spread-eagled legs and growled out his satisfaction. Deep inside her, his cock spasmed wildly and he shot his sweet cum deep into her woman's core.

Chapter Ten

∞

Streams of late afternoon sunlight twinkled through the lush trees overhead as Jacey led Ben along the narrow woodsy trail.

Torment claimed her mind as she relived the gentle way he'd kissed her last night. The excruciating pleasure zipping through her insides from the butt plug. The exquisite way he'd whipped her breasts until she'd shivered with arousal. The violent thrusts toward the end as he'd fucked her without mercy.

Most of all she remembered her screams as body and mind had come apart while she'd climaxed over and over again.

She'd waited all her life to experience this type of sex. None of her fantasies had ever been this good. And yet, within a few minutes, she would tell Ben Hero that they had to part.

The horrible thought made a cry bubble up from her throat. Thankfully Ben didn't hear it, as he seemed to be lost in his own thoughts.

Parting with him was the best thing for both of them. She couldn't stay with him forever. Not that he'd asked. But if he had, she'd have to turn him down anyway. She'd been selfish in allowing herself to divulge in her wildest fantasies. She'd broken so many laws. Laws created by women for women, laws that had stood for hundreds of years.

She'd broken them so easily it made her wonder how in the world she ever thought she deserved to be a Queen.

Because of what she'd done with Ben, she had to return to her hub. She would hold her head high with pride as she explained to her people what had happened. She would force herself to face the dire consequences. And when all was said and done, she would accept her fate, as a Queen should dutifully do.

Last night, while Ben had slept, she'd lain awake. Her mind clouded with guilt at allowing herself to be subjected to such immense pleasure by a male. The prophecy had also run rampant through her brain.

During Queen training, she'd been taught about the prophecy that foretold the coming of aliens to their world. The arrival of people who would eventually develop the technology to find them, people who could destroy their way of life.

It had already started. With her and Ben Hero.

In the past few days she'd grown too close to him. Just thinking about letting him go made immense sadness tug at her heart, but if she didn't send him and the other males back to where they came from, many more males would come in search for them.

Males who might try to dominate once again. The women wouldn't allow it. They would fight to the death. Blood would spill on her land and the males could once again rule the world.

Sending Ben home to where he belonged and asking him not to come back was the best way for everyone involved.

She'd sunk so deep in her sadness, she almost missed the fork in the road.

Ben didn't miss it. He tapped her on the shoulder, calling a halt.

"Which way?" he asked as he stepped beside her and surveyed the two trails.

"The lower one."

He made a move toward the lower trail and noticed she wasn't following.

"You tired? Want to rest?"

Her throat clogged up and she shook her head.

"You're going alone." Those words were the hardest she'd ever had to say in her life.

Ben's brows furrowed with puzzlement.

"What do you mean, alone?"

"The trail will lead you back to Freedom Sea and ultimately to your spaceship. But you must promise me on your word you will do everything in your power to tell the Earth people not to come here."

"I will not promise any such thing. You're coming with me."

Jacey jolted at the anger in his voice, the hurt and betrayal shimmering in his eyes.

"I can't come with you. I'm a Queen. I have to face up to what I've done."

"What you've done? What you've done is make love. You haven't done anything wrong. If your people don't see that, then that's their problem." He made a grab for her hand, but she tugged away from him.

"What about what I want, Ben Hero?"

Her question obviously shocked him. His face paled.

"What do you want?"

Her throat clogged up with tears at his harsh question.

"I want you to go home, Ben Hero. I want you to be safe."

"But what about you? What if you're pregnant?"

Ah, so that's why he was concerned, because she might be carrying his child. Considering males and females were equal where he came from, it would be normal for him to wonder about the fate of his child.

"I'm not pregnant."

"How do you know?" His blue eyes seared right into her very soul, challenging her not to lie to him. She made herself hold his bold gaze as panic knotted her stomach. She couldn't tell him the truth. It would put him into danger. He had to leave. And she had to let him go.

"Because we Queens take monthly birth control measures in case of what just happened to me," she said firmly. It was a lie, but it was for his own good.

"Birth control? Why didn't you tell me earlier? Why did you let me think—"

"I didn't know what you were thinking, Ben Hero."

He sighed heavily and a muscle twitched wildly in his jaw. He was angry with her. Angry and disappointed.

He studied the trails that split into two different directions.

"What about the other trail? Where does that one lead?" he asked. Her heart ached for the lost look splashing against his face, and she felt just as lost, just as alone. She fought the tears threatening to clog up her throat.

"It leads to the front entrance of the Caves of Knowledge, about two miles from here."

"To the High Five."

Jacey nodded. "It's where I must go. One of the High Five is a close friend of mine. I can persuade her to turn off the disintegrating machines to allow you to leave."

Ben shoved a hand through his feathery hair. It was an endearing gesture she really liked, but right now it was ripping her heart to shreds. Letting Ben Hero go was harder than she'd ever imagined.

"We can go together," he stated firmly.

"No. We can't risk getting caught. If I'm alone then no one will suspect anything."

"Then I'll wait here until you come back. And we'll go to Freedom Sea together." Hope soared in his eyes and it made her angry. Why was he making this so difficult?

"I'm not coming back, Ben Hero!"

"What you're trying to tell me is good-bye. For good."

Jacey nodded and blinked back the tears.

"Don't cry, Jace."

"I can't help it. I've grown fond of you, Ben Hero."

"And I like you too much to let you go."

His words tugged the tears from her eyes.

Ben reached out and gently wiped away the hot stream running down her face. His fingers were warm against her skin and she couldn't help but push her face into his hand.

"It's for the best, if you go alone, Ben."

"I don't think I can live the same way I did before I met you, Jace. I don't want us to part."

Her resolve began to crumble. "But I don't know the ways of your people. I wouldn't fit in."

"I can teach you and you'll fit in just fine. And I want you to meet my mom and dad."

His finger traced her lower lip with a sensuous sweep that left her wanting his mouth upon her flesh.

"I can teach you many things, Jacey. Come with me."

"I can't."

His finger stilled. She sensed his hurt and it took every ounce of her being not to reach out and touch him.

"I have to stay here, with my own people. No matter how much I desire to be with you."

"What's really stopping you from coming with me?"

"We don't even know each other, Ben Hero."

"What do you want to know? Just ask. Or I can tell you right now. I come from a family of astronauts. I trained as one for many years and did some space stunts. I'm also a part-time mechanic. When I'm not in space I have my own shop with a tiny apartment over it. When we get back, I'll quit NASA, do the mechanic gig full time. We can live over my shop. It's small, but we'll manage until I can get us a bigger place. I'll never leave you. I know enough about you that makes me sure I want you in my bed every night and by my side every day."

Ben's excitement was contagious and she couldn't help but be swept away in his dreams.

His finger dipped tenderly along the side of her mouth, catching another tear. She licked the salty liquid from his warm flesh.

His masculine scent intoxicated her and his body heat crashed seductively against her skin. How could she part with him?

"I can't."

"Why can't you come with me?"

"I mean I can't leave you," she admitted softly. Just saying the words lifted her spirits to unbelievable heights.

"You've changed your mind?"

Jacey nodded.

Suddenly Ben let out an excited whoop of joy. The sound startled her as well as a flock of nearby birds, who squawked frantically and took flight.

The warm grin on his lips made Jacey's heart beat erratically and before she knew what she was doing she was kissing him. His lips tasted of the sweet fruits they'd eaten for breakfast. They moved over hers expertly, sensuously. Ripping womanly moans out of her chest and into her throat. He captured the moans with the heat of his mouth.

Cupping her bare ass, he pulled her against him. Her body tingled with desire as the thickness of his massive arousal pressed intimately between her legs.

"We can't," she whispered as she broke the kiss. "Not here."

"Let's go deeper in the trees"

"Too close. Someone may hear."

He grinned knowingly and her cunt moistened with the need to have him deep inside her.

Gently he grabbed her hand, intertwining his fingers with hers.

She nodded toward a third trail. It was so well concealed by the oncoming darkness she'd almost missed it.

"Where do you think it goes?" Ben asked.

"Let's go see," she replied as she tugged him toward it.

* * * * *

About a half-mile later, they lay on a soft patch of dry moss that ran along the edge of a grey rock cliff. The sun dropped behind the horizon, bringing with it an unusual quietness that set Ben's nerves just a little on edge.

"I lied." Jacey whispered and snuggled her warm body closer to him, as if fearing he might suddenly bolt.

"About?"

"The child. Queens don't take birth control. I just wanted you to go back to your own people and be safe. There's no life here for an educated male. Only slavery or death."

Her confession brought a rush of emotions cascading over him.

He resisted the savage urge to pull her tighter against him, to wrap his arms around her like a cocoon in order to protect her. He sensed the intensity of his love for her might frighten her away. Anger bit deep in his guts too. Anger that she'd lied to him about something so important.

But most of all, relief poured over him. Relief that she'd cared enough to tell him the truth about her possibly being pregnant and that she wanted to stay with him.

He pressed a finger to her mouth. "Shh. Everything will work out okay, Jacey."

"You're not mad that I lied?"

"I understand why you did."

Suddenly a streak of lightning flickered overhead and Ben cursed their rotten luck.

Jacey giggled beside him.

"What's so funny?"

"Have you ever fucked in the rain?" she asked.

Hot blood pumped through his veins at her question.

"Can't say that I have."

"Neither have I."

Ben gazed up at the now dark sky. "I'm assuming we aren't in The Acid Zone again."

"We're safe here."

"I don't suppose there are any caves or cabins around nearby to take shelter for the night?"

"The only shelter you're going to have is me, covering you."

He groaned when her mouth came down upon his without warning.

Her velvety lips burned against his as she kissed him. Her seductive assault made intense warmth grip his abdomen. Heated blood poured into his cock, hardening him. Readying him to plunge deep into her cunt.

It amazed him how quickly he could be aroused by her. Never in his life had he made love to a woman so many times in such a short period or wanted a woman as fiercely as he wanted Jacey.

Now he understood what his dad had meant that day when Ben had asked him how he had known he was in love with mom. His dad had merely smiled, ruffled Ben's hair affectionately, and said softly, "You'll know when the time comes, son. You'll know."

Damned if his old man wasn't right.

Her kiss grew harder, more demanding, and Ben met her fierceness with an urgent need of his own.

He skimmed his hands along the long column of her graceful neck, over her collarbone, the silkiness of her arms, and then over the side curves of her generous breasts. The silky globes fit into his large hands with such perfection, it seemed as if her breasts were made especially for him. He tugged at her rings and rolled her diamond-hard nipples. She arched her back against him and he caught her aroused gasps in his mouth.

Raindrops seductively kissed his heated flesh, adding to the sexual tension building like a live wire inside him. Her tongue slipped into his mouth.

She tasted sweet. Like nectar from a beautiful flower or like honey. He shuddered with fevered passion and his senses spun as she explored every nook and cranny of his mouth.

Her sexy scent in his nostrils turned him on even higher. The storm inside his body grew frantic. His flesh yearned to be touched by her. His cock hardened to the point where he was convinced he would explode if he couldn't ram himself into her cunt.

He ripped his mouth from hers and gasped into the wet air.

Her mouth slid against his neck, covering his flesh with delicious wet kisses. Her hot hands were everywhere. Touching his nipples, sliding along his hips, squeezing over his ass cheeks.

"I can't take much more of this, Jacey. Take me now or dammit, I'll take you," He was breathing real hard now. He was so aroused he couldn't even think straight.

Against the skin of his neck where her wet mouth touched, her lips curled into a smile.

She pulled away from him. At the same moment a flash of lightning zipped through the heavens and he saw something beautiful shimmering in Jacey's eyes. Something so wonderful that the breath lodged deep in his lungs with the realization of what it was called.

Love.

She'd never said the word love to him. He'd tried getting her to say it by using it as a safe word while he'd seduced her last night. She probably never would say those words, not with her upbringing, but that was okay. It showed in her eyes. That knowledge made the tension in his body mount to an almost panicky state. He had to be inside her now. He needed to show her how much he loved her.

As if sensing his urgency, Jacey wasted no time rising over him. Her luscious body heat swept against him in ferocious waves. He gasped when she grabbed his throbbing rod by the base with both hands and held him steady.

Spreading her thighs, she lowered her hips.

Ben groaned out his pleasure as her succulent cunt sheathed his burning shaft.

A killing ecstasy exploded through his entire body, sending his senses reeling and his mind spinning in all kinds of directions.

She unleashed herself on him like a wanton woman out of control. She rode him violently. Her hips crushed into his hips. Gyrating with a fierce frenzy he hadn't felt in her before.

His rod sunk even deeper into her tight channel. Deeper than he'd ever gone before.

"Jacey!" he shouted her name the instant her cunt muscles began to spasm around his aching cock with her oncoming climax. Her body shuddered violently. His body trembled with anticipation.

She screamed. Once. Twice. Three times, as she came hard.

Her musical voice washed over him in such a seductive assault it made his orgasm twice as sweet. Her silky insides milked him to the point of insanity. The burning pleasure zipped like a lightning bolt up along his entire shaft, crashed into his balls and sunk deep into his abdomen. So deep, the pleasure made his eyes open wide with wonder, and made his shout hitch in his throat.

More forks of lightning splashed overhead, illuminating her.

Her hair was tussled and matted from the rain. Her two silky globes glimmered with wetness and bobbed wildly as she rode him. Her eyes were wild. Lost in an ecstasy so all consuming that he felt sure she'd slipped into another world.

A moment later, he joined her in the fantastic world called ecstasy, as the remainder of his mind splintered and his penis exploded, shooting his hot love seed deep inside her.

Chapter Eleven

ɞ

They'd made love all night as the rain poured down around them, their screams of arousal drowned by the cracks of thunder. Bright flashes of lightning had allowed her to see the exquisite joy on Ben's face as they'd fucked each other.

She was sore and weary this morning but she'd climbed down the cliff to the small river that ran directly below.

She planned on catching fish for breakfast. Although a female cooking for a male was forbidden, she just didn't care any more. She wanted Ben Hero happy and healthy.

She'd snagged two fish with her bare hands and laid them on the nearby bank when she heard the guttural growl. Through the early morning mist, she barely made out the threatening form.

Her breath seized up in her lungs and her blood ran cold in her veins.

A black panther.

She saw hunger in its emerald green eyes. A giant pink tongue swiped across its upper lip.

The creature must have smelled the fish she'd caught and followed its velvety nose to her!

Slowly moving out of the water, she frantically searched the sandy riverbank for some form of protection. Nothing caught her eye and she chastised herself for being so foolish to be caught defenseless.

The giant cat's long tail swayed in anger. Or was it anticipation? Its massive paws padded delicately over the sand as he cautiously treaded closer to her.

Its mouth dropped open, giving Jacey a much too close-up view of jagged and very sharp yellow teeth.

Panic zipped along her nerve endings. The only thing she could do was run, but she knew the creature would be upon her within seconds.

Suddenly, a blur of movement shot through the mist. She blinked in paralyzed fear as Ben Hero appeared. Jumping in front of her, he pushed her behind the safety of his big masculine body.

"Get the hell out of here!" he shouted at her as he wielded a giant tree branch.

Stunned by his appearance and not knowing if he was yelling at her or the panther, Jacey could do nothing but stand and watch the male she loved battle the giant cat. The gnarled piece of wood lifted and came down on the panther's nose. The creature retaliated quickly. Before Ben could bring the branch down again, the cat swiped a massive paw across his chest. Jacey's heart froze at Ben's groan of pain.

He stood his ground, bringing the branch once again down upon the black panthers nose.

This time the cat gave a painful squeal, turned and loped away.

Jacey's heart wrenched in pain as Ben fell to his knees.

Blood seeped from four angry tears in his chest, compliments of the cat's paw.

"What have you done, my fool?" Jacey cried as she slumped down on her knees beside him.

"Are you all right?" he hissed between gritted teeth.

She nodded numbly.

He grinned with relief and suddenly collapsed, his naked body dropping sideways to the ground in a boneless heap.

Jacey closed her eyes, praying to the Goddess of Freedom that she was somehow lost in a nightmare. A split second later she opened her eyes again and realized this was not some horrific dream.

Cold terror ripped at her gut as with trembling fingers she felt his cool clammy neck for a pulse.

He was alive!

Stop the bleeding! a voice barked in the back of her mind.

How? Her mind whirled with confusion. She'd never seen such raw jagged cuts before. Hadn't trained in anything but the basics for medical injuries. It certainly didn't include this!

Blood continued to flow freely from his wounds. She had to do something to stop the flow. She could use her hands!

Her lungs squeezed tightly as she slid her palms across some of the hot gashes. His chest muscles spasmed under her hands and he groaned as she increased the pressure. But the slices were too long. Warm blood oozed between her fingers, making her hands red.

There was nothing she could do to staunch the flow of his life force.

What in the world had possessed him to save her? Why hadn't he just stayed on the cliff where she'd left him, safe and sound?

The thoughts ricocheted wildly through her brain. If only she'd insisted he go along yesterday. He would have been safe. If only she hadn't been so selfish…

Ben's eyes fluttered open and he tried to say something.

"Shhh, Ben Hero. Don't speak. Save your strength."

"Jacey?"

"I'm here. I'll always be here with you."

"I love you," he whispered and his eyes fluttered closed again. A measure of relief slipped through his pain-wracked features.

I love you. The words danced wildly in her head. She grabbed them and tucked them into her heart.

Reality hit like a sledgehammer. If she didn't do something fast, the male who loved her would die.

One choice remained to help him. She made it swiftly.

Throwing her head back, she gathered air into her lungs and screamed like she'd never screamed before.

* * * * *

"Ben? Can you hear me?"

Jacey's voice?

He tried to move, but agonizing pain swamped his senses.

A cool palm touched his burning forehead. Soft. Fragrant. Jacey.

He forced his eyes open. A blurry figure swam nearby. He blinked a few more times and his vision cleared.

"Ben?"

Fear drizzled through him as Jacey's concerned face hovered mere inches away. Tears slid down her cheeks. Her pretty scent washed over him in soothing waves. He wished he could curl his arms around her neck and kiss her. Ease her worries and tell her he was fine, but nothing cooperated. His limbs refused to move. His mouth appeared paralyzed and no words could form.

"We're going to burn the wounds to stop the bleeding. Do you understand me, Ben?"

He nodded. Or at least he thought he nodded.

Someone forced his mouth open and shoved something between his teeth. He tasted wood.

Jacey's soft voice once again drifted through the haze of pain.

"Bite down on this when it hurts."

Dammit! It already hurt.

He struggled to remain conscious and clamped down on the piece of wood.

A soft feminine hand slipped against his palm and squeezed in reassurance. Instinctively he knew it was Jacey. It took all his strength to curl his fingers tightly around her warmth.

She kissed him gently, as if trying not to hurt him. Her lips were a cool salve against his burning mouth and he tasted her desperation, her warmth, her love.

"I love you, Ben Hero," she whispered.

His heart swelled with happiness at the words he thought he'd never hear her say. Closing his eyes, he inhaled her sweet delicate scent and prayed he would live to hear her say those three magical words again.

Without warning, intense pain jolted through him. It sliced deep into his chest, fiery hot, like a blade of lightning. His whole body arched with the blinding pain. Somewhere deep in his mind he knew his wounds were being cauterized but it felt as if the panther's claws were once again scraping through him.

A moment later, more searing pain ripped through his chest. The smell of burning flesh assaulted his nostrils. Nausea rolled over him in giant black waves and he blessed the black haze that carried him into oblivion.

* * * * *

"His fever is gone." Queen Jasmine's full lips tilted into a heartwarming smile as she touched the sleeping Ben's forehead. "I'll order another Quick Healing shot for him for this evening. He'll be good as new by tomorrow."

Jacey sighed with relief. The worst was finally over.

Ben had been unconscious for three days. The only reason he was still alive was due to the quick thinking of the young Queens-in-training who'd been nearby and had heard Jacey's screams for help. Thankfully, Jasmine, her good friend with the High Five and former teacher, had been leading the group. The women had worked quickly under the instruction of Jasmine. They'd cauterized Ben's wounds while she'd watched, a helpless nervous wreck. Then a litter had been quickly constructed and Ben and she had been whisked to Jasmine's private cave.

Upon Jacey's desperate pleas that the young women remain silent about the male and herself, Jasmine had reluctantly sworn the trio of Queens-in-training to remain silent about their unexpected adventure.

Jacey had promised her friend she had a good reason, and by the way Jasmine's smile was quickly disintegrating as she crouched beside Jacey, she knew it was time to tell the High Five Queen the truth.

Despite Jacey's distress, just looking at her friend's familiar shoulder-length red hair and her kind gray eyes made Jacey comfortable with the idea Ben and she were safe, for now.

"What distresses you so, Jacey?" Jasmine asked.

"Nothing," Jacey lied. Suddenly she wasn't sure she was ready to tell Jasmine the truth.

"You've barely eaten for three days. You don't speak. All you do is sit beside the male. Perhaps it is best if I send him away?"

"No! You promised to keep him here. You promised him safety."

High Queen Jasmine's eyes widened with surprise at Jacey's outburst.

"What has happened, Jacey? Why such concern for a male?"

"If I tell you, you must promise me you cannot repeat a word. It is my right as a Queen to ask you of this, is it not?"

"My silence is guaranteed, Jacey."

"No matter what?"

133

"Yes, of course. Not only because I am a High Queen and you are a Queen, but because you are my friend." Jasmine patted Jacey's hand gently. "Now, what is troubling you so?"

Jacey inhaled on a sigh. Where could she start? What should she say?

"Does this have to do with the injured male?"

Reluctantly Jacey nodded.

"I thought so. I've seen the look before."

"What look?"

"The look of a woman torn. Something about him is tearing you apart. What is it?"

"The male slave and I have traveled a few days together."

"Highly illegal for a Queen and a male to be alone together, but you must have a good reason. I know you do. You aren't one to do things without thinking things through first. That is why you were groomed for Queen status and why I hope that one day soon you will take my place as High Queen."

"You think too highly of me, Jasmine." Honor and extreme guilt zipped through Jacey that Jasmine would consider supporting her for her position when it was time for Jasmine to be killed.

A tinge of a smile lifted the High Queen's lips. "Perhaps you don't think highly enough of yourself?"

Jacey gave a strangled laugh. "That's not it."

"Ah, we're back to the slave."

"As I said, we traveled together for several days. We grew close."

"He didn't touch you, did he?"

Jacey couldn't answer, but the tears streaming down her face made Jasmine's shoulders sag in defeat, her face paled.

"What did he do?"

"He didn't do anything I didn't want done."

"That's not an answer."

"It is my answer, Jasmine. I care for him."

Jasmine's sharp inhalation made Jacey laugh.

"I do believe all the years I've known you, I've never seen you shocked."

"Well, you've certainly succeeded." Jasmine said. "Please, continue."

"When I saw him lying on the ground, his life blood pouring from his wounds. I felt a piece of me die inside. I knew instinctively if he died, I would too."

High Queen Jasmine didn't say a word. Her face was furrowed with concern, but there wasn't any judgment in her eyes. It encouraged Jacey to continue.

"He rushed in front of the panther and he saved my life, without any thought for his own safety. I think I love him."

"Love, a forbidden word." Jasmine spat with disgust. "A word once used by males to dominate females. To brainwash women into caring for them. To brainwash women into doing anything males want to do to them."

"No, that's not the true meaning, Jasmine. Love is beautiful. It means you care deeply for someone. It means you can't stop thinking about him. You want to touch him all the time. You can't wait to hear him speak or sing or dance with you. You worship the way he looks at you, with so much caring, it hurts inside. But it's a beautiful hurt."

"He has taken your heart, Jacey."

"Yes, he's taken my heart. I want to be with him but I feel obligated to my people. Obligated to be punished for my crimes."

"If anyone finds out you were penetrated, you will lose everything, Jacey. He is a toxic secret to keep. But as I agreed, I will keep this secret."

"I'm afraid it goes much deeper than that."

"How so?"

"The Breeders know."

"How is this possible? Were you not discreet?" she screeched.

"He...penetrated me in one of the Breeder's stalls, after they captured me. One of the guards watched. On more than one occasion, I'm sure."

"More than once...Jacey, why? Why did you venture away from your hub? You know how dangerous it is for a Queen to be near another Queen's territory."

"My reasons for leaving are purely personal. The fact is The Breeders caught me. Tied me down. He came in and we...he made love to me."

Jasmine covered her mouth to prevent herself from crying out.

"Shocked again?"

"I fear for you, Jacey. Oh, how I fear for you." Jasmine bit her knuckles with worry and Jacey felt her stomach plummet with uneasiness. "There is only one choice left. You must leave with the male. As soon as possible. You can never go back to your hub. You have lost the respect of your people."

"And what about you? Have I lost your respect?"

Queen Jasmine hesitated a heartbeat too long, giving Jacey her answer.

"Above all else, I am your friend, Jacey. I will keep your secrets buried deep in my heart. Now we must make preparations. The instant the male is well you must leave the sanctity of my home."

Jacey nodded. "I understand."

It didn't mean she had to like being thrown out, but she understood the consequences of what would happen to Jasmine if they were discovered here. After all, once The Breeders spread the word, Ben and she would be outlaws.

* * * * *

"Welcome back," Jacey whispered into Ben's ear as his eyelids fluttered.

At the sound of her tender voice his eyes popped open and he stared up at her. Worry marred her features.

"What happened?" he asked.

"You jumped in front of a hungry panther, remember?"

To her surprise, he chuckled. Then grimaced, both his hands clutching the white bandages swaddling his chest.

"Hurt?"

"Damn right it does."

"Good."

His eyes widened with shock. "What's so good about it?"

"It'll teach you to never do that again."

"Don't be so sure I won't, my Queen," his voice was thick with emotion, the sound clutching at her heart.

"You would do it again?"

"Within a heartbeat."

Jacey shook her head in disbelief and feathered her fingers over his forehead making double sure it wasn't a renewed fever talking.

He was cool and totally coherent.

"Where are we anyway?" he said as he looked around at the craggy walls of the cave room he'd been stashed inside.

"We're in the accommodations of one of the High Five, High Queen Jasmine."

Ben visibly tensed at the news.

"We're captive again?"

"She's the friend I was telling you about. She'll keep silent about us for as long as she can."

"Then we'd better hightail it out of here, before she changes her mind." He made a move to get up but groaned and slumped back onto the rough cot Jasmine had reluctantly supplied when Jacey had insisted he have one. Male slaves were required to sleep on the bare ground, despite their condition.

"I think I need a hand up," he groaned.

Jacey found herself smiling at his words, her gaze flying to his flaccid penis.

She licked her lips at a most delightful thought.

"I think you need more than a hand, Ben Hero."

He gasped out loud as both her hands slid under his heavy penis and she clasped his hot flesh.

"What are you doing?" he hissed in apparent shock.

Despite his protest, Jacey could feel his rod thickening, pulsing to attention at her touch.

"I've missed you, Ben Hero. I want to welcome you back. Since the rest of your body isn't well enough to appreciate my sentiments, I'll concentrate on another delicious looking part."

"Are you sure this is the right time?" he gulped.

His Adam's apple bobbed wildly. His eyes darted to the entrance. "There isn't even a door. Someone might come in."

"Let them," she teased.

He blinked in stunned fascination.

Jacey couldn't help but laugh.

"You don't have any choice but to submit. I am the Queen and you are completely at my mercy."

To prove her point, Jacey leaned over and with the tip of her tongue she licked the entire huge length of his silk-encased shaft.

His cock's flesh tasted yummy and stuck straight up like a tree by the time she reached the bulging tip.

When she lifted her head, she saw him biting his lower lip as he stifled a groan. His eyes were scrunched closed from sheer pleasure.

All this excitement from him and with only one stroke of her tongue. Amazing. The last time she'd sucked his cock, she'd been blindfolded, unable to see the desire on his face.

Suddenly, she was desperate to have her lips circling his cock. To have his thickness inside her mouth while she looked up into his face to see what kinds of pleasures she could create. She wanted to see his eyes glaze over with arousal. Wanted to feel his hot shaft pulse against her tongue. She wanted to taste his cum. Wanted his hot semen shooting deep into her throat.

"I've been dying to devour your rod since I first saw you."

"All you had to do was ask, baby," he breathed.

A sharp inhalation from the entrance, made both Ben and Jacey turn around to find High Queen Jasmine standing there.

Her eyes were wide with shock. No one had to tell Jacey she'd heard Ben Hero speaking.

Chapter Twelve

ജ

"But this isn't possible. Males cannot be domesticated." Jasmine sputtered a few minutes later after Jacey had quickly ushered her from Ben's room, urging him to remain calm and to get some rest.

"They can only be taught a few simple lessons," she continued, "Just basic commands. You saw what happened with the Slave Uprising when they are taught more. Needless to say, you've seen some of the Forbidden Pictures during your Queen training. You know what males are capable of. The torture they inflict upon females."

Jacey nodded as she remembered the pictures shown only to those who become Queen.

"And the High Five have discovered more films in the archives. I believe I should show you these new moving pictures preserved by our ancestors to remind you of what they endured at the hands of the males. Come, we will go to the High Five Plex and I will show you why you should not trust this talking male."

Now was not the time to argue with Jasmine. It was in Ben's best interest to keep him here resting for as long as she possibly could. If that meant doing what Jasmine asked, so be it.

"Will the male be safe here?" Jacey asked.

"There is no reason for anyone to come into my cave without my permission. I will lock the main door as we leave."

Jacey nodded and breathed a sigh of relief when Jasmine led her outside, locking the door behind her.

Thousands of stars sparkled brightly overhead in the inky night sky. Neither said a word as they moved silently up the narrow trail that ascended steeply.

Fifteen minutes later, Jasmine led Jacey into the opening of another cave. It was cool inside, cooler than Jasmine's cave.

About ten paces inside the opening a wall of rock stopped them. Lifting a key from the chain of keys she wore around her neck, Jasmine slid it into a nearby slot on the wall.

The rock in front of them disintegrated without a sound.

Jacey's mouth dropped open in surprise.

"I told you that the High Five know more than the Queens." Jasmine smiled shakily. "Come inside quickly."

Jacey followed her inside and watched as the rock wall suddenly re-appeared behind them.

Jasmine ushered her into a rock-walled room. Five comfortable seats lined the back wall and a flat white screen took up the entire front wall.

"Have a seat. I'll turn on the Forbidden pictures in a minute."

Jacey did as instructed and Jasmine slipped through a back door.

A moment later the white screen lit up with moving pictures.

A naked woman wearing a steel collar huddled inside a metal cage. The tormented look in her eyes made Jacey's heart twist with sympathy.

Two men stood in front of the cage trying to decide who would be the first to fuck her.

"She's just been captured. They will eventually turn her into a sex slave." Jasmine explained as she sat down beside Jacey. "The two males are discussing how much money she should bring at the slave auction."

The woman wailed as one of the men opened the door, grabbed her arm and tugged her outside.

She cringed as one man held her arms behind her back making her breasts thrust out provocatively. The other male ran his hands along the outside curves of the woman's breasts making a small moan of arousal erupt from her lips.

The man smiled with satisfaction and nodded to the other man who then turned the woman around and made the woman get down on all fours. He forced her head down toward the ground.

Jacey inhaled sharply.

One of the men tugged down his pants and prodded his thick penis into the woman's anus.

Jacey closed her eyes as the woman's painful screams thrust through the air.

"I know you've been trained in certain aspects of our history, but I'm sure it won't hurt to show you what may be waiting for you if you go with this talking male." Jasmine returned her attention to the screen.

"Toward the end of Male Domination, before the females rebelled against their masters, this is how they were treated. No woman was free, Jacey. All women were captive of the male. Some women were shared with hundreds of men in brothels as our male slaves are currently shared."

Thankfully the picture changed to another scene. But this one wasn't any better than the last.

Images of women wearing clothing from head to toe with only a thick cloth screen to look through walked cautiously and quietly among the streets. Men stood everywhere. Rifles slung over their shoulders as they watched the women.

"Before the Male Domination became unbearable the women were allowed to wear clothes." Jasmine explained.

"She could not show her face. Nor show any flesh. If she did, she was punished by the males."

A woman briefly lifted the heavy veil concealing her face so she could get a better look at the price of a fruit when a male grabbed her by the arm and thrust her into a nearby hallway.

Ripping the veil off her head, he slapped his hand over mouth to prevent her from screaming.

Another male came out of nowhere and began to remove her robe. Her breasts bounced free and the man's hands cupped them. He pinched her nipples, and suckled them, much as Ben had done to Jacey.

The terrified look in the woman's face as the men removed the rest of her clothing made Jacey sick to her stomach.

Pushing her onto the ground, they spread her legs and took turns holding her down while each of them plunged into her writhing body.

"Ben's not like that." Jacey said.

"Perhaps not yet."

"I won't believe he would ever do something like that."

And yet he had, hadn't he?

When she'd been tied down and spread-eagled that first time in the Breeder Stall, she'd seen the lust shine in his eyes at seeing her bound and naked.

Jacey shook aside the disturbing thoughts. That had been different! Very different. She'd wanted Ben Hero to take her. She'd told him to.

"Ben's not like that." Jacey said more firmly this time. "He will never be like that."

"You feel very strongly about this male. I hope you are right."

"I am right. I've seen enough of these forbidden pictures."

"There are many more, Jacey. If you had become a High Five, you would have had to watch these. Study them."

Jacey nodded. Suddenly she was glad she wouldn't have to view them or study them again. Relieved that she wasn't as brainwashed as the rest of her people or angry and frightened of males like Jasmine.

"Do you see why this male must return to where he came from and never come back here?"

Again Jacey nodded.

"And you must come to a decision yourself, Jacey. Let this male go alone or better yet allow him to be destroyed."

Jacey was about to protest vehemently when Jasmine held up her hand to silence her.

"I understand you don't wish that to happen to the male. But at the very least, let him go and you go into hiding. I will help you like I helped you to free Virgin from prison. She's roaming around right now because of us, but if she's ever caught…" Jasmine's words furrowed a hole straight through Jacey's heart.

It was a risk they'd taken freeing Virgin. If she was caught, Virgin may point fingers revealing the identity of the people who helped her escape. But Jacey didn't think her friend would do that. She was an honorable woman.

But should she let Ben go as Jasmine suggested? And go into hiding without him? How? How could she even entertain the thought of leaving him after realizing what he meant to her?

He'd risked his own life to save her from the panther. Her whole body had caved in with fear when he'd slumped to the ground from his wounds. Her mind had been paralyzed when she thought she'd lost him. At that point, she'd even felt a part of her had died.

And now Jasmine was suggesting she should lose him all over again?

Bitter tears dribbled down Jacey's cheeks and she angrily wiped them away.

"I'm sorry but I thought you required a dose of reality, Jacey. I'll go and stop the pictures." Jasmine said softly.

While Jasmine was in the back room, Jacey's thoughts raced frantically to when she'd first met Ben. His magnificent oiled cock all primed and ready to thrust into her.

But he'd seemed genuinely upset that she hadn't been in The Breeder stall of her own accord. What would he have done if she hadn't encouraged him to fuck her?

Deep down inside her heart she knew the answer. Ben Hero would have risked his life by refusing to fuck an unwilling woman. The fact had been plain on his face, by the frantic look when he'd discovered she hadn't been there of her own choice. That led to the question of why The Breeders had brought Ben to her in the first place. Had it been simple revenge? Or a mad territory grab as she'd first thought. Or was it something more sinister?

Why would The Breeders go to the trouble of capturing her? Why bind her to a bed? Why bring her a well-endowed male? Why make all her secret fantasies come true?

And why impregnate her instead of killing her? Impregnating a Queen was surely the best way to discredit her or break the laws. Did someone hate her enough to do such a vile thing?

Was she reading too much into this? Was all this merely a coincidence?

Whatever it was, there was no way she was letting Ben Hero go. She wanted him to be in her life forever.

* * * * *

When Jacey returned from watching the Forbidden Pictures, she'd found Ben fast asleep. Instead of rousing him and leaving immediately, she'd settled into the chair beside his bed with full intention of waking him at first light. But sometime during the night she'd drifted off to sleep.

A rough shove on her shoulder woke her straight up.

"Wake up Jacey!" It was Jasmine. Her eyes were wide with fear, her face pale in the cave light.

"What's happened?"

"The news has been spread by The Breeders. Your hub is searching frantically for you. Your second in command is now in charge. She's replaced you."

"What? Cath is Queen?" The shock of losing her Queen status shook the rest of sleep from her brain. It wasn't as if she hadn't been expecting it. It just hurt more than she thought it would that she could be so easily replaced.

"What's going on?"

High Queen Jasmine's face went paler at Ben's sleepy question.

"Oh sweet Goddess of Freedom, the male is speaking. Please, Jacey tell him to remain silent. I cannot handle more of this."

"Okay, whatever you say." Ben grumbled.

"There's more bad news." Jasmine continued, keeping a wary eye on Ben as he struggled into a seated position. "The High Five has put forth a motion to hunt down the talking males and kill them."

Jacey closed her eyes as dread swamped her. Beside her, Ben cursed.

"I'm sorry but the motion was passed. I had to vote for it or they would surely have been suspicious. You must leave at once."

"I'm sorry we put you in this position."

"No apologies, Jacey. I've already ordered my personal guide to lead you and the male to wherever you wish to go. Wait here a moment, I will see if the guide has arrived."

Jacey nodded numbly and she watched Jasmine bustle away.

Ben still looked a little wobbly as he tried to stand up, but when Jacey curled an arm around his waist to help keep him steady, she didn't miss his cock begin to rise.

He followed her gaze and grinned widely.

"I can't seem to help myself. Whenever you touch me, my body celebrates."

"We'll celebrate later. Come, we have to go, now."

"What about the disintegration machine? We can't get off the planet if it's running."

Jacey cursed at Ben's question. She'd totally forgotten about their dilemma.

"I can help you with that." Jasmine said as she re-appeared at the doorway. "When do you think you will be able to leave the planet?"

Jacey blinked with wonder that Jasmine didn't even seem distressed Ben Hero came from another planet. Obviously the High Fives did know a lot more than the Queens.

"Our ship is by the sea," Ben explained. "It should take us one day to get to Freedom Sea, another day to find the ship and perhaps another day for leeway. In case we've miscalculated something."

"When the departure time is close, instruct my guide to send a signal to me. I will disable the machines. Now, move quickly. Follow this hallway." Jasmine pointed to a cave opening to their left. She then turned to Jacey and embraced her warmly.

"Oh Goddess of Freedom. I can't believe I just talked to a male and he seemed...domesticated." The woman whispered with excitement.

"I'm sorry you didn't have a chance to get to know him, Jasmine."

Jasmine let Jacey go and shook her head. "I'm glad I didn't. I would have had to rethink everything I've been taught. I still might have to. Now go. Be safe."

Jacey nodded and bit back the tears knowing this was most likely the last time she would ever see Jasmine.

Ben grabbed Jacey by the arm and pulled her down the hallway.

"Good-bye!" Jasmine called after them.

Jacey waved and then they rounded the corner of the hallway, and her friend vanished from her sight.

* * * * *

"Jacey, what the hell is wrong?" Almost an entire day had passed and she had remained pretty much silent. When the guide that High Queen Jasmine had sent along with them finally ambled a little further ahead on the trail, he'd tried to kiss her. To his shock, she'd stiffened beneath his touch.

When she didn't answer his question he shoved his fingers through his hair and sighed with frustration.

"You don't want to tell me what's been bothering you. You don't want me anywhere near you. I'm not stupid, you know, I can take a hint. Somehow I've upset you."

Jacey sighed and took his hand in hers. Well hallelujah, at least she still wanted to touch him.

"It's not you directly, Ben Hero."

"Okay, so it's me indirectly? What is it?"

"I'm not sure."

"You can tell me anything, Jace. What do you think is bothering you?"

"I promised Queen Jasmine I wouldn't say anything."

"About?"

She smiled. "You are an amusing male, Ben Hero. I just told you I'm not supposed to reveal a secret and you simply ask anyway."

"So, you've been sworn to secrecy. Why not tell me and swear me to secrecy? No one will know, right?"

She lifted her head to search for the guard.

"She's just up ahead," Ben said. "If you keep your voice down, she won't be able to hear."

She nodded and frowned. Perhaps she should share her concern with Ben.

"Jasmine showed me something last night. Some more Forbidden Pictures that I'd never seen before."

"Forbidden Pictures?"

"Movies that show a horrible part of our history. Of the time of Male Dominance."

"These pictures, they disturbed you."

"Yes, very."

"What kind were they?"

"Males and how they used to dominate the females. How they forced themselves on women. Made them wear too much clothing so no part of their flesh would be shown, and then later in our history when women were not allowed to wear clothing at all. Males could do whatever they wanted to us."

"And you want to know if the men on Earth are the same way."

"Do you deny the males from your planet don't behave that way?"

"Some do."

Her sharp inhalation to his confession made him tighten his embrace on her hand.

"You aren't denying your males do these horrid things?"

"There are all kinds of different people on our planet. Some are bad, but most are good."

"And you will stay a good male, Ben Hero?"

"I would never hurt you, Jacey. Not intentionally."

"But those things we did together, the different positions, the whipping, they are from the Evil Times."

"What we did was fantasy, honey. There's a big difference between reality and fantasy. As long as it is mutual, and we aren't hurting anyone, we can do anything we want with each other."

Her brow wrinkled with puzzlement and then understanding. "Anything we want?"

"Back on Earth we use safe words. Like we did in the cabin, remember?"

"How could I forget?" The sexy twinkle in Jacey's eyes made Ben's shaft harden.

"You think we can ditch the guide for a little while?" Ben whispered.

Jacey giggled. "Do you have something delicious in mind, Ben Hero?"

"Dangerously delicious."

"And what would that be?"

"If I told you, my surprise would be gone, wouldn't it?"

Ben took another peek up the trail. The guide was nowhere in sight. "You think the guide will come looking for us if we disappear?"

"I'm sure she'll realize why we've snuck away." Jacey giggled and then winked. "Besides, when she hears us, she'll know."

Grabbing Jacey's hand, he led her off the trail through a thick stand of bushes. After a few minutes they erupted into a small clearing.

"Oh my!" Jacey exclaimed at the beauty of the meadow.

"Must be fate," Ben chuckled as he took her into his arms. His masculine scent mingled with the flowery perfume of the meadow, making Jacey heady with happiness.

"I've never seen anything so pretty," she said as she watched the fat white daisies and bright yellow buttercups bob their heads in the waist deep green grass.

"Neither have I."

Her pulses skittered at the dark desire sparkling in his eyes. Instinctively she knew he wasn't talking about the meadow.

"Do you really think I'm pretty?" She asked shyly.

"Beautiful. Absolutely breathtaking."

Happiness swelled in her chest as his head lowered and he took her mouth in a heated kiss.

Chapter Thirteen

❧

Ben didn't know how long he lay there relaxing after their fantastic lovemaking. Cuddled in each other's arms and Jacey fast asleep.

But it wasn't long before he felt an angry prodding against his naked hip.

He figured it must be Jacey kicking his thigh in an attempt to tease him. So, without opening his eyes, he shooed her away with his hand. The prodding continued and grew harder making Ben believe the guide must have found them and was pissed off for getting ditched. Reluctantly he opened his eyes, fully ready to apologize for sneaking away, when he saw them.

Females.

Very naked females.

Standing around Jacey and him.

Shit!

"What have we here?" The dark haired woman who'd been prodding him looked somewhat familiar. But the rifle she held in her hand captured most of his attention. A weapon that looked strangely similar to a double-barrel, side-by-side shotgun his grandfather had once owned.

And this one looked just as deadly.

"Good afternoon, ladies," Ben smiled.

The sudden inhalation of breaths made Ben instantly realize his mistake. Males weren't supposed to know how to speak around these parts.

Double shit!

He'd blown his cover by his good manners.

"Queen Jacey and a talking man. How very interesting."

Beside him, Jacey stirred.

Ben nudged her shoulder in an attempt to warn her about their new guests, when something painful slammed into the side of his temple, knocking him out cold.

* * * * *

Ben awoke in what appeared to be a jail cell devoid of anything. Not a bed. Not even a toilet.

He lay naked and alone on the chilly ground where they'd dumped him. Cold metal shackles were clamped over his wrists and legs with one-foot long chains connecting them.

Aside from a lovely headache pounding at his left temple and still feeling a little weak from the after-effects with the panther tussle, he seemed pretty much intact.

Staring at the craggy walls and rock ceiling, his stomach sank at the realization that obviously there was no way out of this place. Not unless he walked through the front door, but that was highly unlikely due to the thick rusty bars barring the way.

"Jacey!" He called out, wincing at the pain his shouting caused.

His voice echoed back to him.

Panic edged into his thoughts. Where the hell was she? Where had they taken her? What were they doing to her?

The woman who'd conked him over the head didn't look the Breeder type. They'd worn nipple rings and clit rings similar to Jacey's. Could they be her people? They wouldn't harm her, would they?

Whoever they were they didn't seem too pleased to find Jacey and him together.

Hell, he needed to figure a way out of this cell, find Jacey and get out of here.

He tried to move, but the pain in his temple radiated throughout his head, stopping him cold.

Okay, so he wasn't going anywhere fast. He had to think of a plan. And from the distinct sound of several approaching footsteps, he better think of one in a heck of a hurry.

Once again he tried to get his butt in gear. This time he fought off the pain enough to get himself into a seated position. With his naked back planted against the cold wall, he braced his feet firmly on the floor and awaited his fate.

Relief swept through him when Jacey, totally naked as he was and wearing shackles around her wrists and ankles, was pushed into the jail cell.

When she saw him, her eyes lit up. The sickening sound of chains rippled through the air as she hobbled to his side.

"Are you all right, Ben Hero?" she asked as she slumped down beside him. Her sweet scent sifted into his nostrils, automatically calming him.

"I am now," he admitted.

"How touching." The woman, clad in a plain green uniform, stood on the other side of the bars glowering at them.

Ben recognized her instantly. The bitch that had conked him over the head.

"Leave us, Cath." Jacey said firmly.

"You can't order me or anyone else around anymore, my Queen," the woman named Cath smirked. "You aren't in charge of this hub anymore. I am. Within hours I will be officially crowned the new Queen and you will be dead." Cath laughed harshly and walked away from their cell.

"What is her problem anyway?" Ben asked, when her footsteps faded away.

"Never mind about her. How are you feeling?" She ran her fingertips along the side of his temple where he'd been hit. He winced at the combination of pain and arousal her delicate touch invoked.

"You've got a bump the size of a chicken egg, Ben Hero."

"You keep rubbing my head like that, I'll be having a bigger bump somewhere else." He wasn't joking either.

The warm scent of her body and the feathery way her fingers ran through his hair was doing a sexy number on his own body, and remarkably making his headache disappear.

"They've injected you with a sex drug," Jacey whispered against his ear. "Just like they did to me."

"As if we need it," Ben chuckled.

"This is not the time to start joking. We are in serious trouble."

"Like in D-E-A-D trouble? What was with that anyways? And why give us sex drugs? Or do I want to ask?"

She didn't answer. Her glazed eyes raked over his solid erection, making every other part of his body awaken with desire.

"I think those sex drugs are kicking in quite nicely," he found himself whispering.

She blinked and shook her head.

"We should concentrate on something else."

"Like?"

"Escaping or maybe figure out who set me up to be captured by The Breeders."

"I think I can help you on who's behind all of this."

The cute way she tilted her head made her brown hair sparkle brilliantly in the dim light of the prison cell and all thoughts of explaining his theory disintegrated.

Her eyes grew fevered. Her nipples looked like two beautiful puckered rosebuds and the dainty way she stroked his injured temple with her soft fingertips and the way the chains between her shackles rattled throughout the silence only increased the volcanic charge zipping through his penis.

"Who do you think is behind it?" she asked.

Her lips were full. Sensually curved. Trembling.

Oh man, he wanted to kiss her so badly. Her intoxicating scent overwhelmed him and in an instant his lips melded with hers.

* * * * *

"What's happening?" Ben anxiously whispered to Jacey as two strong women led both of them, still in their restraints, out of the drab prison into a sunlit yard.

"They're going to kill us." Jacey's voice was calm, matter-of-fact. Apparently she'd accepted their fate. Unfortunately he wasn't quite as accommodating.

Anger rose within him like a violent storm.

"Is this anyway to treat your Queen!" He shouted at the large group of females gathered in the prison yard.

The women, who'd been chattering with excitement amongst each other, all turned around at the sound of his voice.

Their eyes widened with fear. Mouths dropped open in disbelief. Others swayed with shock and yet others smiled lustily at his thick arousal.

Beside him, Jacey swore very un-Queen-like beneath her breath.

"She is your leader, isn't she?" Ben continued, desperation clawing at his insides as they led him closer to an area where he spied four stakes in the ground with ropes tied to them. Nearby, half buried in a log, was a double-edged sharp looking axe. It didn't take a genius to know what fate awaited him. "You're supposed to be faithful to her, aren't you?" he shouted.

The woman named Cath, stepped out in front of him, blocking their way.

"The man speaks words. You can see for yourself, the Queen was found with a talking man. Another reason she must die with him."

Cheers went up through the crowd.

"I'd suggest you keep silent, Ben Hero, or they might cut out your tongue. I'd rather you keep it while we make love."

"Make love? I thought you said they were going to kill us?"

"They are. While we make love."

* * * * *

Jacey's heart crashed against her chest as she watched Ben struggle valiantly against the women who pushed him to the ground. Within a minute they'd expertly lashed his arms and legs to the stakes.

She'd seen this done only a handful of times. The male, who'd usually done something severely wrong, was lashed down, totally helpless. The women would take turns fucking him. When they were sexually satisfied, he was beheaded.

During her reign, she'd never felt the compulsion to order any of the wrong-doing males that her hub possessed to die in that particular way. She preferred a swift death for males, with no suffering.

She prayed to the Goddess of Freedom that Ben would have only *her* before he was beheaded. She didn't think she could stand watching others take him against his will.

Seeing him naked, aroused and splayed out for her, sent raw desire shooting through her insides. The sex drugs were still within her. Still working their wonderful magic. Still effectively clouding her thoughts.

She pushed against the erotic feelings and tried to make her anger work for her. It did work, to a certain degree, but was it enough to keep her from losing herself in the threatening pleasure?

157

If her hands and ankles hadn't been chained, she would have grabbed the nearest woman, broken her neck like a twig and seized a weapon. She would have freed her male, killing anyone who got in the way.

"She didn't break your laws on purpose!" Ben shouted at the women who were leaning over him.

Jacey watched helplessly as he grimaced with embarrassment. Their frantic feminine hands groped his hard penis and testicles. Their eyes were glazed with lust as they tried to arouse him to an even higher level, if that were possible.

"The Breeders were hired to do it." Ben yelled as he continued to struggle against his restraints and the feminine hands roving over his body. "Hired by someone in this hub. And I know who!"

"Cut out the male's tongue!" Cath ordered.

"No!" Jacey screamed, throwing herself forward, trying to intercept a woman who was already heading toward Ben, a shiny five-inch long knife in her hand.

"I know who did it! And I know why!" Ben continued.

"Let the male speak!"

Jacey stared in disbelief as the crowd parted to allow High Queen Jasmine to step forward.

"The male is a brute. He knows nothing!" Cath shouted.

"I know you were the one who hired The Breeders, Cath!" Ben cried.

An excited murmur shot through the crowd.

"Silence!" Jasmine shouted.

The crowd hushed immediately.

"Do you have proof of these accusations, Ben Hero?"

"I saw Cath at The Breeders hub! I thought they were your enemies? Why would she be talking with your enemies? Was she trying to free Jacey? I don't think so. She spoke with the guard who was whipping me. Afterwards, the guard took me to Jacey's cell."

"We're getting off topic here!" Cath interjected. "The fact is Queen Jacey was fucked by a male. The tests prove it. The tests prove she is with child."

Jacey felt as if a fist slammed into her gut. She was pregnant? Her gaze immediately fell to Ben. His expression was of shock also.

"How do you know this, Cath? How do you know Jacey is pregnant?" Jasmine questioned.

"I...one of The Breeders informed me."

"The only time I was tested was in The Breeder's cell." Jacey announced.

"And why would a Breeder, your enemy, tell you, Cath?" Jasmine countered.

"Because I am the reigning Queen. I have a right to know this."

"Not officially. According to our laws, until you are officially crowned, you cannot order this Death Ceremony." Jasmine said firmly.

She turned to the women still crouched over Ben. "Take them back to their jail cell until such a time as this matter can be resolved."

"But High Queen, they are here. Do it now. Why make them suffer longer than they have to?" Cath replied tartly.

"You mean why make you suffer, don't you? The accusations will be investigated thoroughly. Bring them back to their cell."

No one moved.

"I am a High Queen. Do as I say!" Jasmine snapped.

Jacey's legs wobbled with relief as some of the women quickly released Ben from the restraints.

A moment later, still clad in the heavy shackles, they were both led back to their cells.

* * * * *

Ben's hand lay protectively over Jacey's warm abdomen as he watched the slow rise and fall of her tanned breasts. She'd finally fallen asleep after they'd talked endlessly about the baby. He'd reassured her he was thrilled at the thought of becoming a daddy.

He'd also told her he was from Earth. She hadn't seemed surprised at all. But she did seem eager to learn about how children were raised on Earth. So he'd explained how parents were responsible for naming and raising their children. Told her they would have many kids and the boys and girls would all be educated equally.

When she heard that, a beautiful smile had tilted her full lips and she'd cuddled into his arms, and fallen into an exhausted sleep.

Now all he had to do was figure out how to break out of this fine establishment so he could keep that pretty smile on her face.

The sound of a key grating in the cell door made his head snap up. He inhaled sharply at the sight of High Queen Jasmine opening the cell door.

She put her finger against her lips in an indication that he should remain silent. Beside him, Jacey roused. She blinked with disbelief as Jasmine shoved keys into Jacey's shackles, freeing her. Then she started on Ben's restraints.

"Come quickly." Jasmine hissed as the last shackle dropped off his wrist.

Ben and Jacey didn't have to be told twice. Within a split second they were on their feet, following Jasmine down the long corridors of the prison and finally out a back door in the mild summer night.

The same guide that Jasmine had given them earlier stood there waiting for them.

"Go! Now!" Jasmine said as she hugged Jacey.

"Thank you." Ben said as he grabbed and shook the woman's hand. "You may get into trouble if anyone finds out what you've done. You are welcome to come with us."

Her eyes widened with surprise at his offer. "I will be fine. Just keep Jacey and the child safe, Ben Hero."

"I will."

Jasmine hugged Jacey warmly.

Tears glistened in both women's eyes, making Ben's throat tighten with emotion. Obviously the two women were very good friends and he felt a tinge of guilt for having to separate them.

"Follow your hearts," Jasmine whispered to both of them.

Ben nodded and grabbed Jacey's hand. They quickly followed the guide into the nearby darkness.

* * * * *

Jacey grinned at the tall, plump guide who sat on the beach, a few hundred yards away. She'd refused to come any closer to the strange looking silver space ship settled on the sandy shore of Freedom Sea, informing Jacey she would wait right where she was for further instructions.

"You think she'll be okay?" Ben asked as they walked hand in hand toward the craft.

"She'll be fine. She'll stay with us for as long as we need her in order to contact Jasmine about shutting off the disintegration machines. And then we can leave." She stopped abruptly a sudden thought struck horror into her heart.

"What's wrong?"

"The baby. Can our baby travel safely through space?"

"I don't see why not. Many pregnant astronauts travel through space without a problem." Then he chuckled. "You aren't starting to worry already, are you? The kid isn't even born."

"I don't know why I'm suddenly worried. I just don't want anything to happen to the child. I want her or him to be born healthy."

"Spoken like a true Earth mother."

Ben's compliment made her heart burst with love. Actually she didn't think she'd ever been happier in her life. She had Ben Hero and now his child. Things were perfect.

Excitement made Jacey's heart crash against her chest as they ascended the metal steps that led to a platform in front of the ship.

She watched curiously as Ben placed his hand on a console, then gasped in surprise as a door slid noiselessly open.

Ben wasted no time in tugging her inside. Behind them, the door slid closed.

"No one's here," he commented. "Probably out looking for me. I'll check the messages. See where they are. Have yourself a look around."

Jacey nodded as she surveyed the colorful display of lights blinking on the various consoles.

She noted three cozy looking single beds and three green chairs in front of a large window.

"This is where you live when you are in space?"

"Yep, this is our home away from home." Ben said as he slumped into one of the chairs and pressed a button on the chair armrest.

"Welcome back, Ben Hero." A smoky feminine voice echoed throughout the interior.

Jacey's eyes narrowed as she scanned for the voice's body. She saw no one and realized it was a mechanical sound similar to the noise accompanying those moving pictures she'd watched with Jasmine.

"Ashley, are there any messages for me?" Ben asked the voice.

"You have one message, Ben. Dated two days ago."

Jacey immediately recognized the voice of Joe Hero as it crackled through the spacecraft. "Okay brothers, were are you? We've been hanging around here waiting, but you guys aren't showing. We're hiking up the north beach, going to try and track down Buck. He's the one with the most recent footprints. I'll be calling in from the com-link, so if you get back here, stay put. That's an order."

"End of message, Ben." Ashley said softly.

"Thanks, Ash."

Ben frowned and leaned forward, pressing a few buttons on the consul in front of him. "Looks like Buck's missing too. I'm not surprised. Of all my brothers, he's the one who finds trouble everywhere he goes and he doesn't even look for it. Joe sounded kind of pissed, didn't he?"

"If that's another word for mad, I think you're right."

"He doesn't issue orders unless he's pissed. No telling when they'll be back, so we'll just have to stay here and wait."

"I'm sure they will show up before long. Besides, we can always tell the guide to contact Jasmine and tell her everything is on hold."

Ben nodded and stood. He waved a muscular arm at a nearby alcove with green plastic cupboards that lined all three walls.

"Are you hungry?" he asked in a rather serious tone. "We've got lots of nutritious foods in the pantry. Dried peaches. Dried steak and mashed potatoes. Dried vegetables. We just add water and voila, instant meal. You're eating for two now, y'know."

"Now who is sounding worried?"

He grinned. "All Earth dads worry just as much as moms," he explained.

"Good, I'm glad. Then the child will be protected for sure."

163

"So, how about some food? I'm sure the kid must be hungry by now." Ben started toward the pantry but Jacey grabbed his elbow, stopping him cold.

"Actually I'm famished. But it isn't for food."

"Not for food, you say? Exactly what are you hungry for?" A wicked smile tilted his lips, unleashing a strong craving deep inside Jacey's lower belly. Wrapping her arms around his neck, she pulled him against her. The solid impact of his hard body urged many pleasurable sensations to cascade over her.

"I'm hungry for this." She grabbed his thick wrist. Guiding his hand between their tightly fitted bodies, she pressed his fingers against her clit. His hand cradled her cunt intimately, burning her flesh, driving her mad with want.

Then his calloused thumb slipped between her labia lips and leisurely dragged over the tight bundle of sensitive nerves in her pleasure nub, cutting loose the familiar urge to be fucked.

A hot finger slipped erotically inside her vagina and she arched against his hand.

"And this?"

"You certainly got the idea and the touch." Jacey purred.

Her pulse quickened as his head lowered. His mouth, eager and fierce, slid erotically over hers, making Jacey close her eyes as an explosion of emotions firmly gripped her.

Safety. Warmth. Desire.

They were good feelings. Feelings she wished every woman could experience with a male. But she doubted a truce would ever be struck between the males and females on her planet due to the problems in their history. Once trust was broken between males and females, it wasn't easily won back.

She was lucky with Ben Hero. For some reason, she trusted him to protect her and their child from danger. It gave her the strength and courage she needed to travel to this planet called Earth and to give their child a chance at a different life.

The pressure of his thumb increased against her clit. A tiny sob escaped her lips into his mouth as the raw heat built inside her and spread like a fever throughout her body.

Her breath became labored. Her lips burned beneath his seductive assault.

At the same time, his heavy arousal, big and satiny hard, stabbed against her wet cunt. But he didn't enter her. She cried out her protest and he ripped his mouth from hers.

"Open your eyes, Jacey." He commanded.

She did and saw the desire shining in his eyes. Other emotions lay thick in those blue depths. So thick that Jacey couldn't breathe at the intensity of them.

She knew exactly what he was going to say, even before he said it.

"I love you," he whispered proudly.

"I love you, too." Jacey said softly, meaning every word.

He kissed her fiercely and with one swift thrust he buried his throbbing cock into her very soul.

The fit was perfect and she knew her heart would belong to Ben Hero forever.

A HERO NEEDED
&

Trademarks Acknowledgement

The author acknowledges the trademarked status and trademark owners of the following wordmarks mentioned in this work of fiction:

Polo: PRL USA Holdings, Inc.

Chapter One
Hideaway, Maine USA
In the not too distant future…

ဆ

Jenna MacLean couldn't help but shudder in aroused excitement as she watched her ex-boyfriend Sully Hero saunter toward where she sat on the satiny sheets of her lace-canopied, four-poster bed. His six-foot, naked, muscular body looked gorgeously tense, his huge cock fully engorged, eager to impale her.

Behind him she spotted another man silhouetted against the rose-patterned wallpaper watching her, his features blurry, his identity not yet recognizable, but she knew the other would be just as well-hung, just as eager to please her.

Oh, yes! Come to me!

Reaching between her legs, she found her ultra-sensitive clit and massaged it, allowing both men to watch.

Sexy sparks of need flashed through Sully's green gaze and his cock blushed a deep shade of purple—his smooth, mushroom-shaped cock head looked angry and just as purple as it thrust itself from its sheath.

She could smell him. An erotic masculine scent that always played havoc with her senses. Always made her crave the wicked pleasures he gave so willingly.

Heavy, tortured breaths shot through the air as he stood over her bed, his hand stroking the massive eight-inch length of his silk-encased cock.

Stroking. Touching. Preparing.

Oh, God! She'd craved to have Sully back in her life for so long.

Her breathing quickened, met his in the same wickedly quick tempo. His erection seemed so unbelievably long. Longer than she remembered. Thick. Swollen. Ready to pleasure her.

Her finger moved more frantically over her slippery, achy clit, the erotic pleasure spiraled around her, making her whimper and squirm as both men watched.

Desperate hunger blazed across Sully's handsome face. The sight made her cry out her own need.

"I let you get away from me too many times, Jenna," he growled. "It won't happen again. Once you've been initiated into the Ménage Club you'll never leave me." The passion searing his voice made her believe he would stay with her forever. Never leave her again.

His mention of the notorious Ménage Club made shivers of delight shoot through her. The club specialized in bringing couples back together, couples who would otherwise never do so on their own. Couples like Sully and her.

Both men moved closer. Moved toward her like wild predators surrounding their mate. Each ready to take her.

Muscles in their broad chests rippled, lovely tanned muscles in their arms bulged as they both continued to stroke their engorged cocks.

She felt the mattress shift beneath her as the two men came upon her bed.

Oh, God! She'd waited so long for this. Waited too long!

"Okay, what else should I put down in the want ad?"

Jenna MacLean blinked herself out of the wickedly delicious fantasy to find her best friend, twenty-five-year-old Meemee Caldwell, staring at her with blue-gray eyes that glittered with such contagious excitement Jenna had to force herself to steady her breath as she focused her attention back to what they'd been doing.

"What have we got so far?"

Meemee grimaced. Her wine-colored lips dipped into a frown and her straight golden-colored blonde hair swung over her shoulders as she looked down at the napkin she'd been using to write Jenna's want ad.

"'A Hero Needed. White picket fence gal needs a man who loves to walk in the rain.' What else?"

"Okay… I want him to have a nice sense of humor. Must be gentle and caring. Also white picket fence material."

Meemee rolled her eyes, opened her mouth, pretended to stick her finger down her throat and made a gagging sound. "Oh, come on. If you want humor, gentle and caring, and a fenced yard, get yourself a Saint Bernard dog."

Jenna giggled. "Don't take it so seriously, Meems. We're only pretending."

"Me? Serious? Oh, please. Never. You know me better than that. I am the last person on this earth who'd take anything serious. I'm just curious about what kind of guy would rip your soul apart. What kind of man makes your heart pound? Your legs weaken? Makes your pussy scream for his cock. Oh, shit, I forgot to write down he has to be well-hung. He has to have the tool to do the job, am I right?"

Definitely well-hung. Jenna nodded in agreement as Meemee began writing again.

"And make his cock at least eight inches long, two inches thick."

"Now you're talking, Jen. Give me more. Give me your heart."

Meemee looked at her with such sweet desperation flooding her heart-shaped face that it made Jenna a bit uneasy. Meems was definitely looking at this too seriously. But what the heck did it matter? No one would see it. It was just something to pass the time, something to giggle over on their weekly girls' night out.

"So? What do you want in a man, Jen? Spill it."

"I want…" Gosh, what did she want? She found her gaze straying around the cozy western-themed room. It was decorated with several large wagon wheels on the ceiling, rough-hewn, pine-planked walls and tiny, flickering oil lamps set in the middle of white and red checkered cloth-covered square tables.

A rustic red-bricked fireplace complete with a black cauldron hung over it, flickering blue-yellow flames. Nestled in a corner, totally out of its element sat a Fifties-style jukebox, blasting out the latest Shania Twain tune.

Her mouth watered at the tantalizing scents of frying burgers and baking pepperoni pizza. She focused her attention to the two sexy bartenders pouring drinks behind the nearby mahogany bar — in particular to the tall, muscular, brown-haired hunk.

A familiar yearning started deep down in her lower belly.

She wanted him.

She wanted Sully Well-Hung Hero. But he was off-limits. He'd made his decision about them when he'd walked out on their relationship over four years ago. Despite that fact though, she just couldn't seem to stop herself from coming to his damn bar and getting her eye-candy fix of him every week since he'd come back to town.

God, did she have a problem with torturing herself or what?

"Green eyes," she found herself mumbling as she kept an eye on Sully.

The son of a bitch appeared to be flirting with some perfectly thin, leggy, blonde bitch as he poured her a drink from behind the bar. The blonde laughed at something he said and her irritating voice grated along Jenna's nerves, making that familiar, awful jealousy she hated so much spring through her like a heated torch.

He'd been back in town for a month now and hadn't so much as taken the time to say anything more than a formal hello whenever she and Meems came into his newly purchased bar on their weekly jaunt. Not that she expected him to say much to her. Especially after the way they'd left things in the past.

"And he should be clean-cut, have dark brown, short hair...a homebody...maybe a guy who looks like Orlando Bloom." Or Sully. "But he has to be a guy who wants to settle down."

Somebody totally the opposite of Sully.

Maybe she should find a guy not as good-looking as him. A guy who didn't capture every red-blooded woman's attention whenever he passed them on the street. The attention he got from gorgeously sexy women made her feel as if she were too fat for him simply because he was physically fit and she wasn't.

Her pulse couldn't help but quicken at the sight of Sully's shoulder muscles rippling beneath the tight, black, muscle T-shirt that said in bold, white lettering across his wide chest *Sully's Bar & Grill*.

She could still remember how hard those tanned muscles felt beneath her exploring fingertips when they'd made love. How his groans of arousal had made her feel so powerful. Had made her blush as her insecurities about being too overweight to attract such a gorgeous hunk always seemed to blossom whenever she'd been naked with him.

"Okay, so I gather you're stuck about what to put down. How about sexually? Do you want sex gentle or untamed with your man?"

"Depends on our mood. One thing for sure is I want him sexually adventurous so he can teach me to be the same way," Jenna replied, ripping her gaze from Sully and back to her friend.

"Sexually adventurous trainer wanted." Her friend nodded her approval as she wrote it down on the napkin.

Oh, why couldn't she look more like Meems? Meemee was curvy, svelte, blonde and so very pretty with her big blue eyes and a gorgeous body that attracted delicious-looking hunks who seemed to flutter around her like butterflies. Hunks she used to satisfy herself with sexually and then tossed aside.

Although Meemee had never told her, Jenna suspected her friend had the hots for Tony, their lifelong friend and Sully's part-time bartender and best friend.

Tony's sharp angular features, short, feathery black hair and bronzed skin didn't betray his Greek heritage. He was also the man who had created and owned the Ménage Club. It wasn't just a swinger's club where men and women ventured to for sex. It was a relationship club. A place where couples could face their worst fears, and she definitely had some issues she wouldn't mind working on.

God! They were both so pathetic in drooling over men they couldn't have. Try as they might not to venture into Sully's bar, one or the other always mentioned it after they'd seen their weekly movie or after a shopping spree. "And he has to be romantic. Sex toys would be nice too. He's got to like sex toys."

"Sex toys. Now you're talking, woman," she giggled, and kept writing, leaving Jenna to remember the first time Sully had mentioned they should try toys to allow them to enjoy sex in a different, exciting way. Back then, though, she'd been unable to accept them as a natural part of their relationship. She'd been so inexperienced. Insecure and no confidence in herself as a woman. She still couldn't understand how Sully had even been attracted to her with her size eighteen, sometimes twenty, sometimes sixteen-sized body.

She had big breasts, a wide waist and a big butt. Yet he'd pursued her. She'd been twenty and he'd been twenty-one. Sully had been her first lover and after their breakup, he hadn't been her last. She'd slept with two more guys. Guys she'd cared about. They just hadn't been as passionate in bed or as tender as Sully.

Jenna sighed.

Saying no to sex toys with Sully had been a big mistake. It had been an even bigger mistake letting him go so easily. But back then she'd adopted her grandmother's frame of mind that a couple in love didn't need arousal by artificial stimulation. That their bodies should have been enough to keep each other satisfied. On top of that, his mention of sex toys had made her feel insecure about her sexuality. Made her think if she was truly satisfying him in bed, he wouldn't be thinking of other ways to get aroused.

As she'd grown older, her craving to have Sully back had changed her tastes and beliefs. She'd begun to realize she'd taken on her grandmother's excess baggage, had stifled her own natural need to explore her sexuality.

Now that her grandparents were dead and she was finally out from under their overly strict rules and living on her own, Jenna felt more open to new ideas about sex. Okay, so she was a lot more open to sex and what it stood for in a loving relationship.

"And he's got to be into anal play," Jenna found herself whispering, trying out the new territory on her friend. To her surprise, Meemee held a straight face as she kept pen to napkin.

"And he has to be interested in light bondage."

"Meaning he has to like it on himself? Or on you?"

"Both of us."

Meems nodded. "Nice. Very nice. Hero has to be into mutual light bondage."

"Definitely ménages…to keep the sex life spicy," Jenna continued as her thoughts flew back to the exclusive Ménage Club. Indiscreet research through friends had revealed the secret club consisted of a group of men and women who swore they could help troubled couples get together again with the help of a third.

"Ménages are welcome," Meemee said as she wrote quickly. "What else?"

Jenna sighed and tried to put Sully out of her mind. It didn't work. They'd fought much too often during their relationship. Broken up more times than she could count and now, years later, she was more than willing to join the Club, to watch the enjoyment flash across his face, to watch his cock harden while another man pleasured her. To try and use the Club to patch things between them. Unfortunately, now that her interest in sex had finally broken free, it looked as if he'd lost interest in her.

"That's about it. But at the top of the list he definitely has to be a white picket fence kind of guy."

Meaning a man who wouldn't run out on her no matter how badly they fought. A man who wouldn't walk away no matter how many times he said he loved her.

Jenna sighed wearily. Again, he needed to be a man totally opposite of Sully.

"He sounds absolutely delicious," Meemee cooed. "Not many of those types around these days."

"Can I get you two ladies anything else?"

Sully Hero's deep voice sailed through the air and gripped Jenna's veins, heating her pussy so wickedly she almost moaned aloud. God help her, she always reacted so deliciously toward his masculine voice, even after all this time apart.

"I'd like another beer, Sully." Meemee grinned. "And please don't call us ladies. There are no ladies in this booth."

Sully's intense green gaze zeroed in on Jenna. "You sure about that?"

Jenna got his meaning loud and clear. As far as he was concerned, she was a pure lady, no wildcat in her. "So, Sully," Meems said quickly. "Take a look at this ad Jen and I are working on. Give us a man's opinion. If you saw it in the newspaper, would you answer it?"

Horrified, Jenna helplessly watched as Meemee, with a sly grin plastered across her face, handed Sully the napkin with the ad on it.

Meems had set her up! Bitch!

"A Hero Needed," Sully read, and cocked an eyebrow at Jenna.

"Jenna came up with that one."

"She did, did she?" His hot look rammed into her and practically ripped her breath away.

"Actually, the ad is hers," Meemee admitted, and winked at Jenna.

Satisfied pleasure zipped through her as his eyes widened. Obviously he was shocked at what Meemee had written for her, proving yet again his opinion about her being straightlaced hadn't changed.

"The ad is private. If you wouldn't mind…" She held out her hand, expecting him to give the napkin back, but he ignored her and kept reading.

"White picket fence-type, old-fashioned gal needs a man who loves to walk in the rain…" He continued on in silence then cleared his throat, and said in a somewhat strangled voice, "Must be well-hung. Eight inches at least."

Oh, heavens! Was this embarrassing or what? Was he remembering the one time she'd mustered up the courage to measure Sully's cock just for fun? He'd been exactly eight glorious inches long and two inches thick.

She threw Meemee a hateful glance. A look that promised her best friend she was in big trouble. Meemee, however, seemed unfazed and smiled wickedly.

Damn her!

"Sex toys, huh?" Interest tinged Sully's voice.

Heat sparked her cheeks and curled like wildfire through her from tip to toes.

Oh, boy, it was getting too hot in here. She needed another beer. An ice-cold one. A frozen one would be even better. Then she could roll the frosty bottle over her suddenly too-tight breasts and aching nipples. Not to mention sliding it against her suddenly feverish pussy.

But until that could happen, she'd settle for grabbing her ice water glass and resting it against her flaming cheeks. She eyed the glass on the table and the delicious-looking, half-melted ice cubes floating around at the top, resisting the urge to dip her finger inside, grab a cube and run it between her hot pussy lips.

"Someone to teach you to be sexually adventurous?"

There was that tinge of surprise in his voice again. A sudden inhalation of his breath as he continued. "Romance, light bondage, anal…"

He stopped—obviously he was reading the "ménages are welcome" part.

Would he think she was being too promiscuous by mentioning all those things? Or would he take the hint that she was now interested in being with him and willing to join the Ménage Club to fix their nonexistent relationship?

She felt her face heat even harder.

"So? What do you think, Sully?" Meemee asked, thankfully coming to her rescue. The tone of her voice sounded so sweetly innocent, as if she hadn't set the whole thing up.

"I'm sure there would be lots of guys answering this type of ad," Sully replied, and placed the napkin in front of Jenna. She didn't hesitate to snap it up and crunch it in her hand, hiding it from his smoldering gaze.

"You sound like every guy's wet-dream girl…but can you deliver if someone answers the ad?"

His bold question made her stiffen in her seat. The son of a bitch had just insulted her by insinuating she wouldn't deliver.

She forced herself to relax. Sully had no intention of answering her ad — he was too busy flirting with his big-boobed, leggy, blonde bitch clients at the bar.

"Oh, I'm sure whoever answers my ad will be quite satisfied," Jenna purred, enjoying the wild spark flaring in his eyes. "It's just too bad my hero hasn't come along yet. He's missing out on a lot."

"Perhaps," Meemee broke in softly as she thoughtfully fingered the mouth of her almost empty beer bottle, "her hero is standing right beneath her nose and she doesn't even know it yet?"

Good one, Meems. She threw Meemee another hateful glance. The last complication she needed in her life was sexy Sully Hero. He would have her in his bed twenty-four/seven just as he'd tried to do years ago. Not that she would necessarily mind this time around. This time she didn't have her overly protective grandparents waiting for her to come home. They'd always asked her where she'd been and what she'd been doing. Their relationship hadn't been an open one about sex, so she'd always lied and said she'd been out with Meemee. Although she'd been twenty at the time when she'd met Sully, she'd still been living with her grandparents and feeling it was her duty to help her grandmother take care of her grandfather after he'd suffered a devastating stroke several years prior.

Now as he stood beside the table, she found herself eagerly awaiting his answer. None came as a pretty, long-legged blonde waitress suddenly interrupted them.

God! What was it with Sully and all these blonde women?

"Boss, the cook is threatening to quit again."

Sully looked as if he might say something to Jenna and she found herself holding her breath, anxiously waiting like a pathetic dog for him to give her a glimmer of hope that they just might have another chance. Instead, he simply nodded and left with the waitress.

"Shit, Jenna. He is so fucking hot! Why you let him go is beyond me."

"Meems, please, I already told you why we split up."

"Yeah, I know you said it was all those fights you two had. For instance, *your* hang-up about your weight—*your* insane jealousy about other women who looked at him—*your* inability to enjoy sex without feeling a tad guilty whenever he wanted to try anything but the missionary position. But Sully came back *here*, Jenna, after saying he'd never come back. And he even bought the bar. Maybe he came back for you?"

"You're dreaming, Meems. He didn't come back for me."

If he had, he would have approached her by now. Wouldn't he?

"Then why would he come back here of all places? Why return to the one place he swore he'd never come back to when you two broke up?"

She'd been thinking about that herself. "I'm sure his reasons are personal."

"Meaning?"

"I mean it is none of our business why he came back here, understand?"

"Loud and clear." Meemee grinned wickedly. She sucked back the last of her beer, leaving Jenna with the idea her friend had something else up her sleeve. Something she wasn't going to like.

* * * * *

A Hero Needed

White picket fence-type, old-fashioned gal needs a man who loves to walk in the rain. Must be well-hung. At least eight inches long. Two inches thick. Sharp green eyes. Clean-cut. Dark brown, short hair…a homebody, white picket fence type of guy.

Sexual requirements – gentle yet untamed lover. Sexually adventurous who will train to be same.

Must be romantic, enjoy sex toys, into anal play, interested in mutual light bondage, ménages are welcome.

Sully lifted the crinkled napkin off the night table from where he'd left it before taking his cold shower and pressed it against his nostrils, inhaling Jenna's sweet, seductive scent. He found his heart picking up speed and his shaft hardened with exquisite need.

Christ! Her feminine aroma always did that to him. Always made his mind whirl out of control, made him want to tangle his fingers through her luscious, tangled reddish-brown hair, made him want to stare into her bright blue, sparkling eyes that reminded him of storm clouds every time they'd fought – and they'd fought a lot.

Nonetheless he'd never gotten enough of staring into her eyes, never got tired of stroking his hands along her voluptuous, silky, plus-size curves and sinking his fingers into her fleshy hips when he thrust his cock into her tight pussy.

Her sexy, feminine scent always sent his senses spiraling into alert mode. She made him want to explore her every curvy crevice. Taste every part of her. Tonight at the bar he'd watched her perfectly shaped eyebrows arch with irritation as he'd read her Hero Needed ad. He'd wanted to grab her, tug her upstairs, throw her on his bed and lose himself inside her tight pussy. Just as he'd been able to do in the past.

Being away from her had been hell. He'd found that fact out shortly after he'd left her.

Even with NASA inventing spaceships that could use small amounts of hydrogen to fuel rockets into exploring space, allowing him to travel extensively throughout the galaxy and do what he'd always dreamed of doing, he'd missed her. The new, safe rockets as well as the invention of hyperspace travel had made it easy for NASA to put out the call for men and women who were interested in space exploration to join the NASA team of astronauts. Training was minimal, training pay fantastic and the computers took care of everything on the spaceships. All he had to do was make sure the cameras recorded everywhere he went on the planets.

Although training was exciting and the subsequent contract of space exploration had been intriguing, he hadn't been able to get sexy, shy Jenna MacLean out of his mind. He'd barely gotten through the past four years without wanting to pick up the phone every day and talk to her but, of course, that had been out of the question. They'd broken up and the last things they'd said to each other hadn't been pretty.

Recently, when a plum, top secret NASA assignment to explore the newly discovered planet named Paradise using a highly specialized warp speed, hydrogen spaceship was dropped in his and his cousins' laps, he'd found himself backing out at the last minute—backing out and coming back to Hideaway to plunge his entire life savings into this bar and securing the help of Tony and his Ménage Club to help him get Jenna back.

He blew out a frustrated breath as he drew the scented napkin away from his face and once again read the scribbled words.

The physical description on the ad was definitely him, but what about the rest of it? Had the two women simply been goofing around? Or had Jenna left it on the booth table for him to find on purpose? Or maybe she'd simply forgotten to take it along with her after the girls had left?

Jenna wanted a white picket fence kind of guy. By purchasing this bar and preparing the apartment upstairs, would she consider him white picket fence material? Would she ever trust him not to leave her again? He'd seen the pain, the hurt in her eyes every time she looked at him.

The mistrust made his gut twist in agony. So much so, he couldn't even bring himself to apologize to her.

Could he trust himself not to impulsively take off again if things didn't work out between them? Jenna had a jealousy streak that had made them fight like cats and dogs. He knew it stemmed from her insecurity of being overweight and the fact that he had tons of women who were his friends. But that's all they were—friends.

She hadn't been able to get used to the idea that he wanted *her*. Only her. No matter how many times he'd told her he'd always been physically attracted to plus-size women, the green-eyed monster of jealousy had just sat between them.

He'd watched Jenna tonight. Snuck peeks at her as one of the women from the Club had flirted with him. He'd seen the way Jenna's blue eyes had sparked with that familiar anger when she'd looked his way. Obviously her jealous tendencies still hadn't changed. If they got back together, it would only be a matter of time before they were fighting again. It would just be the same old song and dance. Fights just weren't his cup of tea.

One thing he knew for sure though, he wanted Jenna with his very heart and soul.

One thing he didn't know for sure was had he done the right thing in asking for help from the Ménage Club without asking her first?

He eyed the phone and resisted the impulse to pick up the receiver, call her and ask if she was still as interested in him as he was in her.

Maybe he should just throw the want ad napkin away? Maybe he should just sell the bar and get the hell out of town?

Maybe he should just go and take another cold shower.

* * * * *

"Dammit! Where is that napkin!" Jenna hissed as she rummaged through her bag after she'd plopped it onto the bathroom counter. She was sure she'd dumped the napkin into a side pocket of her purse right after Sully had left the booth. But now it wasn't there.

Shit!

Unfortunately, the remnants of his heated looks were still playing tease with her body. Her nipples ached to be touched and her clit needed to be soothed desperately — all because of Sully Hero.

Why in the world had he come back here and not gone off to God knew where with his astronaut cousins? And why did she insist on going to Sully's bar every Friday night and submitting herself to this torturous, sexual hell every time she came home without him?

That son of a bitch! He was probably screwing the blonde bombshell who'd been flirting with him. Just the thought of him being in another woman's arms made that familiar roar of red-hot anger grip her.

Oh! She hated feeling this way. Hated the idea that Sully might prefer a skinny chick over her. Hated the idea that she still cared about him at all.

Looking at herself in the mirror, she slipped off her blouse, unlatched the front clasps on her bra and watched her generous 36D-sized breasts fall free. Her globes looked heavy and swollen, her large, pink, lollipop-sized nipples appeared taut beneath the glare of her bathroom lights.

Damn Sully Hero for making her react this way every time he was merely in the same room as her.

Glancing lower, she noticed her thick waistline bulging slightly over her size sixteen skirt.

She frowned. Okay so she was still as overweight as ever. It wasn't as if she hadn't tried to lose the freaking flab. She ate relatively well, exercised almost every day with brisk, early morning walks and yet she never lost weight.

Her grandmother said it was in their genes. MacLean women were good farm stock material. Always on the big side. Big-boned, big-boobed and big-assed.

Even her grandmother had been overweight all her life, and pictures of her late mom showed her being overweight too.

When Jenna had been younger, she'd tried to defy her heritage, gone the diet route, laxatives, played a little with the bulimia stuff and tried to shed her pounds that way, but all it had gotten her in the end was sick as a dog.

She'd finally accepted herself as being a plus-size woman. Destined to be a size eighteen, sometimes size twenty, sometimes size sixteen, bouncing between a hundred and sixty and a hundred and ninety pounds for the rest of her life. She'd thought she'd gotten used to the idea, thought she'd finally felt comfortable in her own skin, that is…until sexy, well-hung Sully had sauntered back into town and conjured up all her insecurities again. Stupid, immature insecurities that whispered to her he was just too good-looking for big, tubby her.

Frig!

Why should she even care that he talked to other women more than he did to her? Their relationship was in the past, but those intense sexual sensations she got whenever she was around him or smelled him wasn't history. Those feelings were alive and eating her up—making her feel like a firecracker about to explode.

Frowning, she reached into a nearby drawer and pulled out the weighted nipple clamps she'd ordered through her favorite sex toy Internet site. According to the site, these clamps were made for beginners, the tension being adjustable and the grips rubber-tipped. She'd worked her way up to wearing them at tighter and longer tension levels until she now craved a harder grip. But these would do until she could get online and search for new ones.

She inhaled softly as each clamp bit into her tender, aroused nipples and she allowed the foot-long chain with the crystal stone weight to dangle between her breasts. The sight of her breasts being decorated in this way turned her on, adding to the already lusty feelings roaring through her at the thought of Sully being there in the bathroom with her, watching her, wanting her.

Ignoring the painful pleasure-pinch of the clamps, she unzipped her skirt and let it fall to the ceramic floor with a soft rustle, then pulled down her thong underwear and stepped out of them. From the same drawer she withdrew the glass dildo wand she'd bought at the same time as the clamps.

Dubbed the Long Dong Torpedo, it consisted of a nontoxic, red liquid glycerin compound that generated unbelievable heat just as a man's cock did. Eight inches long and two inches wide, it fit inside her pussy nice and snuggly, just as Sully's penis once had.

Slipping her free hand between her widespread legs, Jenna bit her lip to keep from crying out as her finger eagerly pushed past her swollen pussy lips and slipped inside her vagina to collect some moisture. Gliding back out she then began a slow, erotic slide of her wet finger over her aching clit while watching her reactions in the mirror.

This is what Sully would see when he watched another man touch her.

Half-lidded eyes, her full, red lips slightly parted as the increasing aroused bliss blew around her, her pink nipples growing darker beneath the sharp pinch of the clamps.

At the beginning, when she'd first started playing with the clamps, she'd kept them on only for five to ten minutes at a time, allowing herself to get used to the pleasure-pain, allowing her nipples to receive its much-needed blood supply. But now, she'd graduated and could keep them on for up to thirty minutes inside her comfort zone of pleasure-pain.

Her clit pulsed and sent shimmers of delight outward as she feverishly moved her wet finger over her swollen, tender nub.

In the mirror, she watched the length of silvery chain sway between her big breasts as she inhaled harshly, the heavy stone trying to drag her nipples down.

Would Sully enjoy watching the pleasure skim across her face as another man ran his finger over her engorged clit, making her moan and whimper her need for more?

Jenna drew more moisture from her ever increasingly wet vagina and rubbed harder, faster. She could feel the familiar sexual tension grip her. Could see her eyes begin to close. Heard her breathing grow heavy and tortured as her want for pleasure increased.

Grabbing the huge glass wand, she imagined it to be Sully's hot cock as she plunged it into her vagina in one quick thrust, burying it into her wetness.

Oh, yes! So hot! So big!

Keeping both hands moving, one finger eagerly rubbing her clit, the other sliding the dildo in and out of her, she scrunched her eyes tight and allowed the pleasure to burst over her.

Within seconds she became lost in the frantic, erotic waves of bliss.

Chapter Two

 හ

Jenna hadn't been kidding when she'd told Meemee to write down she was a white picket fence kind of woman, Sully thought as early the next morning he gazed at the newly painted white picket fence enveloping the cozy century home on the corner of Lilac Lane and Peppermint Trail. A colorful sign, splashed with the words *Jenna's Antiques and Collectibles* hung over the fancy, white screen door.

The house looked vanilla yet sexy at the same time.

He'd passed by the place many times since he'd been back, but he'd never gone inside. Not until the time had been right, and today…it was right.

He'd known she'd dated several local guys while he'd been away. Letters from Meemee had kept him up to speed about Jenna MacLean, whether he'd wanted to hear about her or not.

When his contract with NASA had been finished, he'd come straight back to Hideaway.

Back to Jenna.

But try as he might, he hadn't been able to seek her out and apologize for breaking up with her the way he had, for leaving her and for crushing the promises he'd made to her.

Apologies had always been hard for him. Stubborn Hero pride, his mother always called it. She'd warned him many times his pride would get him into trouble.

Looks like she'd been right.

Sully's heart picked up a mad pace as he caught sight of the two white-painted, fan-back settees on the front porch and the twig heart busting with ivy hanging on the wall between

the chairs. It looked like a nice place for a couple to sit during romantic evenings. His cock hardened at the thought of Jenna and himself sitting there, talking of what they would do with each other when they hit the sheets for the night.

He shook his head in frustration. He had no business chasing after Jenna MacLean. He didn't need her, didn't need the complication of love in his life again. Nor did he need the pain of a broken heart should she choose not to give them a second chance and that was only if he ever gathered up the nerve to ask her to take him back.

And then there was the Ménage Club. The possibilities of pleasuring Jenna using the club were endless.

Although she'd mentioned in her ad she would participate in ménages, if they got together and she discovered he wanted help from a third in their relationship from the Club, would she tell him to go to hell?

Or would she submit?

They'd been apart for so long. It was obvious from that napkin she'd changed, matured. Did she even want him back in her life? Was it not crazy of him to think they could simply pick up where they'd left off? To give their relationship another try based on a club that used extreme techniques to bring a couple back together?

He should just keep on walking. Pass the cute, little antiques shop and the life she'd built without him, and never look back.

Sully frowned as delicate perfume wafted up from the carefully tended flowerbeds. Once upon a time, he'd dreamed of a place like this. Dreamed of a woman like Jenna.

Old-fashioned yet sexually adventurous.

And then he'd met Jenna and his dreams had come half true, but because of her jealousy and his inability to reassure her she was number one in his life, he'd turned his back on her. He'd joined NASA's new astronaut training program that had promised great pay, big space adventures, astronaut training and a way to forget about Jenna.

Yeah, he'd gotten the great pay, space adventure and training, but his heart and bed had been empty without her. Maybe it was better for her if he just stayed away. Maybe it was best if he just kept on walking and walked right out of her life.

* * * * *

The sound of the bell jangling against the front door to the store made Jenna lift her head from the items she'd been unpacking in the back room.

"I'll be there in a minute!" she called out and returned her gaze to the yellowware dish set. The set was fantastic and in prime condition. She already had a buyer for it. She would get a great profit since she'd gotten it for peanuts. Not to mention the other goodies she'd purchased. A 1740s pewter cupboard, the Connecticut saltbox that was used as a hideout for the Tories during the Revolution then used to hide the Civil War slaves, and many other items that would sell like hotcakes this summer when the tourists came to the quaint little town of Hideaway, Maine.

Taking a quick sip of her strawberry cooler, she then made her way to the main room.

Hmm…no one here. They must have gone into one of the other areas in her shop. She'd arranged the entire first floor of the old century house using a theme for each room. The living room was the first room the customers saw when they came in. She'd crammed it with antique wingback chairs, a gorgeous sofa, a fish-packing crate she'd found at an out-of-town antiques fair. Among other things, she had a variety of antique kerosene lamps strewn about for effect, spinning wheels, late nineteenth-century cast-iron urns, a weaver's frame with hand-carved spools for the wool and tons of vintage bottles that cast jewellike hues as they sat on glass shelves in the numerous windows.

190

As she zipped through the kitchen, she couldn't help but glance at the decorative yet old copper pots and pans hanging from a hook lamp, the bright antique pottery displays sitting on the kitchen countertops or her prized possession—a cast-iron beauty of an aged stove made in the early 1900s.

She peeked into the various other rooms before spotting someone in the back bedroom. Ah, so this is where her customer had gotten off to. He stood with his broad back to her and even before she recognized his dark brown, short hair and the confident way he stood as he surveyed the 1890s canopy bed she'd decorated with a late nineteenth-century, finely stitched tulip quilt, her pulse was already racing.

"It must have taken a lot of work to put this place together," Sully said.

He didn't turn around when he spoke. Instead, he reached out a large hand and ran his fingers tenderly over the quilt.

Jenna swallowed at the sensual gesture.

Suddenly wished for his fingers to touch her heated skin, cup her breasts, rub her clit.

Oh boy! Not good.

"May I help you?" she found herself whispering in a somewhat sultry voice. She forced herself to quickly clear her throat, to push aside the wicked sensations running through her as she stood in a bedroom with her sexy Sully.

"Actually, yes. There are a few interesting items here I could use in my bar…as conversation pieces."

He strolled to a nearby Pennsylvania cupboard where she had housed some of her antique erotic toys. She'd debated long and hard whether or not to invest in such intimate items. To her surprise, they were some of her hottest sellers.

Most people bought them as keepsakes to remind them of the old days or like Sully, who wanted them as conversation pieces.

Now as he touched her sex toys, he was turning her on big-time.

Good grief, just looking at his broad back, the arrogant slash of his bristled jaw, the gentle way his fingers wrapped around the wooden egg-shaped item as he scooped it into his large, calloused palm made her mind scramble into a whirlwind of thoughts.

What if he decided to throw her on to the bed and have his way with her? What if she broke down and asked him to take her back? Told him she really wanted to be with him. To experiment with him at the Ménage Club. A club that was rumored to have a 100% success rate for bringing together old lovers who'd sworn never to get back together again.

"What's this?" he asked as his hot, green gaze slammed into her, making her catch her breath.

Damn him for being so curious.

She should tell him it was a Fabergé egg, just to be rude or to tease him, but he was a potential customer and she needed to keep herself in business mode.

Sully Hero was a well-liked man in this town and if he could spread word about her antiques shop, it could only be beneficial to be nice and pretend her insides weren't shaking with both lust and fear that he would recognize she wanted to reignite the passion they'd once shared. But she couldn't afford to have him break her heart when he took off again. Maybe next time he'd be gone for good.

"It's a Victorian-era butt plug," she admitted.

"Really?" One side of his luscious mouth quirked upward and her heart went into hyper mode. He'd always looked so damn cute when he threw her that teasing smile. It just about made her knees melt.

"Yes. A European doctor invented this particular shape. He prescribed them to couples as a kind of fertility aid to help prevent sperm loss. The idea of the inserted egg into a woman's anus would make her vagina tighter and this butt plug would make the sperm head toward the woman's reproductive organs."

He merely nodded, acting as if speaking about butt plugs were a perfectly normal event for him.

She, however, could feel her face heating up. Whether from excitement or embarrassment, she wasn't too sure. And sweet heavens she couldn't believe she was speaking so casually about sex toys with him. In the past, it had been a topic of conversation she'd avoided like the plague...until she'd read on the Internet that sex toys were a perfectly natural addition to millions of couples' sex lives and it wasn't something shameful or scandalous as her late grandmother had made her believe when she'd discovered the tiny vibrator in Jenna's room — the vibrator Sully had bought her.

"And what's this?" He picked up a long, thick, ivory item.

Oh, God!

"A...a Renaissance Italian dildo." Have mercy, now it really was getting hot in here!

"Tell me more about it."

Keep it businesslike, Jen. If he buys one, you'll be making a tidy profit.

"Well...back then they were called *diletto*, which means delight. Skilled craftsmen made them out of stone, leather, ivory and wood. Olive oil was used as a lubricant."

She could literally feel her pussy spasm at the thought of Sully inserting the dildo into her eager and craving vagina.

"And this?"

Oh my! Her throat suddenly grew dry as he set down the dildo and picked up an ivory ring.

"It's from the 1600s."

"Exquisite carving...looks like a dragon."

"It is." To her horror her voice cracked. She cleared her tight throat and forced herself to remain calm. Heck, she wasn't doing a good job of it, at least not by the look of her reflection in a nearby mirror.

Oh, God! Her cheeks were pink and her swollen breasts were heaving wildly against her suddenly too tight granny dress. Not to mention her pussy was creaming up a hot storm.

"What was it used for?"

Use your imagination! she wanted to yell. Instead, she found herself explaining, totally mesmerized at the lusty interest sparkling his eyes.

"Men would slip it over their...erections in order to hold them longer."

Sully moved closer to her, his gaze narrowing as he looked more closely at the object.

"An antique cock ring. And what about this nub here? It looks like a clitoris stimulator."

Her pussy creamed harder as she imagined slipping the cock ring onto Sully's penis. Imagined his huge cock sliding in and out of her quivering vagina for hours as the cock ring maintained his erection, the nub on the end of it massaging her into one mind-blowing orgasm after another.

Suddenly she noticed how good he smelled. His masculine scent teased her senses, made her want to inhale deep and hard, made her want to melt against him and feel him rub that big bulge in his pants against her pussy.

"Jenna?" His sexy voice shattered her fantasy.

She blinked and looked into his eyes. They were dark with sexual intent.

Hunger and raw, fierce need grabbed her. Instantly she was lost in sensations. Lost in lust. Lost in love.

Good grief! Was she nuts? Sully was no good for her! She'd taken years to get over him...hell, who was she kidding? She'd never gotten over him. Their years apart had only made her crave him more, had made her study sex toys and their history just so she would be ready for a moment like this. Now that the time had come, she wasn't prepared for the sparks of attraction bursting between them. Nor was she prepared to lose herself inside these wonderful sensations.

Her nostrils flared at his primitive, male scent. Her breasts felt all tingly as his gaze drifted to them. She managed to take a step backward and felt the bureau press erotically against her ass. Her face grew warmer as he watched her closely. Too closely.

"Yes, the nub would rub against the woman's clit," she admitted.

It would rub against her clit. One brilliant orgasm after another while Sully watched.

"Enhancing her pleasure, no doubt."

"No doubt," she agreed.

He grinned. The intimate smile sunk deep into her very core, making her body hum. He placed the item back on the shelf, only to pick up yet another toy.

"What would this be used for?" he asked as he lifted the rubber penis-shaped item and examined it. "It's hollow. Wide opening. Wide enough to slip over a man's cock. Is it a cock massager of some sort?"

Sweet heavens! She couldn't hold out too much longer against him.

"Actually no, it's The Penis Stiffener, patented in 1907 in the United States."

"Exactly what's that?"

"It was used by men with…erection problems." Of which, Sully still had no problem in that area, if the huge, quickly growing bulge between his legs was any indication.

"And the smaller opening at the other end?"

"To allow the sperm through and into a woman's vagina."

"Very nice invention. Which leads me to my next question."

"Wh-What's that?"

He'd placed The Penis Stiffener onto the bureau and maneuvered himself in front of her. His body heat slammed into her like a seductive lover as both his arms came around to her sides, his hands settling on the bureau, effectively holding her hostage.

Oh boy.

"Why the interest in antique sex toys, Jenna? Why the ad on the napkin last night?"

Your sexual tastes have changed. Big-time! Are you dating anyone special? Will you let me fuck you right now, right here? Or will you turn me away? He hadn't said anything, but she could literally hear his unspoken words and questions sizzle through the air between them.

"Actually, it really is none of your business."

His scorching gaze once again traveled to where her breasts were pushing violently against her granny dress as she tried desperately to inhale fresh air. But his strong, masculine scent was everywhere, calling to her, telling her to move closer to him.

"Actually, I think it is my business," he whispered.

His large hands suddenly lifted and she found herself exhaling a slow, aroused breath as he ran his fingers through her hair, holding her head hostage.

Her heart thumped as his lips parted. "As a customer, I have every right to know where you get your information from and why your interests lie in antique sex toys."

He leaned closer. Her pulse skipped erratically and she received an awesome view of the gold flecks in the dark green of his eyes. His erotic scent swarmed her. Encouraged her to part her lips in answer.

He was a bastard to do this to her. But what a hunky bastard.

He came down.

His lips were warm. Oh, so damned warm. His mouth smoothed over hers in such an intimate caress she found her knees weakening.

In a split second she was torn. Torn by her need to be with him again. Torn by her fear of being hurt again. Her need won out.

Wrapping her arms around his neck, partly to keep herself from dropping to the ground as her knees continued to melt, but mostly because she didn't want him to pull away.

She loved the silky feel of his short hair brushing against her hands. Enjoyed the way her fingers tingled as she touched the bare flesh of his sinewy neck, the hot, male muscles of his strong shoulders.

His mouth savored her. His carnal-shaped lips sliding, tasting, exploring, sending raw desire coursing through her mouth. Her breasts. Her pussy.

Damn! He made her feel so aware of her sexuality as his tasty mouth held hers captive. She was enjoying this so much it made her feel heady. Made her want to hop up onto the bureau. Made her want to spread her legs and allow him to come inside her.

"I've missed kissing you, Jenna," Sully whispered as he licked her now tingling lips with his moist tongue.

Before she could tell him she missed him too, his mouth latched onto hers again. His strong, delicious tongue pushed past her lips and slid against her teeth. His breath was so hot against her face. The yearning to have his cock buried deep inside her grew even stronger.

She should be pushing him away, pounding against his solid chest with her fists, demanding to know why he'd come back to town when he'd told her he would never return.

Instead, she felt herself melting against his hard length. Responding. Returning a tentative kiss. As she kissed him back, he groaned a virile sound of unleashed passion. Jenna's pussy pulsed at the erotic sound.

His hands slid from her tangled hair and his long, tender fingers trailed down the side of her neck. A moment later, she could feel his fingers fumbling with the granny buttons on the front of her dress. She wanted to help him, but his intoxicating kisses kept her from moving, kept her trapped and at his mercy.

Mild air pressed against her bare shoulders and she realized he was trying to push the garment down her shoulders. Reluctantly she let go of his neck and dropped her arms, splaying her hands onto his narrow waist, allowing him easy access.

Her breath stilled as his big fingers worked the front clasp on her lacy bra. When her breasts fell free, hot hands cupped them. The sensual touch fried her blood. The heat of him made her cry out. He quickly drowned her sob as his mouth captured hers once again.

Instantly any resolve she may have had about not letting him near her vanished as his masculine burn zipped through her flesh.

"You're tense, Jenna. Too tense. Are you afraid of me?" His softly whispered words against her tingling mouth made her shake her head in response.

"Do you mind me touching your breasts?"

Again she shook her head, staring into his startling green eyes, wondering why he was being such a darned gentleman when, instead, she wished for him to be fierce with her as he'd been in the past, craving him to caress her breasts and take her roughly the way he'd always done.

He pressed the top of his forehead against hers, a past indication that she should look down. Watch what he did to her breasts. The gesture was all too familiar and suddenly it felt as if they'd never been apart.

Oh, God, she should be pulling away. Telling him exactly where he should go. Instead, she found herself looking down as she'd always done in the past. Looking down and watching the erotic sight that had always sent hot, jumbled need shooting through her.

Her body shook with remembrance as his palms held her breasts captive. His fingers and thumbs tweaked her aching nipples, drew them out until they were rosy red. Until exquisite pleasure-pain erupted. Until she felt that invisible line of erotic longing burn straight down her lower belly and deep into her clenching pussy.

The son of a bitch always knew just what buttons to push to turn her on or, in her case, what nipples to squeeze to make her hot and hungry. To make all coherent thoughts fly to the wind.

Oh, yes! This felt so heavenly! Much better than her nipple clamps.

His long fingers massaged her mounds, traced her areolas until Jenna swore her breasts felt twice their normal size and her nipples were peaked, aching to be touched some more.

He licked her lips, her cheeks, her neck, moving due south. Long, erotic strokes, his moist tongue dabbing at her flesh like little blades of fire. Wet fire that also erupted inside her pussy.

When his tongue swiped across one of her nipples, her bud tingled from the warmth. The need to have his mouth feast upon every inch of her flesh was so great she could literally feel the raw tingling sensations of need slide through her, take her over.

His luscious mouth quickly latched onto a lollipop-sized nipple.

"Oh, sweet mercy!" she couldn't help but cry out as intense heat zapped through her nipple sending her senses into hyperawareness. She bucked against his face. Instinctively she rubbed her breast against the roughness of his five o'clock shadow until her flesh burned and ached.

Until she breathed rapidly. Until lust ravished her senses.

God! He'd always made her feel so incredibly horny. Always made her lose control.

The sucking sounds of his mouth feasting upon her breast intermingled with the faraway sound of jangling bells. The sound barely registered upon her senses. At least not until she felt Sully's lips stiffen against her aroused breast. She cried out in distress as his succulent mouth let her nipple go with a pop, and it slowly registered through her erotic haze exactly what the jangling sound entailed.

A customer.

Oh, my God!

She'd become so lost in her arousal she'd forgotten anyone could come into the antiques shop.

She pushed Sully away, trying hard to ignore his amused grin.

Anxiety gripped her as her gaze flew to the bedroom door, fully expecting someone to walk in on them. God! Wouldn't her customer be shocked to find her there with her breasts hanging out of her dress, her nipples red and swollen from Sully's suckling?

"I'll take all of the items we talked about." Although he sounded all business, as if nothing had just happened, she could hear his harsh breathing, could see the blush of redness in his lips, the swelling from their kisses. Her mouth probably looked the same.

And, good heavens, she could see the intense erection pressing against his jeans. Her customer would know what they'd been doing!

Get a grip, girl! Your grandmother's stern principles are rearing their ugly head again. Who cares about what the customer thinks!

"Are you sure?" she said, her face heating as with trembling fingers she hooked up her bra and buttoned her dress, avoiding his searing gaze.

"Very." He grabbed the cock ring and the other items he wanted to purchase and cradled them in his arms. He acted as if he belonged there, as if it were perfectly normal for him to come into her shop, feast upon her breasts and stand there with an armload of antique sex toys.

Confusion slammed into her.

For goodness' sake! She'd just let Sully Hero seduce her breasts with his mouth! Why? Why had she allowed him to do what he wanted to do so damned easily? She should have protested. Should have pushed him away or, at the very least, slapped his face for making her succumb to these fantastic desires once again.

"We'd better hurry. You have a customer," he prodded.

Shit! Her customer!

She had better get her ass in gear and quit lounging around in the bedroom, craving more of these unwanted attentions from him.

She had to act like a professional. This was a small town after all. If a client even suspected she and Sully were doing something inappropriate in one of her antique-laden bedrooms, it would be all over town within minutes.

She forced herself to snap into business mode. "If you'd like to follow me, I'll ring up your purchases."

"Sure thing."

Jenna could literally feel his scorching gaze caress her ass as she walked down the hallway. A wonderful splash of excitement gripped her at the thought of him finding out she wasn't as prim and proper as she'd once been. The thong she wore beneath her granny dress and the belly button ring she'd given to herself as a birthday present last year would attest to that fact. Stronger waves of desire swept through her at the thought of him pressing the egg-shaped Victorian-era butt plug into her virgin ass, as per the European doctor's instruction. And then her Hero sliding his big, rigid cock into her.

Pressing, pushing, pumping. Frantically thrusting his hips as he led both of them toward an exquisite orgasm.

Suddenly Jenna found herself craving that frozen bottle of beer she'd been wanting last night in Sully's bar when he'd read her ad on the napkin.

"Hello, Jenna, Sullivan," came elderly Mrs. Hero's soft voice as they erupted into the living room where she kept the cash register just beside the front entrance of her antiques shop. She noticed Sully's grandmother's eyes widen with surprise and his grandfather's knowing smile when they spotted their grandson following her, his arms laden with antique sex toys.

Jenna's face grew even hotter.

Shit! Was this embarrassing or what? Sully's own grandparents witnessing what he was purchasing. He, however, didn't seem the least bit fazed by their appearance as he grinned happily and dropped the toys onto the counter. He quickly gave his petite gray-haired grandmother a big bear hug and slapped his tall grandfather on his shoulder with affection as they greeted each other warmly.

As quickly as she could, Jenna grabbed the erotic toys and settled them on a chair behind the counter, out of sight. The last thing she wanted to do was mortify the couple, especially since they came from the same generation as her grandmother, where sex hadn't been as free as it was today.

"Please, there's no need to be embarrassed, dear," Mrs. Hero said. Jenna felt her face literally burn as three sets of Hero eyes looked at her. "We've been married for more years than either of your ages. Nothing surprises us, especially the fact that our grandson is purchasing such interesting items."

She turned to look up at Sully, who towered over the petite woman. "Shouldn't you be purchasing modern sex toys instead of antique ones?"

His grandfather chuckled as Sully frowned. Was that a blush teasing his cheeks?

Jenna bit her lip to prevent herself from laughing out loud. Confident, sexy Sully Hero could actually blush.

"I take it you've been keeping Jenna busy with those toys?" Mr. Hero, an elderly version of Sully's sexy looks asked.

Oh, God! These folks sure did have an interesting sense of humor. They didn't seem the least put off at Sully's interest in sex toys.

"We've been having an interesting time of it. We were getting...reacquainted."

"How exciting!" Both Mr. and Mrs. Hero grinned with approval.

Oh, God! She needed to change the subject and fast. The last thing she wanted was for them to get their hopes up. They'd always treated her so kindly, had expected she and Sully would eventually get married. They'd been devastated at the news of their breakup.

"I'm glad you came in," Jenna said quickly. "I was going to call you, Mrs. Hero. About the yellowware set you were enquiring about a few weeks ago."

"You found a set?" Her eyes twinkled with happiness.

"It's in the back, if you'd like to take a look at it. I can bring it out as soon as I ring through Sully."

The elderly lady clasped her hands together with obvious delight. "Oh, I'm so excited."

"If I'd known you'd get excited over a yellowware dish set, I would have bought you one," Mr. Hero chuckled, amusement flashed in his eyes.

"You already bought me one shortly after we were married, don't you remember?" Mrs. Hero frowned with obvious disappointment.

"Oh, yeah, whatever happened to it?"

"I threw the dishes at you that night you came home drunk without a paycheck."

Sully a quick wink.

"I can't seem to remember that." He threw Jenna and
Sully a quick wink.

"Don't be fooled by him. He remembers and he never did
that again. It was during the Depression. He'd been laid-off for
months and just called back to work. It was his first paycheck
and he'd gotten drunk and gambled it away."

"Actually, I gambled it away then got drunk on the last
dollar."

Mrs. Hero grinned at his admission and, to Jenna's
surprise, she wrapped her arms around the tall man and gave
him an affectionate hug.

"When he came home and explained what happened, I
threw every piece of the yellowware set at him. Broke
everything. The way I saw it, if there was no money for food,
why bother to have any dishes?"

"I learned how to move really fast that night," he said,
returning her hug. The elderly couple gazed into each other's
eyes, seemingly oblivious of Jenna and Sully watching them.
Or at least Jenna had been watching them. When she looked
up, she discovered Sully's hot gaze traveling down the length
of her body then drew back to connect with hers, sending a
lightning storm of heat zipping through her.

Irritation nibbled at her nerves. She shouldn't be reacting
this way every time he looked at her. She should be immune to
his hungry gaze, to his hot, wild kiss, to the erotic way his
sensual mouth had just latched onto her nipples only moments
earlier in the bedroom.

"They never go to bed mad at each other," Sully
explained. She detected anger beneath his controlled voice.
Anger directed at her, no doubt. They'd had many fights when
they'd gone out together. She didn't like the fact he had
women friends and he didn't like the fact she was sexually
uptight. He'd wanted more than she'd been willing to give at
the time. They'd both been too proud to apologize after their
fights, until the need for the fantastic sex they always

experienced together had arisen, then they'd always managed to run into each other again and make up.

Unfortunately having great sex didn't a relationship make…at least it hadn't worked for them in the past and she doubted things had changed very much between them, especially at the fact of her red-hot anger popping its nasty little head up at seeing him talking with that blonde beauty last evening at his bar.

"On our wedding night we vowed to never go to bed mad at each other, no matter how big the fight," Mrs. Hero explained.

"We were both too stubborn to break that promise," her husband chuckled. They were still locked in an affectionate embrace.

"That's the secret to our long marriage," she smiled.

"It's a lovely tradition." Jenna grinned, feeling the warmth of their happiness sift through her. However, her warmth disintegrated at Sully's cool voice.

"Too bad more couples don't adopt that tradition."

His searing gaze once again traveled over the length of her, leaving her both breathless at the intensity of his scorching look and also insulted at his words. Not to mention she was getting the distinct feeling he thought their final breakup was all her fault.

"I've got several errands to run. Can I pick the stuff up afterwards?" *So we can pick up where we left off?* He didn't need to say it, she could read the lusty message flashing in his eyes. But she was pissed off at his comment about adopting a tradition of not going to bed angry at each other. The dissolution of their relationship hadn't been all her fault. Besides, she was not in the mood for "making up" and starting the same pattern as they'd done in the past.

Fighting. Having great sex. Fighting. Having great sex.

"You can pay upon delivery. I'll drop it by the bar tonight," Jenna told him tightly, suddenly eager to get rid of

Sully before her temper exploded and they started rehashing old times in front of his grandparents.

"Okay, I'll see you at the bar, tonight." Sully turned to his grandparents and smiled warmly to the elderly couple. "I'll see both of you later."

His grandparents didn't seem the least bit put off at the tension zipping between Jenna and Sully as he bid them goodbye.

The minute the bell jangled his exit Jenna knew exactly what question was coming.

"Are the two of you back together?" Mrs. Hero asked, hopefulness washing across both their faces. Guilt slammed into her and she almost lied. Almost told them that Sully and she were on friendly terms again, but Sully's little snap a moment earlier had just bought all the hurt and frustration to the surface. Hurt because it seemed he thought everything had been her fault and frustration because she thought that too. It had taken her four years to realize when a relationship broke up it wasn't just one person's fault.

It takes two to tango. Her best friend Meemee had told her that over and over again every time Jenna broke it off with a local guy—especially after things started to get a little too serious for her comfort.

She forced herself back to the present. Back to reality.

"No, we aren't back together and don't expect us to, either."

Both of them looked devastated. Oh, God, now she felt really bad.

"But at least we're on speaking terms, that's a good sign."

"You're more than halfway there," Mrs. Hero burst out.

I wish you were right, Jenna thought to herself, suddenly wishing she and Sully were together again, but that could never happen, not unless they got a miracle. Sully was obviously still carrying around anger toward her because of the way things ended between them, and she seemed to always sense it in him and became angry herself. It was a no-win situation.

"I'll go get you that yellowware set so you can take a look at it. Back in a minute."

Besides, she thought as she hurried toward the back room, she never wanted to experience the searing hurt she'd gone through after their last and final breakup. As far as she was concerned, that fact alone should be enough of a reason never to let Sully Hero back into her heart...or her bed.

Chapter Three

က

"So? Did you go and see Jenna?" Tony asked as Sully threw himself into the secluded booth of his bar so they could talk.

"And did you find the napkin with her ad?" Meemee asked as she made a mad grab for the frosty beer he'd just brought her.

"Yes, on both counts," he admitted.

"And?" both of them asked at the same time.

Sully couldn't help but laugh at the excitement these two shared in helping to get Jenna and himself back together. For good this time.

"Easy, guys. One at a time."

"Me first," Meemee said quickly. "Did you get the napkin I left?"

"You left it?"

"Jeez, don't sound so disappointed." Meemee threw him her famous pout. Her full, red lips going into a downward spiral. The sight of her doing that consistently seemed to cheer him up. She was always such an outgoing person and even when she tried to pout, the happiness in her just seemed to shine through, giving her an even cuter appearance. He was sure guys she dated loved to tease her just to see that sexy pout.

"No, it's not that... I..." *He had hoped Jenna might have left it for him to find.* "Yes, I got it."

"Good, then you know what's she's looking for. Now all you have to do is supply it."

She made it sound so damn easy. She was such a romantic. She'd been an avid fan of Jenna and him getting back together. She'd almost given him a heart attack with her excitement when he'd called her, told her he was coming back for Jenna and wanted the help of the Ménage Club that Tony not only created but also ran out of his beach house.

He'd hurt Jenna terribly by running off the way he had. She was an extremely sensitive woman, especially about her weight and ultra-sensitive in the way he kidded around with his women friends. It wouldn't be easy to regain Jenna's trust. But he knew in his heart he wanted her, loved her, and this time around, he was willing to go to extremes to get her and to keep her.

"So? How did your meeting with her go this morning? Did you start phase one of the body seduction?" Tony asked. Sully ignored the way Meemee leaned closer, her eyes wide with expectation. She was also a member of the Club, helping couples through their troubled relationships, but she'd kept her membership a secret from Jenna and him until she'd finally mentioned she was a member in the last letter she'd sent to him.

"Normally, I'm not a guy who kisses and tells," he said truthfully. "But since the Club's motto is to be honest at all costs… I had her in the palms of my hands…literally."

Tony grinned. "You work fast, my young apprentice."

"I fucked up."

"How?" Meemee asked.

"When I left her, we were both pissed off. Just like old times. It's like we can pick up on each other's moods or something, and then we both act on it."

Tony nodded. "You two are both on the same level. So in tune with each other. It may not seem like it now, but in the future, as you learn to trust one another, this gift will cement your relationship."

Jan Springer

"Did you speak to her about the Ménage Club?" Meemee asked.

"No, like I said, I got sidetracked and then we got interrupted."

"Well, she is a beautiful, curvy woman," Tony said. "I can see why it would be hard to keep your hands off her, but you must remain focused on our goal. You must remember what you've been taught by us. The whole theory behind the Ménage Club is to discover both of your underlying fears and bring them to the surface. To treat these fears in a world of pleasure and affection. That will make each of you vulnerable and open to the other. Then and only then will you both be able to change and ultimately trust each other. In short, capture her body first, her heart will quickly follow and, eventually, you will win her trust."

"All this ménage stuff is just almost too unbelievable to work, it just seems all backward. I mean you're supposed to fall in love first and then have sex, and then maybe a ménage if both parties agree but this..." He shrugged and cursed silently at all the insecurities starting to flood him.

"That's the old-fashioned side of you talking. You want Jenna, don't you?" Meemee grinned, knowing what his answer would be.

Frustration grabbed at his gut making him wince. "With every breath of my being. But—"

"No 'buts', Sully," Tony broke in. "As you've told us, your old-fashioned ways haven't worked for you—it's time to try our techniques. Remember we've been 100% successful and we sure as hell aren't going to let you two be the first to break our record."

"If the Ménage Club is so successful, then why aren't the two of you hitched?"

A dark frown of pain flashed between the two of them leaving Sully wishing he hadn't asked. Both of them had lost the loves of their lives. Meemee's fiancé had run off with

210

Tony's fiancée while Tony had been away on his last space assignment.

"That's why we're there, Sully," Tony replied. "Why I gave up NASA and created the Club. To help others get back together. We've all lost someone we love in one way or the other, with the barest of chances to get them back. While we train with couples, we learn about relationships ourselves. When we think we are ready, we pursue the partner we wouldn't have had a chance with otherwise."

"Enough about us," Meemee broke in. "We need to figure out another way for you two to meet."

"She's making a delivery to the bar tonight with some stuff I bought at her store."

"Good. Are you ready for her?" he asked.

Sully nodded and fought against the excitement that was quickly building at the thought of his next meeting with Jenna.

He found himself grinning at his two friends. "She won't know what hit her."

* * * * *

Despite her earlier sane ideas of not jumping back into bed with Sully, Jenna's heart picked up a mad speed as she swung her truck into the dark lane that led to the back entrance of Sully's bar. She'd opted to come this way in order to avoid the crush of people who were sure to be there. All she'd have to do is slip in the back door and find Sully, which should be easy enough. Ever since he'd bought the place and reopened last month, the few times she'd come there she'd seen him flirting with some long-legged woman or another at his bar. A fissure of jealousy slithered through her at the thought of finding him amusing himself with yet another woman. He seemed to do it easily enough, had given her a firsthand look as he'd so efficiently kissed her breathless back at her antiques shop. Before she'd known it, he'd unbuttoned her dress and had had his way with her breasts.

She moaned out loud as she remembered the seductive way his lips had clamped and captured each of her buds, teasing them with his raspy tongue, tormenting her until she was a torrid bundle of need.

Bastard! He was good. So damn good. He'd always known her weakness for sex even when she'd denied it to herself. Truth be known, she craved to be pleasured by Sully.

But not tonight. Tonight she'd be as solid as a stone toward him.

Yeah, right. That's why she'd changed into a sexy black dress that flattered her generous breasts and made her big butt look just a tad thinner. Not to mention her pussy was trembling with anticipation as she hungered to see his eyes flash with lust the instant he saw her.

Cursing herself for being so damned weak, she parked her truck, hoisted the small box containing his toys into the crook of one arm and got out of her vehicle. Except for the screen door, the back entrance was open. She'd expected to hear rowdy music drifting out, but she heard nothing as she opened the door and let herself inside.

There was also an absence of people talking and she wondered what the hell was going on. The hallway looked ultra-clean and smelled really nice too as she walked farther into the establishment.

"Hello! Delivery from Jenna's Antiques and Collectibles," she called out, her voice echoing through the silent hallway.

"Back here, in the kitchen!" came his shout. "Just set it on the bar, I'll be out in a minute."

Gosh, he even yelled good. His smooth, rich voice just made her skin tingle wonderfully all over.

She entered the bar area and frowned.

Empty. The dammed place was empty! That meant they would be alone.

Oh dear.

Insecurities pushed away the confidence she'd had building throughout the day. Maybe she should get out of there? Maybe she really wasn't prepared to be alone with him again?

"Gone out of business already?" she couldn't help but tease and settled the box on to the counter. "I'll just leave it on the bar. You can catch me with the money another time."

The faster she got out of there, the safer her heart would be.

Before she could spin around and leave, he appeared in a nearby doorway, totally shirtless.

Oh, double dear.

His gorgeous shoulder muscles rippled as he dried his hands on a towel and her attention immediately drew to his chest, to the soft dusting of curly hair and the smooth bunch of muscles swelling there.

"My cook just quit on me and the water main broke. No water. Had to close the bar."

"Oh."

Talk about a wonderfully sculpted chest. She found herself wondering if that soft-looking, downy chest hair was still as soft and silky as she remembered.

"Thanks for bringing the toys, Jenna."

He smiled as he walked toward her. The smile didn't reach his eyes. Instead, raw, burning lust burned there. Lust and affection and appreciation.

"You look really hot in black, Jenna."

She did? She pushed aside her self-doubts. Of course she did! That's why she'd picked this dress.

"Thank you for noticing," she found herself whispering, eagerly accepting his compliment.

Whew! He looked hot himself in the way he moved. Sexy. Sensual. A man on a mission of seduction perhaps?

Her pulse fluttered at the idea.

His long fingers popped open the box containing the erotic toys and he examined each one. His large hands handled the items gently, intimately.

"I put a cabinet in the corner for these toys," he said softly, and pointed to the secluded corner near the jukebox.

Anyone using the music machine would certainly get an eyeful when they passed the glass-enclosed cabinet.

"Want to help me arrange them? I could use a woman's touch."

She bet he could. His piercing gaze made her catch her breath.

He was topless, wearing a scorching gaze—not to mention they were totally alone—and he was asking her to stay.

God, she wanted to stay. To see where things would lead. To have some red-hot maintenance sex with him and then simply walk away, but she could see herself falling head over heels for him again.

"Jenna? You okay? Looks like you zoned out on me for a second."

"I'm fine, just fine." She plastered on a fake smile, although she could feel a hand squeezing her heart for what could have been between them.

"You sure?"

Damn him. He'd always been so in tune to her feelings. What else would he guess?

"I should leave."

"Meaning you don't really want to."

Bold son of a bitch, wasn't he?

"C'mon, let's set the toys up."

To her surprise, his fingers intertwined with hers.

Hot was her first thought as his grip tightened around her hand. He picked up the box she'd just delivered and pulled her toward the cabinet. *Desperate* was her second thought as she noticed the delicious bulge pressed boldly against the prison restraint of his pants.

Whew! Warm in here, wasn't it?

He let her go and tilted the box on the jukebox. Cupping the Victorian-era butt plug, he lifted it out of the tissue paper.

"Top, middle or bottom shelf?"

"Middle shelf. Most people probably wouldn't know what it is, so it's best to put something more recognizable at eye level on the top shelf."

"Oh, yes, I forgot to tell you. They'll know what these antique items are and where I got them." He reached into his back pocket and produced some of her fancy little business cards. She hadn't noticed he'd picked some up. There were some index cards too.

"You remembered everything I told you," she laughed as she read each of the cards stating the information she'd told him about the European doctor's butt plug and the other items he'd purchased.

He grinned as he positioned the items on the shelf where she suggested and she placed the appropriate card with the item.

"I'll have to come over for more sex toys," he said softly after he was finished. Now why did she get the feeling he wasn't talking about her antique sex toys but her personal toys?

She inhaled sharply at that thought and smelled his masculine scent.

Strong. Powerful. Sensual. Her body clenched erotically, heat gripped her veins, preparing her.

"Maybe you've got some anal beads or a vibrator lying around in that store of yours?"

He'd come closer. God! When had he come so close? They were practically touching each other.

Lusty sensations swept around her. She could hear her breathing quicken. Could see his eyes darken with need. Dilate with desire.

Oh, sweet heavens, help her. She didn't want to be swept away with this need of being in his arms again, didn't want her nipples tightening with the delicious craving of having his hot, succulent mouth on her breasts again, his thick, hard cock penetrating her, her self-control vanishing...

She swallowed against the ache of touching him, tried to dampen the desire swirling around her.

It didn't work.

She dropped her truck keys. Barely heard them clatter to the floor as his mouth came down hard on hers. Harder than the gentle kiss he'd given her in her shop earlier that day. The erotic sensations threw her off balance and instinctively she melted against him.

Gosh! This was the Sully she remembered.

Demanding. Seductive. Fierce with his need to pleasure her—to take pleasure from her.

His lips claimed hers, kissed hers until any focus she might have had disintegrated. Until fire raged through her. Until her knees wobbled and her legs gave out.

On her cry, he caught her. Caught her in his strong, naked arms and carried her to the bar where he hoisted her onto the counter.

She reached out and curled her fingers over the strong, sinewy muscles in his shoulders, spread her legs quickly as his hands touched her knees and he pushed her dress up around her waist.

His hot gaze immediately zeroed in on her belly ring and the tiny gold chain she'd strung through it and wore around her waist. The chain always made her feel feminine and pretty. Always gave her that little satisfaction she knew something that no one else knew about her.

Until now.

Her body hummed at the sight of dark lust splashing in his eyes. His Adam's apple bobbed as he swallowed. She found herself holding her breath as he slipped his little finger through the ring and pulled gently, forcing her to move even closer to him.

Masculine heat splashed all around her, his sexy scent made her so hot for him she had to blow out a breath.

"I love this new, daring side to you, Jenna."

"I do too," she found herself admitting.

His finger let go of the ring and he traced a scorching line down her abdomen to touch her thong.

"I've wanted to do this for so damn long," he whispered as his fingers clenched the material and he quickly removed the garment from her, baring her pussy to him.

He swore softly as he noticed she was nude down there. She'd taken to shaving only recently. Perhaps because deep down in her soul she'd held hopes that this day would someday come. Now it was here and her heart hammered violently in her ears and frantically pounded against her chest.

His hands softly stroked her inner thighs, moved inward to her pussy. Sharp sensations ripped through her and she trembled at the intense arousal his tender touches created. Her mouth dropped open in a silent gasp as a finger slid over her sensitive clit.

Immediately she creamed.

He grinned.

Bastard!

He continued.

Slowly sliding. Making her cream harder.

Watching. Pinching softly. Watching.

She burned. Oh, God, did she burn.

Her breath went ragged when his finger slipped inside her wet pussy.

She shivered, overwhelmed by his touch. He collected her juices. Used it to massage her ultra-sensitive clit.

She could feel the orgasm coming already. So quickly.

He shifted and she blinked against the carnal haze enveloping her, moaned as he sat on the barstool, his hot breath exploding against her quivering pussy as his head came down between her spread legs.

Her lips parted in a satisfied gasp and she could hardly breathe as his tongue slipped inside her vagina.

Touching, stroking, probing while his finger continued the wicked seduction of her clit.

Oh, my God! It felt so good!

Her body tensed as he worked her. Her eyes closed as the pleasure waves cascaded nearer. Her pussy contracted around his tongue. She could hear his guttural moan. In response, she clamped her legs around his head. His tongue branded her vagina—his finger tortured her clit.

She came hard.

Thrusting her pelvis forward into his face, she gyrated her hips as the pleasure assaulted her.

She shuddered, cried out, and simply went with the carnal sensations. Her body tightened into one solid ball of pleasure as contractions crashed through her and washed all around her.

When it was over, she allowed her head to loll. Allowed her legs to be pried from his head.

She sat there on the bar, breathing in and out as she tried desperately to catch her breath.

Man, she felt so weak.

Damn! That felt so good!

"You always were as weak as a kitten after a climax. It always tamed you, allowed me to do whatever I wanted to you on those occasions when you let me."

She was surprised by the anger etching his strangled voice. "The things I've wanted to do to you, Jenna. Things you wouldn't let me do." *Until now.* He hadn't said it, but the silence that followed said those two words for him.

From somewhere far away, outside her increasing erotic haze, Jenna could hear a phone ringing. Could hear a familiar man's voice echo on the answering machine, a voice she couldn't quite remember.

"Sully? You there? Come on. Pick up the phone, I'm in trouble."

"Ignore him," came Sully's strangled voice as she pulled her fingers from his burning flesh.

"Sully, answer the damn phone. I need your help. I'm in jail." There was a pregnant pause and that's when she realized who was calling. It was Tony, Sully's best friend. Tony was in love with a woman who wanted nothing to do with him and was now with another man. Sometimes he ended up in jail when he drowned his sorrows in booze and became uncontrollable, even violent.

"Come and bail me out, will you? You gotta come fast. You know how I hate spending the night in jail."

Sully frowned and cursed, his heavy breathing split the silence of the barroom.

"You better answer." Jenna said softly as her bearings slowly returned.

"If he's in jail, I bet there's a woman involved," Sully growled as he slipped off the barstool and headed for the phone.

Probably a redhead. Tony had always preferred redheads. Especially the one he let get away.

"I'm going to have to bail him out, Jenna," Sully growled as he dialed. "Feel free to stay." *So we can pick up where we left off.* Again he didn't say the words, but his carnal look told her everything she needed to know.

"It's better if I go," she found herself saying. She needed to be alone, needed to think things over.

"I'm sorry." He looked it too.

She hopped off the bar.

Her legs trembled terribly as she slipped into her thong. Adjusting her clothing, she couldn't stop a wave of anger whispering over her.

He'd already started chatting to the police on the phone and she felt...dismissed. She searched the nearby floor for her keys, found them then headed toward the back door, chastising herself for giving in so easily to her lusty cravings for him. If her grandmother were still alive, she'd be horrified at what she'd let Sully do to her. As it was, she was probably rolling over in her grave.

"I'll walk you to your truck."

He'd come up behind her, his hand braced against the small of her back as he followed her out the back door.

"I want to see you again, Jenna. I'll be in touch."

Before she could so much as mount a protest, his hot mouth seared against hers, capturing her in such a tender kiss that her legs just about gave out. She could taste herself on his lips, a cinnamony-sweet mix she found rather erotic.

He broke the kiss and if he hadn't helped her up into her truck, she surely would have sprawled to the alley pavement.

Sweet Mercy! He knew how to kiss!

"Go home. Get some sleep." *So you're well-rested for what I plan to do to you next time we meet*, his eyes said.

He tapped the hood of her truck and waved. With shaky fingers, she turned on her ignition and watched as he sauntered back into his bar. Heat radiated all around her as she watched him.

Blowing out a tense breath, she pressed her hot forehead against the cool steering wheel. Once again hot moisture was pooling between her legs and her pussy throbbed where his face had just been. Her inner thighs burned, compliments of where his five o'clock shadow had brushed so erotically. She resisted the urge to press her legs together, to bring herself off.

God! She'd just been eaten by Sully Hero!

What had gotten into her? And now she wanted more from him. So much more.

My, oh, my. She was in big trouble.

* * * * *

"Jenna MacLean, special delivery."

Jenna looked up from the day-old blueberry muffin she'd been staring at while reliving the other night's adventure with Sully to find her best friend Meemee grinning at her from her back room doorway. She wore her professional, homemade courier uniform, tan slacks and a tan shirt with a colorful nametag proclaiming *Meemee's Courier*.

Gosh! She'd been so deep in thought, wondering why she hadn't heard from Sully in the couple of days since their rendezvous on the bar that she hadn't been aware of the jangle of the bell, signaling someone entering her shop.

"Hey, Meems, what's up?"

"This." She held up a small, slender package of about seven inches long by three inches thick.

Meemee was an entrepreneur in Hideaway. A jill-of-all-trades. Her self-employment jobs included a taxi service, gardening service, as well as the town's only courier service. "The sender requests you open it immediately."

"Who is it from?" Jenna asked when she found no return address on the lightweight item.

"You'll know when you open the package."

Oh, really? How intriguing!

Eagerness to see who was sending her a parcel had her virtually ripping the brown wrapping paper from the box. Who in this town would send her a parcel and instruct her to open it immediately? She did a mental check of the many antiques purchases she'd made. She had plenty on the way but none this small.

Jenna smiled. It had to be from Sully's grandmother. The other day when Jenna had brought out the yellowware set, Mrs. Hero had clasped her hands together and fallen in love with it. Even Mr. Hero had sparkles in his eyes, no doubt remembering the early years of their marriage. They'd purchased the set along with the pretty tulip quilt she'd placed on the canopy bed, the bed in the same bedroom Sully Hero had had his way with her breasts.

God! Just thinking about him made her horny.

She redirected her thoughts back to the parcel. Had Mrs. Hero sent her some of those fresh-baked cornmeal muffins she was so famous for? Her mouth watered at the idea of having a couple of cornmeal muffins instead of the stale blueberry one she'd brought along for brunch.

Even as she opened the box, she knew it wasn't from Mrs. Hero. It was way too small for muffins. Her mouth literally dropped open in shock as nestled snugly in blue tissue paper was a slim six-inch long, one-inch wide fuchsia-pink butt plug. On the side, written in bold black letters were the words MÉNAGE CLUB INITIATION.

"Oh, my God," she found herself whispering. It had happened. She'd received an invitation to join Sully at the Ménage Club.

"All right, confess, girlfriend," Meemee said softly as she too peered inside the box.

"He answered the ad," Jenna replied as her heart slammed up against her chest with such excitement she thought she would pass out.

"What ad?"

"With that cocksure grin plastered all over your face, Meems, I believe you know very well who answered what ad.

And you are probably the one who took it out of my purse and gave it back to him."

Meemee shrugged her shoulders and threw Jenna her famous pouty look. "I can't help it if you disappear to go to the bathroom and I happen to need a napkin and look through your purse for one and find the one with your ad and accidentally left it on the table."

"I should have known you were the one who took it!"

"What? I did something wrong? Oh! And look the plug comes with instructions."

A cat-got-the-canary grin splashed over Meemee's face as she quickly changed the subject and delicately lifted a paper from the tissue. "This heated, self-lubricating, six-inch butt plug can inflate to eight inches long and to two inches wide," she read. "New superior technology allows the plug to quickly and comfortably inflate and deflate several hundred times a day, allowing a woman's anal muscles to quickly become accustomed to the maximum size within a week."

Meemee blew a stray blonde bang out of her eyes, fanned herself and looked down at Jenna with wide eyes. "Have mercy, best girlfriend, but he is well-hung. I'm so glad he fits at least that part of your ad."

Jenna snatched the paper away from her and read the instructions. Oh, God! Meemee wasn't kidding. There it was in black and white. *Superior technology allows the plug to quickly inflate and deflate...self-lubricating...*

She swallowed at her suddenly dry throat and her ass muscles clenched in wicked anticipation.

"So? Why send you a butt plug? I mean you two split up like years ago. Why is he sending you something so intimate in the mail?"

"It all happened so fast," she confessed.

"What happened so fast?"

"I brought over the erotic toys he'd purchased at the store."

223

Her eyes widened. "He bought some of your sex toys when he was here? And you just forgot to tell me?"

"It happened so fast."

"God, woman! What happened that he would send you a butt plug instead of roses?"

"Stuff happened. On his bar."

Meemee wiggled her eyebrows in amusement. "*On* his bar? Way to go, Jenna! So? How was it after all this time?"

"Meems, please. What should I do about the plug? Should I send it back?" Even as she asked, she knew she wouldn't send it back. She wanted like crazy to join him for a ménage at the Club.

"No proper gentleman sends a woman a butt plug as an invitation to a seedy club instead of roses."

"I'm not looking for a gentleman, Meemee." *I want Sully.* She wanted to be able to trust him not to walk out on her again. She wanted him to be the man she was looking for in her "A Hero Needed" ad.

"Newsflash, girlfriend. White picket fence guys are gentlemen. Tell you the truth, I'm disappointed in Sully for not sending you roses. That's just not romantic. Maybe he's not the guy for you."

"Oh, cut the reverse psychology, Meems. It won't work. I know you want us back together."

"Okay, so what happened on the bar? Oh, jeez, don't tell me. Oh, God! Please do tell me."

"He went down on me."

Meemee's mouth dropped open in apparent shock. "On your first date?"

"It wasn't a date."

"Well then, girlfriend, that was some business trip. So are you going to wear it? Are you going to accept his invitation?"

Jenna picked up the plug. In the box, it had looked small but now, as she felt the weight in her hand, it seemed a little too big.

"Aha, a note!" Meems cried out, and she snapped up a small piece of light blue paper from the box. "He says he wants to meet you in a week. At his bar, after closing. Wearing the plug. Are you going to do it?"

"I don't know, Meemee. What do you think?"

"I'd hold off until he sent me the roses."

Jenna rolled her eyes. "A lot of help you've turned out to be."

* * * * *

"I think she's taken the hook...er...I mean the plug," Meemee's cheerful voice echoed through the tiny, hot bar kitchen as Sully tried to balance two platters of chicken fingers in one hand and two platters of fries in the other.

Yes, the cook was back and, yes, he was threatening to quit again if Sully didn't get him help pronto. In an effort to stall the cook from walking out, Sully had thrown in to give him a hand tonight. Cripes! Was it his fault that the bar was growing leaps and bounds, and not one reliable person had applied for the cook's helper position?

"Hello! Sully! Did you hear me?" Meemee cried out as she sidestepped the angry, red-faced cook and followed Sully out of the kitchen into the noisy bar.

"Sorry, Meems, it's a bit hectic around here tonight. You really think Jenna is going to wear it?" Doubts had been circling ever since he'd sent that package off with Meemee. He still couldn't get over the fact that Jenna had allowed him to go down on her the other night. Things were happening a hell of a lot quicker than he'd thought they would.

Jenna *had* changed. Had become more at ease with her sexuality, and it just seemed to make her that much more attractive to him.

She'd been so sweet and succulent when he'd sucked her pussy juices into his mouth. The taste of her had just about driven him wild. Now he wanted more from her. A hell of a lot more. He just hoped he was doing the right thing in pushing her so fast. But it was the Club's rules to move swiftly on a woman. Not to allow her too much time to think or react with her brain but to instead respond with her body.

"You don't sound too happy. Don't tell me you're actually nervous about your next meeting with Jenna?" She giggled from behind him as he settled the plates in front of his customers.

"Nothing has really happened between Jenna and myself, Meems. Why are you so damned cheerful?" he asked as he headed back to the kitchen for yet another order.

"Because life is beautiful, my young apprentice. Especially when I see my uptight best friend finally melting in her attitude toward you."

Jenna was melting? Sully closed his eyes and said a silent thank you.

"Now we'll just have to wait and see if she shows for your meeting," Meemee continued. "When she does, then we move quickly on to the next phase. Have you got it all planned?"

"I do."

"Good…" She made a move to go but turned around again, her facial expression anything but happy.

"Sully?"

"Yeah?"

"No contact with her for the next week before Initiation. We want her all primed and eager for you."

"I know the rules, Meems."

She nodded. "Great stuff. Oh! And congratulations. You're already halfway into the Ménage Club. Because of the plug, she's aware of your intentions. Now all we've gotta do is persuade Jenna to join you for that one, hot Initiation night. I'm sure she'll not only go for it but she'll enjoy it as well."

"You think so?"

Meemee sighed wearily. "Those doubts are showing again, Sully. You've got one week to work on that problem, okay? You're going to have to be certain that this is the way you want to go."

"It is the way. I don't want to lose her this time around." Or ever.

"You stick to the plan and she'll thank you forever. Trust me—once she's Initiated, there won't be any looking back for her or for you."

He could hear the smile in Meemee's voice and found himself nodding in agreement.

Yes, Meemee was right. Once Jenna accepted the invitation to be initiated into the Ménage Club then she would be his to pleasure.

His to pleasure forever.

Chapter Four
One week later…

෨

"The way she keeps twirling her fingers through her hair makes me think she's a little bit unsure of herself," Tony said as he watched Jenna where she sat in a far corner booth while Sully, at Tony's request, mixed a banana daiquiri for the cute little redhead sitting alone at the end of the bar. Thankfully, Tony wasn't drinking himself. Last week when he'd gotten Tony out of jail, he'd made his friend promise not to get drunk and cause a disturbance every time he saw a redhead. Hopefully, Tony would hang onto his promise—at least for tonight.

"It's natural for her to be that way," Tony continued. "There's that trust barrier to break through. From everything you've told me about your relationship in the past, I'd say she's most likely afraid you'll leave town if you have another fight. And like she's said many times during your fights, she's afraid you'll leave her for some skinny chick, maybe even one of those endless ladies who you call friends."

"They *are* just friends, Tony."

"I know it, but she still doesn't believe it. You told me yourself she seemed pissed off when one of our Club members flirted with you right here at the bar the other week. Anyway, I'd be worried if she wasn't nervous. This indicates she's interested in getting back together with you, to make things right between you two, but she still has insecurities." At Tony's words, a memory zipped through Sully.

A memory of the summer he'd come to stay with his grandparents. Initially he'd come to help them with their bakery during the busy tourist season and to ponder on whether he should join NASA's new training program with his three cousins. Meemee and Tony also worked at the bakery. The three of them had become fast friends. It had been at Tony's twenty-first birthday bash when he'd first seen plus-sized Jenna. The instant he'd walked into Tony's apartment he'd been floored. Her adorable, wide blue eyes, sassy auburn curls and her shy, yet sexy smile had made his cock and the rest of him take immediate notice. He'd always been attracted to plus-sized women and he'd made it a point to get introduced to her. She'd seemed surprised when he'd quickly invited her out for coffee with Tony and Meemee after the party, and he'd been thrilled when she'd accepted.

Tony, Meemee, Jenna and himself had been inseparable that summer. Not a day went by that the four of them didn't get together for some reason or another. And not a day went by that he didn't have the urge to find out everything about Jenna MacLean. He also found himself wanting to kiss her soft-looking, cupid-shaped, luscious, ruby-red lips, or want to do the naughty things to her plump, sweet-smelling body. Delicious things he'd heard his cousins brag they did with their girlfriends. It hadn't taken him long to figure out Jenna was sexually shy. The moment he'd met her grandparents he'd known why. Her grandmother had been strict, religious and controlled Jenna's every move.

No wonder she had hang-ups.

Jenna's mother and father had been killed in a car crash when she'd only been two years old and her grandparents had taken over raising her, had imposed curfews on her, had made her quite uptight sexually. But with Meemee's help, Jenna had been able to go out often, under the guise that she and Meemee went to the movies or to the fair or shopping. That's when he'd hook up with Jenna and they'd go off by themselves.

Kissing her had been torturous — guilt had always brewed in her eyes afterwards. It had been frustrating to say the least, but he loved Jenna MacLean and he could be patient as hell.

He'd vowed he would wait until she was ready. He'd wined her and dined her that summer, introduced her to his grandparents, who'd absolutely fallen in love with her during the fun Sunday dinners his grandmother loved to throw.

One hot summer night as they'd walked arm in arm down along the sandy beach watching the moonlight sparkle off the ocean's whitecaps they'd gone further than just kissing. Their touches had turned hungry. Desperate. Frantic.

They'd both been so turned on and she'd asked him to fuck her right then and there on the beach. It hadn't been the romantic way he'd planned to make love to her for her first time but he just hadn't been able to refuse that hungry, passionate look in her eyes or the delicious way her feminine fingers had shyly slipped into his pants and explored his cock.

Thank God, he'd had a condom in his wallet.

They'd consummated their relationship in a secluded grassy area near the beach's park gazebo beneath the twinkling stars. His heart had soared as he'd unleashed the passionate woman ripping her very soul from her every time he'd made her orgasm. Unfortunately, after their lovemaking session and many more after that night, he'd seen guilt and shame shine brightly in her eyes. Guilt and shame that her religious grandmother had no doubt instilled in her. Because of her guilt, he'd become angry. They'd fought frequently.

They'd also fought because he had quite a few friends who also happened to be women. She'd told him it wasn't proper for him to have so many women friends. In other words, she didn't trust him. Didn't believe him when he said he loved her and wanted only her in his life.

Frustration had begun to gnaw at him.

He'd even given her a vibrator. He'd figured it would help her explore her own body, her sexuality.

Toward the end of summer, her grandmother had found the sex toy and had freaked-out. Jenna had been in tears the last time he'd seen her. They'd had the big fight that night.

She'd told him it wasn't proper for a man and woman to use sex toys.

It had just been too much. Bitterness and frustration had overwhelmed him and he'd told her he was leaving town.

Swore to her he'd never come back to Hideaway or come back to her. He'd left town with Tony and joined NASA's new training program.

That's why the advertisement Meemee had written on the napkin on behalf of Jenna had come as such a shock.

Anal. Sexually adventurous. Ménages. And not an ounce of that guilt he'd come to hate so much had sparked Jenna's eyes when he'd read the ad and looked at her. Where once there had been shyness, there was now hunger. Where there once had been hesitancy, there was now a refreshing boldness.

Shit! Her heated looks and the ad had turned him on so bad he'd needed to take several cold showers since then.

Sending her the butt plug had been a bold move. A test to make sure she would come here tonight. To prove to himself she really had changed. To ask her a question that could change their lives and hopefully bring them back together again.

And here she was.

Near closing time. Casting shy, yet eager glances his way.

Did she have that inflatable butt plug buried up her cute little ass as he'd asked her to wear? Or was she here to tell him to take the plug and shove it up his own ass?

"I remember her being quite the innocent," Tony said as he lugged back a root beer. "Her grandmother made her that way. The old bitch sure had sexual hang-ups. It was a wonder she'd even let her husband near her to have a kid of her own."

"Don't speak ill of the dead, Tony," Sully teased, then walked the few steps to deliver the banana daiquiri to the redhead, who accepted the drink with a smile. She nodded her thanks to Tony, as well, and sent Sully back to him with an answer.

"So what did she say?" Tony eagerly asked when Sully returned.

"She said thanks but no thanks. She's not into men."

"Shit!" Tony said softly. "Another wasted drink."

Tony's gaze swung to Jenna again.

"With Jenna's grandmother out of the way, I wonder how much she's changed?"

"How do you mean?" Sully poured another beer for yet another waiting customer and pretended not to know what Tony meant.

"I mean, has she dropped her sexual shield? By the way she's squirming around on that bar seat, I'd say she's over her shyness and she's got that butt plug buried up there, making her pussy nice and tight. And the way her nipples are poking against her blouse makes me think the plug has turned her on, despite the intrusion up her sweet ass."

Sure enough, Tony was right. There was a cute blush to Jenna's cheeks, a sparkle in her eyes he'd never seen before.

"Sexually adventurous," Tony said again. "I'd even bet she's been fantasizing about a ménage. She's had a week to think about it."

Sully nodded his agreement. Jenna had mentioned light bondage in her ad. Mentioned ménages. But when it came right down to it, was she serious? Could he use her fantasies to get her to join the Ménage Club? Could he show her just how much he wanted her in his life?

He handed Tony another root beer and looked at his watch. Almost closing time. His gut twisted with anxiety. Soon he'd have his answer. One way or the other.

* * * * *

Shards of silver rain were slapping against the windows of Sully's Bar & Grill when the last customer left.

Jenna was so nervous she almost left too.

Since shortly after she'd arrived, both Sully and Tony had been casting scorching glances her way. She didn't have to be a genius to know they'd been talking about her. Maybe even making plans for her?

Pushing her fingers anxiously through her hair, she watched Sully disappear into the back room.

After she'd received the sophisticated Ménage Club Initiation butt plug from Sully, she'd been plagued all that day by doubts. Should she try it? Should she send it back to him? By the end of the day, her brain had been fried from all that thinking, and finally excitement about trying it had prevailed. After closing her shop that night, she'd followed the directions. After turning the toy on, she'd watched how the plug had generously lubed itself.

Unbelievable technology!

The plug even felt contentedly warm, yet strange, as she'd inserted it slowly inside her. She'd found herself gasping at the odd pleasure-pain as her firm muscles at first tried to reject the intrusion. But after relaxing herself and with some gentle prodding, her sphincter muscle had given way and the toy slid in with fairly little pain after it having been so liberally self-lubed. To her surprise, the plug felt relatively comfortable as she'd worn it off and on over the next week. She'd scarcely even known it was there, had barely felt the gentle stretching motions as the plug had slowly but firmly inflated, gently massaging her anal muscles, prodding her wider—readying her.

Jenna blew out a breath and swallowed at the nervous tightness clogging up her throat. She'd missed Sully terribly over the past week. Had even picked up the phone many times to call him, but she'd persevered and each time hung up.

Now she was here at Sully's Bar & Grill and was actually being turned on by the scorching way the two men were looking at her. Their hungry gazes made her feel desirable, sexy, and at the same time scared the shit out of her because she was actually fantasizing about having sex with Sully *and* Tony.

She'd be lying if she told anyone that the thought of a ménage turned her off. Even if she and Sully never got together, she really wouldn't mind experimenting in a ménage à trois with him.

At the very least, her searing curiosity would be quenched...at the very worst, she'd become addicted to ménages...and isn't that what she'd heard the Ménage Club had been created to do? Make the intended couple become addicted to pleasuring each other long enough for them to stay together and work through their problems.

Oh, she'd heard the rumors. Heard about how the men and women at the Club captured their lovers through arousing their bodies. She had friends who swore ménages wouldn't work if the couple's relationship was in trouble. They said ménages were the ultimate trust factor between couples. That it should only be tried when a couple's relationship was clearly established because in some cases bringing a third into the bedroom broke a relationship.

Sully and she weren't even in a relationship so she really had nothing to lose if the idea was proposed.

What if Sully didn't propose the idea? Maybe she'd been misreading the signals those heated masculine looks had thrown her way? Maybe her instincts were just fantasy?

No, her instincts were spot on with that butt plug he'd sent to her.

She'd been doing a lot of fantasizing since her grandfather and grandmother had died. As long as both of them had been alive, there had been some sort of unbreakable bond—a rope that had kept her on the straight and narrow. Kept her from fulfilling her wickedly delicious sexual fantasies.

They'd passed away within weeks of each other. She'd grieved their loss for several months and, call it morbid, but after the grieving process had lifted, she'd actually felt liberated. A newfound guilty happiness had replaced the guilt of wanting sex with a man. It had almost seemed with her strict, religious grandparents out of the way, she'd entered a new life and she'd begun dating men.

Begun experimenting with sex on a whole new level. But her sexual and emotional experiences with the local guys had always been lacking. It hadn't taken her too long to figure out she'd been comparing her men to Sully. Sully, her first man. The only man who'd made her orgasm.

"I think I'd like to join you in those carnal thoughts, Jenna."

Her head snapped up to find Sully standing over her, a most gorgeous grin on his face, and he was holding out his hand. "But first let's go for a walk."

"A walk? But it's raining out there."

"I know." He wiggled his fingers and without hesitation, she placed her hand against his firm palm.

Immediately he pulled her from the booth and against him. She couldn't stop the violent shiver of excitement as his hard bulge pressed intimately between her legs. Her thighs clenched with need, a fiery wetness spilled from her vagina and dribbled along her inner thighs. Tonight she'd purposely not worn underwear, eagerly anticipating a repeat performance of that gut-clenching oral session on the bar over a week ago.

"You look really nice in that dress, Jenna. Hot. Sensual."

She tingled at his warm words. Tonight she'd opted to wear a cream-colored lace dress with a halter bodice, which accentuated her breasts, tied at the waist for shaping and a billowy skirt that flowed with her body as she walked.

"Come on, I've got a little surprise for you," he whispered softly. A beautiful smile whipped across his lips and a sharp tug of warmth yanked at her heart.

"What are you up to?"

Suddenly everything about him seemed to intensify. His eyes became greener, his breathing faster.

"There's only one way for you to find out. Are you game?"

For a split second she hesitated. His question whirled around her senses. Instincts told her if she went with Sully Hero now, then there would be no turning back. She'd lose her heart to him all over again.

She thought about saying no. That she wasn't game for whatever he had in mind for her.

"I'm game," she found herself whispering, desperation and curiosity allowing him to lead her down the hallway.

At the back doorway, he pulled a thick green sweater off a hook.

"You're going to want to wear this, it'll get chilly where we're going." She slipped her arms into the sleeves of the sweater. The material felt warm and snug as it wrapped around her. It smelled deliciously of Sully too.

He removed an umbrella from a stand and once they were out the back door, he popped the umbrella over them. It wasn't much protection from the warm spray of the late spring rain slapping her face as he led her down the dark alley. The rain did nothing to cool the heated excitement building inside her as Sully and she walked across the secluded street and into the local park that hugged the ocean beach where they'd first made love.

In the distance, she noticed the white gazebo near the beach edge. It was well-lit, twinkling with pretty, white miniature lights indicating something was going on at this late hour. Maybe a party in the rain?

She drew her attention to Sully.

Silver raindrops glistened on his tanned arms, beaded his sexy five o'clock shadow, and landed on his full lips. Her nipples pulsed at the sight, remembering how wonderful his mouth had felt on her breasts when he'd suckled her in her shop. Her pussy trembled as she remembered the scorching touch of his mouth suckling her clit, licking her pussy lips, his tongue dipping into her vagina.

Suddenly he let go of her hand and turned to her.

She gasped as he dropped the umbrella and the rain came down on her, the unexpected wetness took her breath away. Without warning, his large fingers speared themselves into her tangled hair and he eased her head backward, exposing her lips for him. Hard heat from his body slammed into her as he pulled her against him.

"Jenna," he whispered roughly. His hot breath caressed the cool raindrops on her lips as he brushed his warm mouth ever so slightly against hers.

The erotic touch made her knees weaken and she found herself wrapping her arms around his strong neck. He groaned as her fingers stroked the back of his head and she pulled gently on the wet strands of his short hair.

Oh, yes, she'd missed this. Missed touching him, being close to him, feeling safe and loved in his arms. She missed the sexy, masculine scent of man that was so distinct and unique to him.

"Widen your legs for me, Jenna."

Her head spun against his words as she did what he wanted. Her legs trembled with need, with excitement, and she couldn't help but moan softly as she felt his warm fingers slip up her dress and glide along the insides of her thighs.

He touched her labia, tenderly circled her clit until she was breathing harshly. Then he touched the plug.

"You wore it." There seemed to be surprise lacing his voice.

"Yes," she whispered.

"You understand what wearing the plug means? That you've agreed to be initiated into the Ménage Club? That afterwards you'll be asked to make a commitment to the Club and to me?"

Oh, sweet mercy, he was actually talking the commitment word, even after they had been apart for so long.

She nodded, pushed her lower half closer to his stroking fingers.

"Despite the Club, you're mine, Jenna. No matter who else takes you, understand?"

She understood what he was saying. He would be bringing her to that exclusive club where she would be expected to be intimate with a third.

"But first we need to talk."

Frustration grabbed her as he pulled away. Once again he clutched her hand, his hot palm seared into hers.

"Sully?" What the hell was going on?

"Let's go see the surprise I have for you."

Shit! She thought his touching her, fucking her in the park in the rain would be the surprise.

He settled the umbrella over them again and led her down the path, all the while his masculine scent mingled with the fragrance of rain. The dual scents wrapped around and created tension in her pussy.

Through the silvery rain, she noticed that well-lit gazebo again. As they drew closer, she could hear the buoys clanging out on the water and the ocean waves crashing over the nearby sandy beach.

Was this the surprise? Making love in a gazebo that overlooked the ocean beach where they'd first consummated their relationship?

That certainly would be romantic. Not to mention they were walking in the rain. Both were prerequisites for the hero she was looking for in her napkin ad.

Her heart picked up a mad tempo when they stepped up the wooden stairs, out of the rain, and walked into the windowless structure. She stopped short at the tiny, intimate table for two placed in the middle of the gazebo. The table setting looked absolutely gorgeous splashed with silver cutlery and a bright red tablecloth. In the middle sat a bottle of pink bubbly and beside it a clear crystal vase laden with ruby-red tulips.

She swallowed. Red tulips were her favorite flowers.

"Oh my gosh, what's this?"

"Looks like some couple is getting pretty romantic," Sully whispered as he pressed closer against her backside and snapped the umbrella closed. Rain poured past the openings in dripping sheets and echoed noisily on the roof making her realize they were isolated.

Isolated and in quite an intimate setting, because from here, she could almost visualize the dark patch of grass hugging the beach, mere feet away, where they'd made love for the first time.

It brought back a rush of memories. Of their naked bodies intertwined beneath the summer moonlight. Her cry of pain when he'd first entered her tight vagina, the wickedly delicious sensations that had followed.

She also remembered their fights and it suddenly made her feel very unsure of herself. Maybe she'd made a mistake by coming here? Maybe things couldn't be worked out between them?

"We should get out of here before the couple comes back," she whispered.

She made a move to go but his fingers intertwined with hers, holding her firm. "No need to run. The couple is already here."

Shoot! Why did she know he was going to say that?

"Sully —"

"Shhh, let's just eat and talk."

That's the last thing she wanted to do right now. Part of her wanted to run away, part of her wanted to stay and ask him to do naughty things to her... Heck, her mind was twisting with confusing thoughts. Had he forgotten about the butt plug buried in her ass? Had he forgotten what had happened between them in the past?

He slid out a chair and gestured for her to sit. Suddenly he looked way too serious and fear dashed through her. Now that it was finally happening—that Sully was finally going to talk about them—she was unsure of what she wanted.

Did she want to join the Ménage Club? Did she want another man touching her? Did Sully want that? Would a third person in their relationship actually help to get them together? Could something so controversial as the Ménage Club actually work and keep them together?

With all those questions fluttering around in her head, her brain said "absolutely not". Joining a club was not the answer. On the other hand, her heart and her body were saying something totally the opposite.

Yes, she wanted to learn to trust Sully. Yes, she wanted to try ménages with him. And what better way for her to learn to trust him again than by having a third in their bedroom? Gosh, it sounded so crazy that it just might work!

Then there was that 100% success rate she'd heard about.

"This all seems so…extreme for me," she admitted, feeling a wee bit overwhelmed that Sully Hero was actually talking to *her* about reigniting their relationship.

"Just hear me out, Jenna. If you don't like what I have to propose, you can walk."

She nodded and sat down, the butt plug pushing up her behind ever so slightly, reminding her of what she'd agreed to do just by wearing it and coming here.

Beneath the table, she intertwined her fingers nervously.

"You said we'd talk, so talk."

"Let's eat first." He made a grab for the chilling champagne bottle.

"No, Sully. You talk or I walk." There was no way she was going to fall for this romantic dinner. She needed to hear his proposition. Needed to make herself believe she wasn't dreaming.

"Okay, but first let's have some champagne."

"You're stalling, Sully."

He smiled. God! He looked so damn sexy, with his hair all wet and curly, as if he'd just stepped out of the shower and his hand... She watched his long fingers wrap around the bottle of pink champagne and imagined him touching her, parting her pussy lips, his head lowering between her legs as he'd done back at the bar last week. Jenna stifled a moan and swallowed at the carnal flutter rippling through her lower belly.

He filled both their goblets and handed her one.

"A toast. To pink champagne and romantic red tulips." His eyes were dark and sparkled with lust and something else... Love?

A voice of reason told her to get the hell out of there before she entered a world of ménages. A world she knew nothing about. Instead, she clinked her glass against his then sipped the sweet, cool liquid.

Very nice. She sipped some more. The bubbles burst against her tongue with wonderful explosions and she closed her eyes, enjoying the fruity palate. She could already feel the alcohol warming her blood, making her flush. Champagne always did that to her, even with just a few simple sips.

"Let's see what kind of food we have for our dinner, shall we?"

"Sully..." More stalling!

He lifted the elegant silver lid holding her plate hostage and she couldn't help but gasp in surprise at the luscious-looking, steaming hamburger, fries and a sprig of decorative parsley.

"No way," she found herself laughing.

"What? You expected something else?" He sounded hurt, but amusement played in his eyes.

"Anything but your grandmother's famous burgers and fries." Another favorite of hers. When Jenna and Sully had gone out together, having dinner at Sully's grandparents every Sunday was a fun time. His grandmother always made delicious burgers, fries and salads.

He folded his muscular arms over his wet shirt, illuminating his nipples beneath the wet cloth. Oh boy. The erotic way those muscles played as he moved made a dangerous wave of desire race through her.

Rein it in, Jen. Rein it in.

That's when she realized where his lust-filled eyes had strayed to.

She looked down and realized she hadn't buttoned the sweater. It hung wide open, revealing her own damp clothing hugging the generous curves of her breasts. Her peaked nipples were also outlined, special thanks to the rain that had whipped against them earlier when he'd lowered the umbrella to kiss and touch her. She hadn't worn a bra tonight, had wanted to make it easier for his hands to touch her, so he was getting a real eyeful.

Her face began to warm at the sight of her large nipples pressing against the cream-colored dress—she could even see the dark outline of her areolas.

She should be over this shy bit with Sully, shouldn't she? She wanted him. He obviously wanted her. So why was she feeling…embarrassed?

"I'm starved," he said. His voice sounded low, husky and seductive as if he were saying he was starving for her, not food. To her disappointment, he picked up his burger and started munching away.

This time it was her turn to watch him. To stare at the scrumptious way his lips wrapped around the burger, the seductive way the tips of his mouth curled upward as he smiled at the taste of it, obviously enjoying the robust flavor.

Her tummy growled.

He laughed.

"Come on, eat. Why are you so tense? I won't do anything you don't want me to do."

Great! How was she supposed to eat after he said something like that?

Her stomach growled again.

Sully lifted an eyebrow. "Are you going to eat? Or do I have to feed you myself?"

Oh wouldn't that go over well, having his long, luscious fingers touching her mouth as he finger-fed her bits of burger and fries. She could literally feel the need to have his fingers in her mouth, the need to suck his fingertips, to lick the taste of him from her lips.

Oh boy.

His eyes twinkled darker with amusement.

She picked up her burger and started eating. Flavor she remembered so well slammed against her taste buds and she couldn't help but moan her gratitude.

"Nice sound," he whispered. "You should do it more often."

"Shut up, Hero, and eat your food."

And that's what they did. They devoured the food Sully's grandmother had prepared for them and, to her surprise, it felt as if she were sinking right back into old times. Chatting with Sully, finding out about his astronaut training, digging around for information on any girls he'd dated in between assignments while he'd been gone. His playful avoidance of her questions about those girls seemed, oddly enough...reassuring and relaxing, maybe even enjoyable—that he'd taken her feelings into consideration and not talked about them. It allowed the same familiar roar of sexual tension to hum all around them that had been there years ago during their time together.

As he related his experience with NASA, she noticed he was suddenly frowning.

"And then NASA asked us if we might be interested in a top secret assignment. My cousins were totally gung ho about it. I wasn't."

"I find that hard to believe. I know you were thinking of joining the team when we first met. Your desire to go out into space. Why'd you change your mind? Why did you come back here?" That last sentence slipped out even before she realized she'd been thinking it.

Sully sighed heavily. It was a ragged, uneven breath of intense frustration. The sound squeezed her heart and made her burst with pain for him. Obviously, his space adventures hadn't turned out the way he'd thought.

"Have you ever left something behind and then later realized it was the most important thing in your life?"

She'd realized what she'd lost when Sully had left town and because of the pain she now experienced at his sigh, she wasn't sure how to respond so remained silent.

"It's because I left you behind that I realized how important you are to me, Jenna. You've heard about the Ménage Club," he said. It was an unexpected statement, not a question. Surprise almost made her choke on her food at how quickly he'd broached the subject, but she managed to gulp it down before he noticed her reaction.

"Yes, about how it brings estranged couples back together—" she swallowed at her nervousness "—with the help of a third and sometimes a fourth."

She managed to act nonchalant, as if what they were discussing was an everyday occurrence to her. To her satisfaction, she even managed to take another bite of her burger despite the wild pounding of her heart beating against her chest.

"I know what we had together could be classified as a summer fling."

A summer fling? God! Was that all she'd been to him?

"But for me it was more than that."

"For me too," she admitted.

The tips of his mouth turned upward at her words and for the first time she saw hope flash in his eyes.

"And we have this overwhelming sexual attraction that seems to have stayed with us over the years."

"But a relationship can't be based on sexual attraction alone," she voiced, hoping he felt the same way.

"I realize that we've got a lot of work to do, and the way we left it between us… It shouldn't have happened that way. I apologize. I shouldn't have let my anger blind me toward my love for you and it isn't a love based on sex."

"I know. There's something else between us. Even though we fought, we always seemed to get back together…except for that last one. I'm to blame too. Don't you see? It was my upbringing. I was tied too much to my grandparents. They were both very strict with me… You have to understand—" she took a deep breath and continued "—and I kept thinking you were fooling around on me with all those women friends of yours."

"I wasn't. I still have those women friends, though. I won't get rid of them just because of your insecurities. They are friends, and that's all they'll ever be."

The flare of anger reared its ugly head again, but it quickly disappeared at his next words.

"I came back to Hideaway for you, Jenna. I wanted to come back sooner, but I had a contract to fill and I was out of this world…literally." He grinned. "I was halfway across the galaxy when I realized being an astronaut wasn't for me. I realized not having you in my life wasn't for me."

His confession made a wave of warm happiness spill through her but they still had so much to work through.

"There's something you should know…" Since he was being honest, she may as well be too. "Because of what happened, because of the way you left… I can't trust you not to do it again. How do I know that with our first fight or some disagreement down the line, you won't leave me?"

"I was young and immature back then, Jenna. I'm a man now. A man with responsibilities, a business… Maybe I'm not the white picket fence kind of guy like you want, but I know that I want you, Jenna. I want you to learn to trust me again. I want to make you happy and, as crazy as it sounds, I want our relationship to start off on a sound footing. Our past pattern hasn't been very good so I went looking for help from the Ménage Club. Meemee said it would work—"

"Meemee! You based your decision on Meems? She doesn't know anything about the Club or ménages for that matter." Did she?

"She's in it, Jenna. She's one of the instructors."

She blinked as both shock and hurt knifed through her.

Her best friend was a part of the notorious club and she hadn't told her? She should be more upset than this, shouldn't she?

"The Initiation is tonight, Jenna. One night of pleasuring you with a couple of others from the Club. No strings. After that, we can talk again. If you want to walk, then you can walk. But, Jenna, know that I can't go back to the way it was between us. I can't fight with you anymore when you get angry with me. I won't, because I can't hurt you again as I did in the past. It would kill me this time around. So? Are you in?"

He held out his hand to her.

His hand resembled a bond. A bond she never wanted to break with him.

She found herself nodding as she placed her hand into Sully's outstretched one.

"I'm in."

Chapter Five

ഇ

"Meemee! I am going to kill you!" Jenna spat at her best friend. It was a mere few minutes later and Sully had dropped her off at Meemee's place, but not before giving her a searing kiss, which reminded Jenna of exactly why she wanted Sully back in her life.

Now she stood with her friend inside a closed lingerie store down the street from Meemee's apartment. Apparently, the Ménage Club had given her friend a key to this place and instructed her to help Jenna get ready for her Initiation.

"What did I do now?" Meems asked as her hands scrambled between a shimmering blue chemise and some skimpy red outfit.

"You never told me you belonged to the Club," Jenna hissed as she stood beside Meemee wearing nothing but her thong and a warm terrycloth towel Meemee had given her after instructing her to take off all her damp clothing in the store. She didn't feel the least bit self-conscious or embarrassed at having Meemee seeing her partially nude or totally naked for that matter. They'd seen each other in their birthday suits off and on ever since they'd decided to be best friends in kindergarten.

"So? You never told me Sully was so well-hung either," she giggled.

"Meemee, please be serious. Why didn't you ever tell me? Why the big secret? We're supposed to be best friends. We're supposed to share everything."

Meemee turned from the rack of sexy clothing and winked at her. "Even best friends have secrets, sweetie. Now how about this outfit? It's a hot red, baby doll satin and lace with open bust and strapless, and it's cute with these frilly ribbons and it's crotchless... Your face isn't giving me the 'okay, this is a great outfit' signal... What's the matter? Have you changed your mind about the Club?"

Sweet heavens! No! She'd never been so excited in her life! Just thinking about actually having sex with Sully along with others participating — not to mention the Club's unbeatable success rate of getting troubled couples back together and staying together — how could she even think about changing her mind?

"It's not sexy enough. Besides I don't think I look so great in red."

"Hmm, okay, give me an idea of what you're looking for," Meemee said as she chewed her lower lip thoughtfully.

"I want something daring," Jenna admitted, her heart was thumping a mile a minute at what she envisioned herself wearing. "Something that Sully won't expect. Something that will blow Sully's mind...and get him so horny he wants to take me right there and then. Something that will complement my figure."

"Newsflash, Jen. He wants you no matter what you look like." She threw the red outfit back onto the rack and turned to Jenna, a scolding tone to her voice. "Woman! He is in love with you! L-o-v-e! Or haven't you figured that out yet? Why the hell do you think he came back to Hideaway? Why would he join the Club? Why would he agree to this Initiation? He's not willing to go the regular route of trying to get back together with you because it's failed in the past. During your relationship, you broke up so many times it had my head spinning. I can only imagine how he felt or you, for that matter. Am I not right? You two kept getting back together and just kept on fighting and breaking apart again."

"Yes, but—" She wanted to tell Meems Sully had already told her all this and that she eagerly looked forward to what was going to happen tonight, but her friend seemed to be on a roll, and when she wanted to get her point across, she wouldn't stop talking until she had her say.

"He knows you both have problems that don't have an easy fix. Sure, maybe relationship counseling might help your jealousy issue about him being so hunky gorgeous. And it might help your problem that you don't feel as if you deserve such a good-looking guy, even if you aren't svelte and drop-dead gorgeous like those thin, anorexic models in those lousy glam-glam magazines. But, Jenna, our way at the Club proves that everyone is equal. Fat, skinny, short or tall, we all want to be loved, and to have sex and be pleasured without feeling guilty about our sexuality or whatever the hell problem some couple is working on. The way they do it at the Club is a hell of a lot quicker in helping to repair a relationship than traditional counseling. And it's a heck of a lot more fun. Ménages, when used right, are the ultimate trust factor in a relationship. Are you getting my meaning?"

"Think sexy, Meems. Sexy, hot, something flattering. What do you wear to the Ménage Club when you want to grab a man's attention?"

Jenna hid a smile as Meemee emitted a frustrated curse. "Haven't you been listening to me? He doesn't care what you look like—"

"Every word, Meems. Now move aside so I can see what else is on this rack."

* * * * *

Sully's heart was pounding a mile a minute as he stepped out of the shower adjoining the lavish bedroom they'd be using at the Ménage Club, which was actually in the basement of Tony's secluded, beachfront, three-story home a few miles outside Hideaway, Maine.

"You're looking more nervous than a virgin bridegroom on his wedding night," Tony chuckled from the doorway.

"In a way I am, aren't I?" Sully said as he grabbed a towel and began to dry himself off, being extra careful around his rock-hard cock. "It's been years since I've made love to her. I've almost defied the Club rules several times and shown her how much I want her back."

"But you didn't defy us and now, tonight, you will show her what she'll have in store for the rest of her life…if she so chooses to accept the rules of the Club."

"It's been killing me not to be intimate with her, Tony. I mean intimate the old-fashioned way…one-on-one."

Tony's expression softened. "All in good time, Sully. All in good time. I know it's been hard staying away from Jenna. When a man is in love with a woman, he wants to express it by making love to her, but that would have repeated your old pattern."

Tony was right. Sully knew it, but it didn't mean he could easily turn off the way he was raised. His mother had always told him that love between a man and a woman would solve all problems. Too bad she'd been wrong in this case.

Sometimes outside help, no matter how extreme, was needed to repair a relationship and regain the trust of the woman he loved.

"Here's a little something to keep you going for Jenna. It's state of the art. New on the market," Tony said as he placed something on the bathroom counter.

Sully's eyes widened and his cock immediately pulsed as he recognized the item he'd seen advertised on the Net and had been meaning to get. He blew out a breath as he examined the supple leather item and the bronze ring. He knew full well he'd need the help of this device because without it, he was so hot and horny, he just might explode before Jenna was ready for him.

"Thanks, Tony. I appreciate it."

"Hey, what else are best friends for?"

* * * * *

"Shit, Meems. I'm getting nervous," Jenna admitted as Meemee ushered her down the elaborate marble staircase that led to Tony's basement. She'd never been to his beach house, or maybe castle was a better word for it. She'd never realized such an extravagant house actually existed so close to the pretty little tourist town of Hideaway. Tony had built both it and the Club a couple of years ago when he'd come back from one of his astronaut missions. She'd been invited for the housewarming but had to decline because she'd been busy getting her antiques shop in working order.

And now, here she was...under totally different circumstances. Totally erotic circumstances.

Shit! She couldn't believe this was actually happening. She was actually going through with this Initiation.

Sweet mercy! Had she flipped her lid? Was she so desperate she'd try anything to be with Sully? Or was she finally loosening up and letting her true sensual nature shine through?

"Girl, I'd be nervous too."

At her friend's words her nervousness only increased. "Gee, thanks for helping."

"C'mon, Jen, I'm joking. There's no need to be anxious. You'll be fine, and remember Sully will be with you every step of the way."

Strangely enough, having her say that, actually calmed her a bit.

"Thanks, Meems."

"Hey! What else are best friends for?"

Suddenly Jenna realized she'd been focused so much on herself tonight she hadn't even realized when Sully had dropped her off at Meemee's she'd been dressed in a flirty, one-shouldered minidress with a keyhole bodice and buckle trim. The midnight blue dress contrasted so beautifully with her long, straight blonde hair that the familiar tinge of wanting to have the same perfect body as Meemee's crept into her mind.

Jenna shoved it aside. No use wanting to be someone else. She needed to stay comfortable in her own skin. That's where her happiness lay.

That, however, didn't stop the guilt from sweeping in around her. "I ruined your evening, didn't I, Meems?"

Meemee looked surprised and shook her head. "Ruined my evening? What makes you say that?"

"You're dressed to kill and now you're bringing me over here, so I'm making you late for your date."

"I always dress this way when I come to the Club."

Dressing for Tony perhaps? Tony was an idiot if he hadn't noticed Meems by now, and joining a club just so she could be with Tony was kind of stupid, wasn't it?

Jenna stifled a laugh at that thought. She was doing the same thing just to be with Sully so who was she to cast stones?

"Which reminds me, best friends aren't supposed to have secrets. Why didn't you tell me you joined the Club?" Focusing on her friend might take her mind off what would be happening soon. Unfortunately, Meemee wasn't in the mood for talking about herself.

"This is the bedroom you'll be using," she whispered as she grabbed Jenna by the hand and giggled as she pushed the oak door open to present the awesome sight.

"Oh!" was all Jenna could say as she surveyed the bedroom suite decorated in misty blue and gold highlights. In the middle of the room was a wrought iron canopy bed where a fluffy blue and white square comforter was folded back to reveal midnight-blue satiny sheets and matching pillows.

The walls were virgin white with gorgeous, tastefully framed pictures of nude sex scenes, most of them shots of group sex that made Jenna's pulse race with both excitement and a tinge of anxiety. Perfectly normal under these conditions. Especially when she was going into a world she didn't know too much about except for what she'd researched on the Net and that was totally different than what she would be experiencing tonight.

She was glad she wore the sparkling, white leather chemise with lace trimming at the half-cups and hem. It made her fit right into this gorgeous, sexy scene. The instant Jenna had spied the outfit, she'd known it was what she'd wanted. It hugged her plus-size figure to perfection, the underwire cups cradled her large breasts, allowing ample cleavage, and the material dropped over her rounded belly, hiding it nicely.

The clothing gave her a sexy, flirty, feminine kind of feeling and that's what she wanted for Sully. It also had a provocative slit that went right up her sides, giving a great view of her bare legs and hips, allowing the men to realize she wore no underwear, making herself easily accessible.

She'd removed the plug as per Meemee's instructions and her ass now throbbed and ached to be filled again.

Jenna found herself swallowing against a flutter of nerves as the lights suddenly dimmed and soft, romantic music floated through the room. Behind her, the door softly clicked shut.

She turned around and found Meemee gone.

Shit! Some best friend! Deserting her in her hour of need. She made a move to follow Meemee when nearby another door she hadn't noticed opened.

Jenna did a double take as Sully strolled into the room. He wore a two-tone charmeuse robe, dark forest green accented with emerald green. The coloring of his robe enhanced the green hunger in his eyes as he saw her standing there.

"Jenna, I'm glad you could make it," he whispered as he came toward her. His hair was damp, curling wildly, and made him look so damn sexy that for a split second she thought she just might be having an erotic dream about him.

His eyes shone brightly with desire, hunger splashed across his handsome face. The sexy way his nostrils flared as he caught the scent of his favorite perfume she'd dabbed behind her ears had her own breath backing up in her lungs and her physically backing up as well. She hadn't even realized she'd been so overwhelmed by the erotic sensations spiraling through her that she'd backed into the door, the coolness of the oak smacking against her bottom.

"I've waited a long time for us, Jenna. A long time to finally be with you."

"Me too," she found herself whispering, reacting to his touch as his hands came to settle at her elbows.

His fingers slid with featherlike strokes along the sides of her arms and awareness coursed through her.

"Are you sure you want this?" he asked. She could see the need to be with her so clearly now as he looked into her eyes.

She nodded, suddenly unable to speak, mesmerized by the tingling sensations sifting up along her arms as he continued to stroke her flesh.

"You look absolutely beautiful in that outfit." His words warmed her, his soft touches set her on fire.

"Thank you." She'd never been much for compliments, but his always made her feel so nice.

"They've given us a little time together. Time to get to know one another a little more intimately."

His hand dropped down to brush her wrist. Erotic sensations spiraled through her at the intimate caress. Lacing her fingers with his, he led her to the bed.

He kneeled on the mattress and climbed on. She followed suit, finding the mattress soft and welcoming beneath her hands and feet.

"Come closer. Onto your knees. In front of me," he said softly. She couldn't believe she was actually shivering with so much anticipation as she did what he asked. Nothing had even happened yet and there she was trembling like a freaking virgin on her wedding night. In a way she was, wasn't she? She hadn't made love with Sully in years.

She inhaled sharply as he lifted his hands and speared his fingers through her hair. His touch was gentle, loving, and the sensations running through her scalp felt so…erotic.

"I've missed you so much, Jenna. Missed touching you. Loving you. Being with you."

"Me too," she whispered enjoying the sensual way he played with her hair.

"Touch me, Jenna."

Her fingers sifted through silk as she touched his scalp. He gave a primal growl. The sound made her heart pound with maddening speed.

"Do you see how your touch affects me, Jenna? You've always made me feel like no other woman has ever has."

At the mention of another woman she couldn't help but tense, the familiar pang of raw anger sifted to the surface. He noticed her reaction but said nothing. Instead, his fingers touched her scalp, massaging in soft, sensual circles that had her momentary anger melting away.

Suddenly she felt as if she were a nervous new mare in a stallion's harem. The stallion brushing against her, testing her willingness to mate, smelling her, wanting her, but also sensing he needed to go slow so as not to frighten her off.

"You will always be the only woman for me, Jenna. Even when I'm with others at the Ménage Club, you will be number one."

God! Why was he doing this to her? Why was he talking about other women when he knew it upset her so badly? Again that familiar raw anger she'd never cared for but couldn't seem to stop seeped through her. She felt an instantaneous need to bolt or, better yet, slap him for even thinking about other women when he was there with her.

"Shh, Jenna. Easy. Remember why we are here. This is how it will be if you join the Club, sweetie."

His masculine fingers were still stroking, trying to soothe her as he massaged her scalp in erotic little circles. Tender touches that sent delicious little tingles down the back of her neck and into her shoulders. Shoulders she hadn't even realized were tense.

"The Ménage Club deals with exposure therapy, Jenna. Exposing us to something that bothers us. Exposing ourselves over and over again until all our insecurities are gone and we are both immune to the thing we feared the most. Do you understand?"

She nodded, but damned if she wasn't still pissed off at him.

And getting just a wee bit turned on at the sensual way his fingers were now brushing the sides of her face and tracing her lips.

"Did you know that our mouths are one of the more sensitive parts of our body? Kissing someone combines three of our senses. Taste, touch and smell."

Jenna swallowed as he leaned closer. His green eyes were sexually charged, his lips parted slightly.

"You smell so good, Jenna. Sweet and sexy like my woman should smell."

Her heart thumped out of control as with the tenderest of touches he held her bottom lip while he kissed the sensitive inner curve between her neck and shoulder. The featherlight touch assaulted her senses.

"You're soft as velvet and you taste like candy — very addictive candy."

"Keep those compliments coming," she found herself murmuring as the familiar slow burn unraveled between her legs. She arched closer to him, allowing him to plant tiny erotic kisses along her collarbone until she was whimpering beneath the electrical sensations flaming through her.

This was one of the reasons she'd never been able to stay with a man for too long in relationships after Sully. None of them ever made her feel as he did. None of them could make the hot need for sex race through her veins like Sully could.

"Keep touching me," he whispered. "This Initiation is for both of us."

She blinked, suddenly realizing her hands were still tangled in his soft curls.

God! She'd been so selfish! Taking from him and not giving anything back.

Following his lead, she began her own technique of soft, little massages against his scalp that had his breath quickening just like hers.

She smiled at how easily he responded to her touch. How easily he radiated love when he looked at her. How easily he made her body ache for him.

Angling his head between her shoulder and neck she watched as he ran a pink tongue along the top of her shoulder, caressing her skin and leaving behind a trail of wet fire.

Jesus! That felt good!

He eased away from her. She found herself leaning toward him. Tasting his broad chest, kissing one of his puckered brown nipples. His breath caught and she shyly drew the tight bud into her mouth, gently laving it with her tongue, exploring the tiny ridges until the nub felt hard and hot inside her mouth.

"Jesus, Jenna."

His hands were on her shoulders, easing her sexy garment down her arms and over her waist, his fingers instantly heating everywhere he touched. She enjoyed the tingling sensations of his intimate caresses and could not stop herself from kissing the soft, damp curls on his broad chest and inhaling his intoxicating scent deep into her lungs.

He'd always smelled so manly. Tonight was no exception.

She hadn't even realized her breasts had burst free from her cups until his warm hands palmed them. Looking down, she found his thumbs rasping her nipples. Her thighs tightened in response. Her pussy clenched in wicked anticipation. She felt so hot and wet. So on fire. The incredible sensations made her moan.

"You sound so sexy when you make that noise, Jenna. I want to bring more of those sensual sounds out of you tonight. Every night."

His hands roamed over her breasts, exploring her generous curves, his thumbs moving rhythmically while his mouth locked over hers in carnal, possessive movements pushing more cries from her. He slid his tongue into her mouth, caressing her gums, avoiding her own eager tongue.

The avoidance only made her want him more.

Splaying her hands against his chest, she loved the way his damp, hot muscles moved beneath her fingertips. She slid her hands onto his hard, muscular shoulders and eased his robe off, allowing it to puddle around them on the bed.

He returned the favor and slid her chemise off her. She wiggled her legs and feet until it slipped onto the mattress.

"I'm going to make love to you like I've never done before, Jenna," he breathed against her lips. Then he was easing her down near the foot of the bed and close to the side edge. It was an oddly curious position and, before she could ask why she was being placed in this way, his succulent mouth fused with hers once again, the heat of his upper body washing intimately against her. His hands released her breasts and smoothed over her rounded belly curling into her belly ring. He pulled gently, just enough to bring an erotic chord of sensation shimmering through her tummy.

"I'm going to brand you tonight. Make you mine. Mark you for the Club," he said. As he moved closer, he sucked a nipple into his mouth. He wasn't gentle as he'd been in her antiques store. Instead, he was eager and harsh, his tongue moving in seductive swirls against her hardening bud.

"Oh, God!" She just about came off the bed as his sharp teeth suddenly nipped at her tender flesh and his fingers tweaked and plumped her other nipple.

He kissed the aching tip then sucked it into his mouth again. His tongue laved it, washing away the pleasure-pain. He did the same to her other nipple, nipping and laving, leaving her hot and bothered, pleasure washing through her. He lowered his lethal lips over her belly, making her clench her tummy muscles as he headed for parts south.

Her hips arched to him as he spread her legs and climbed in between them. His eyes were so dark and fierce she could barely breathe.

She'd expected him to go down on her, to dip his head between her legs and suckle her clit and pussy, but to her disappointment he didn't. Instead, she noticed something in his hand.

A vibrator! And straps dangled off it.

She swallowed as her mind exploded with delicious scenarios along with a touch of fear.

The vibrator was huge. Just as big, if not bigger than his cock.

"Just so you know, the vibrator is self-lubricating so I can use it in your sweet ass later."

Oh boy.

"Your pussy is so beautiful, Jenna," he whispered as he positioned himself between her widespread legs. "Flushed red like a tulip with luscious, silky petals waiting to be opened."

Wicked sensations tore through her as he touched her. His possessive fingers parted her labia, the warm head of the vibrator slid into her wet vagina. She fought for breath as the item filled her, stretched her, sank deep inside her. Closing her eyes, she moaned softly as the clitoris stimulator pressed snugly onto her aching flesh. A moment later soft straps went around her thighs holding the sex toy in place.

Instantly the toy began an erotic pulse, making her vagina clench and cream with heat. He was now sliding his hand up her right arm, his gaze holding her, mesmerizing her. His fingers tingled against her flesh. Curled around her wrist, bringing her arm above her head.

He kissed her on the nose, his eyes twinkling with arousal as he brought her other arm up over her head pinning both her wrists beneath one hand. Holding her there. Holding her captive.

Reaching above her head, he seemed to search for something beneath the covers.

"Sully?" She wanted to know what he had there, the curiosity burning her alive.

"Shh, don't talk. Just feel, Jenna. Let your mind soar. Let your body respond."

Something soft snapped around her wrist and then the other. She heard the clink of chain, knew instinctively he'd bound her.

Light bondage, just as she'd asked for in her "A Hero Needed" ad.

"I love you, Jenna. Now I'm going to show you just how much."

Tears sprung to her eyes and joy shot through her heart. Sweet Jesus, she'd waited so long to hear him say those three words again. She wanted to tell him she loved him too when she felt the mattress near the top of her head move.

Someone had joined them!

She angled her head up and found Tony looking down at her. His straight white teeth flashed against his tanned face in a wide smile of approval. Lust gleamed in his dark brown eyes. She could swear her flesh tingled as his searing gaze raked along her naked length, taking in her plus-sized curves, her belly button ring and to the vibrator inside her pussy. "You did well, Sully. How are you feeling, Jenna?"

Aroused? Excited? Confused at being so eager to see Tony there with her?

All of the above?

"At a loss for words?" Tony chuckled. "Just relax, Jenna."

Relax! My God! Her breath was coming faster as she caught sight of his bare chest, naked abdomen and...

Tony's calloused palms shocked her flesh as they slid over her collarbone then slipped over her swollen breasts. His masculine fingers knew exactly where to touch her, how to squeeze her nipples in such a beautiful way that pleasure and pain mixed perfectly.

She found herself looking down and saw Sully's eyes sparkle magnificently as he watched Tony touch her. Her breasts tingled beneath Tony's sensual massage and a line of arousal zipped from her nipples right down to her sex toy-filled pussy. In response, her quivering, wet vaginal muscles clenched tightly around the vibrator nestled deep inside her.

"Go ahead, Sully," Tony whispered.

Sully's Adam's apple bobbed up and down as he swallowed. He kept his eyes on her as his own breaths came through his open mouth in short, raspy gasps. In an erotic slowness that had her mesmerized, she watched Sully get off the mattress. He stood at the foot of the bed in front of her and unsnapped the side snaps. His thong loosened and fell away, making her eyes widen at the spectacular sight.

Sully's cock was already well-engorged and stiff with arousal. His mushroom-shaped head was fully released from its sheath, flushed purple with a dot of pre-come at the slit. But that's not what captured her immediate attention, though. What really gripped her and her soaked pussy was the fact Sully's cock was nestled in full bondage gear.

* * * * *

He'd never seen anything more erotic in his life. The woman he wanted with every breath of his being was splayed out in front of him, his best friend's hands roaming over her breasts like a seductive lover's, ripples of muscles clenched in her belly and a vibrator was tucked snugly inside her vagina keeping her on edge while he prepared for the next phase of their Initiation. The way her mouth was slightly parted as she panted harshly through her arousal had his cock pulsing against the restraints of the cock cage Tony had given him.

The leather cock strap was worn behind his balls with a divider strap that separated his scrotum enhancing his two perfectly shaped swollen spheres. The harness and divider were made of soft, supple black leather with a chrome cock ring that he'd slipped over his shaft before coming into the room. The ring held his erection tightly and prevented him from coming right on the spot. The cock cage as well as the cock ring also had a new state-of-the-art feature. Both would expand and grow with his cock if it became necessary, the erotic grip was rumored to allow him to keep a hard-on for as long as he needed without spewing or injury to his cock.

It was a great invention, allowing him peace of mind. He needed the time because he wanted to make love to Jenna until she was screaming and begging to join him in the Ménage Club and pleading to give their relationship another try with the help of a third.

As he heard a nearby door whisper open behind him, he couldn't stop himself from tensing. The next few minutes would be the most important part of tonight's Initiation. If they were to continue their relationship, now was the time for Jenna to face her worst fear.

Would she bolt? Or would she accept what was about to happen to him?

Jenna was thoroughly enjoying the sultry sensations of Tony's hands smoothing over her breasts, the slow, erotic tremors of the vibrator buried deep in her cunt and the gentle yet erotic pulse of the clit stimulator massaging her clitoris. Everything kept her aroused, sexually tense and on the edge.

The thing that turned her on the most, however, was the way Sully looked at her with a combination of such love and lust it made happiness hug her heart.

And then she detected movement behind him.

Noticed a pair of feminine arms clad in black fishnet curl over his shoulders, reaching for his nipples.

A tingle of uneasiness zapped through her as one of her worst fears was suddenly staring her right in the face.

Another woman had her hands on her man! And Sully appeared to be enjoying it!

She tried to calm the frantic beating of her heart as she watched. Whoever stood behind Sully, whoever was touching him so sensuously, tweaking his nipples until they became erect and red and hard, and had him moaning with arousal, wasn't showing herself.

Hurt slashed through her at the thought that someone else besides herself could bring out those sensual moans. But when she looked into his eyes and continued to see the love shining there just for her, despite another woman touching him, she began to feel something else nudge away her anger.

Anticipation.

A craving to join the woman in pleasuring Sully. She found herself trying to get up, to break free of the bonds that held her wrists captive, but the soft binds only dug into her flesh, preventing her from going to him.

In response, Tony's hands simulated what the woman was doing to Sully. Pleasure-pain burst through her as he pinched her nipples. Perspiration dotted her forehead as the vibrator, as if sensing her increase in tension, began a mad pulse, effectively taking her thoughts off Sully and the woman, and back to her own sensations. The increased stimulation made her cry out, made her legs spread wider, her hips arch higher in anticipation. She hoped Sully would see her distress and come to her rescue by plunging his cock into her.

He didn't come.

She could tell he wanted to. Could see him move his wide chest against the woman's exploring hands, watched the woman holding him back.

She'd expected to feel hatred for the mysterious woman. Instead, she felt joy at the pleasure splashing across Sully's face. She expected to feel anger at Tony for not releasing her bonds and allowing her to go to her man, instead, she felt immense pleasure beneath his hands.

God! This Ménage Club sure knew what they were doing!

When the mysterious woman finally showed herself, Jenna exhaled a sign of relief. It was Meemee! And she'd changed from her flirty dress into a seamless, black fishnet, open-crotch body stocking that illuminated all her sexy feminine curves.

Despite her wanting not to feel anger toward her best friend at roving her hands over Sully, now that she knew the identity of the woman, Jenna felt the sharp blade of pain and betrayal slip through her. To her surprise, it wasn't as bad as she'd thought it would be.

She could handle this. She could handle whatever was coming next.

Chapter Six

✍

Sully could feel his need to get to Jenna growing as Meemee's seductive touches slipped downward. When her long, slender fingers gently cupped his rock-hard balls, he heard both himself and Jenna cry out.

He hadn't even realized he'd closed his eyes but, at the sound of her outcry, his eyes snapped open and he sucked in a hell of a sharp breath.

Tony had maneuvered himself between Jenna's legs. He'd removed the straps from the vibrator and was now plunging it slowly in and out of her tight slit.

Jenna's face was contorted in erotic bliss. The sight of her squirming beneath Tony's ministrations, unable to break from her bonds, made his breath come faster. The smell of her arousal made him swear softly.

Never in his life had he ever wanted a woman like he wanted to be with Jenna now.

As if sensing his need, Meemee's fingers wrapped tighter around his balls, holding him in place, preventing him from rushing to Jenna, preventing him from pushing Tony aside and plunging into her, bringing her the relief they both craved.

The look of mixed pleasure and desperation splashed on Sully's face tortured her, burned her with a need so deep she swore it shot straight into her very soul.

Although another woman was stroking his cock, making him swell and grow hard with arousal, he still kept looking at her, the lust and love mingling in his eyes. Lust and love for her!

She could see Sully's hands were clenched. Noticed he wasn't touching Meemee. Why not? Why was he refusing to bring Meemee any arousal?

Jenna watched the sensual way her best friend moved her fishnet-clad breasts against Sully's sinewy arms, the way her eyes were glazed over as she looked at Tony between Jenna's legs as he continued to plunge the vibrator into her.

Despite Sully's inattention, she could see Meemee was highly aroused.

Jenna held her breath as she watched Meemee's fingers grope Sully's rigid, captive cock. His flesh seemed a darker purple with the bondage gear. Even his eyes were a darker green than she'd ever seen before.

She whimpered through a growing sensual haze as Meemee's aroused gaze crashed into hers. They held eye contact for a moment and, within that short span of time, Jenna felt happiness, gratefulness and thankfulness that her friend would actually do something so extreme to help Jenna get over her jealous tenancies, helping Sully and her get back together. She also gave a silent thanks to the Ménage Club for being considerate enough of her fears in not throwing a perfect stranger at her and Sully during their first night there.

Best of all, no negative feelings lingered as she watched her best friend step to Sully's side. Meems brushed her curvy breast like a wanton hussy against Sully's muscular arm.

Meemee kept watching her. Gazing at her as if she were testing her to see if Jenna was angry or not at seeing Meemee with Sully.

When Meemee gave Tony a nod, Jenna felt the mattress move and realized she'd passed the test. At least this time.

She whimpered at the sensitivity in her breasts as Meemee left Sully and both she and Tony came to her sides, each latching their hot mouths onto her nipples.

Oh, God! She'd never felt anything like it. Pleasure coursed through her as their tongues swirled around her buds, their teeth nipped gently and suckled hard, making her just about climax on the spot.

She needed Sully between her legs now.

And she meant now! Wanted Sully whispering endearments into her ear. Thrusting his rigid cock into her. Telling her he loved her.

Through her erotic haze, she saw Sully come toward her.

She groaned at the sight of him.

Powerful. Strong. Magnificently aroused. And he wanted her!

She couldn't stop herself from whimpering. Couldn't stop the flames engulfing her as Sully came over her. His fingers wrapped around her ankles bringing her legs up and spreading them wide allowing her feet to dangle over his shoulders.

She cried out as he removed the soaked vibrator from her pussy. A moment later she felt the lubricated vibrator slip into her ass. It entered easily thanks to the self-lubricating feature Sully had mentioned and the state-of-the-art butt plug she'd worn for most of the last week in preparation for this night. The vibrator filled her anal canal with such heated pressure she couldn't help but blow out a breath. Sully wound the straps around her thighs, again holding the vibrator securely inside her. The item shivered to life, sending tremors of pleasure and pressure shimmering inside her.

Oh, God! That felt unbelievably good!

He didn't need to arouse her any further. It was as if he knew it.

With a wicked grin, his fingers sank into her thighs like heat-seeking missiles and he spread her legs wider, thrusting his large, thick cock into her in one swift plunge.

Magnificent explosions rattled her.

She screamed. Came apart.

As she cried out her release, Sully's immense thrusts became harder and, with Meemee and Tony's mouths sucking her nipples, Jenna could do nothing but rock with the pleasure.

His thrusting increased.

Sensations continued to spiral all around her.

She moaned.

Heard Sully groan.

Heard Tony groan also. Felt his mouth leave her breast. Heard a cry from Meemee as her friend's mouth left her other breast.

The mattress beside her began to move. She could hear Meemee whimper. Heard flesh slapping against flesh and assumed Tony was now fucking her best friend on the bed beside her.

As she came down from her climax, she could barely open her eyes, the sensual haze draped so heavily over her. Yet she was able to watch as Meemee, her fishnet-clad body on all fours, was being fucked by Tony.

God! What an erotic sight!

It only added to her pleasure and she found herself rocking her hips as yet another climax gathered speed.

She trembled as she watched Sully. His eyes were mere slits, heavy with lust. His chest muscles heaved as both the vibrator and he continued to piston his delicious cock into both her openings, stuffing her as she'd never been filled before.

Her vagina tightened again, began to spasm. She couldn't keep the erotic sensations from coming.

And, boy, did they come.

She came again. Her mind shattered. Her body exploded in a carnal bliss that was even more powerful than the last orgasm.

She rode the magnificent waves.

Rode them hard.

From somewhere far away she heard Sully shout and felt his gush of release as he came inside her.

* * * * *

"Wake up, sleepyhead," The soft sound of Sully's voice made her grin. She loved it when he sounded so quiet and gentle. It was a direct contrast to the way he made love to her.

It was a wonderful combination. A combination she absolutely adored.

Stretching her sore limbs, she smiled at Sully Hero as he lay beside her on the bed watching her. There was no sight of Meemee or Tony. They were thankfully alone.

She needed to discuss what had just happened. Needed to tell him she'd enjoyed it immensely. Wondered if he had too.

"Was it as good for you as it was for me?" he asked. Reaching out, he skimmed a calloused finger along the side of her chin. Her skin tingled at his touch and she wanted more from him. Knew instinctively he wanted more too.

"I can't believe I've missed this sort of pleasure all these years," she admitted, reaching out to touch his firm lips. Lips meant for kissing, for suckling, biting.

He grinned and dragged her against him, kissing her mouth, possessing her, making her feel like she was his princess. His mate.

"Me neither," he breathed as he broke the intoxicating kiss.

"The pleasure can be yours for at least another year," Tony's voice drifted through the open bedroom doorway.

He was fully dressed. Wearing an expensive-looking pair of brown slacks and a Polo shirt, he looked quite serious. Meemee stood there also. Fully dressed in a pretty, flowery dress that enhanced all her feminine curves. It made her look really sharp, yet she had the same serious look on her face as Tony.

For a brief moment embarrassment flushed through her. Both Tony and Meemee had kissed her breasts, suckled her nipples. Her friend had watched as Tony had done intimate things to her.

Both had heard her cries of passion as Sully had made love to her.

However the embarrassment quickly dissipated as she told herself they were all perfectly healthy adults looking to help Sully and her get back together using unconventional means.

"As you know, Jenna, Sully came to the Ménage Club to ask us to help make your relationship last forever."

She snapped her gaze back to Sully, who smiled and nodded his head.

"The reason he did it was so he could not only get you back into his life but he also wants to learn how to keep you in his life and how to keep you happy. If you wish, we at the Ménage Club will proceed with both of you over the next year until you both are comfortable with your sex lives as well as the rest of your relationship."

Wow! Getting mind-blowing sex like she'd just experienced with Sully would be awesome. She'd never felt so good. So relaxed. So eager to be with him again.

Unfortunately, the excitement she felt didn't reflect on his face. He wore the same somber expression as Tony and Meemee.

Her tummy rolled. Obviously, what they were offering her was too good to be true.

"What's the catch?"

They all smiled and immediately her tenseness evaporated.

Tony held up some papers. "In my hand I have two contracts. One for you. One for Sully. What I am about to ask of you both will require an impulsive answer. There will be no time to discuss it amongst yourselves. Little time to think.

Little time to react. Only time for a quick decision based on your primal instincts — instincts that will come straight from your hearts and not from your brains. This decision will be in effect for one year. This contract I am about to ask you to sign is what makes the Ménage Club 100% successful with bringing impossible relationships together."

"Gosh, you make it sound so serious," Jenna whispered, suddenly feeling the need to hold Sully's hand. It was as if he were thinking the same thing and intertwined his fingers with hers. She felt his power soar through her and knew instantly she could handle anything as long as she had Sully with her.

"What's the question?" Sully asked. His voice was a low whisper tinged with anxiety and hope.

"First, I will give you all the details. Each of you will be asked to sign a contract I am holding. As I mentioned, it will be in effect for one year. You will be asked to remain quiet about this club. Anything that is said here stays here. If you meet someone you feel may benefit from the Club, you do not automatically tell them about this Club nor do you invite them here. First, you must come to one of us and we will discuss it amongst ourselves and give you an answer. Is that understood?"

Both Jenna and Sully nodded.

"Good. Okay, the contract will be between each of you and the Ménage Club. If you sign these papers, then for one year you will come to the Club every night and experience what you've experienced here tonight. You will be required to pleasure each other with the help of a third and sometimes a fourth. Sometimes it will be me, sometimes it will be Meemee and then when you are both comfortable, others will also help. We at the Ménage Club each have our own specialties. You will experience them all...if you sign the contract. During the year, if either of you or both of you decide not to pursue your relationship, it will mean you have broken your contract as well as your mate's contract. This means dire consequences to both of you. It will be in both your interests to not break the contract once it is signed."

"What's in the contract, Tony?" Sully asked.

"If you and Jenna sign it, you will in effect be agreeing to what I've mentioned. Coming here for a few hours every evening. And I mean every evening. Days and the rest of the nights will belong to the both of you. You will do with that time what you wish. You can see each other or not see each other outside of Club hours. You can fight as much as you wish, but in the end, you must come to the Club and learn to pleasure each other and discuss your relationship and the reasons for your fights with the third and/or fourth assigned to you at that particular time. Statistics have proven that many fights and disagreements between couples have been worked out during their sex sessions. In your case, you will have a third with which to discuss any personal problems."

"Like our very own marriage counselor?" Jenna asked.

"Exactly," Tony agreed. "But before you agree, you must also realize you will face many challenges with a third. Questions will arise. Both of you will wonder if the third is a better lover than you are? Is he or she a better conversationalist? A better problem solver? These are just a few of the questions and insecurities. They are perfectly normal. Bring any problems you encounter immediately to light to your partner and with your third. Do not let it fester. You will be much better off in the long run. Trust will be learned and earned during this year. Pleasure will be learned. Our research has indicated that thrusting a third into your particular relationship will eventually allow you to trust each other. We gave you a taste of it tonight."

Making love to Sully every night didn't sound fatal. She could do that. She loved him. Had loved him for years. Wanted to learn to trust him. Yes, she would welcome counseling from a third in the bedroom and out. The Club had an unheard-of success rate. They couldn't lose.

"Do not answer me right this instant. You will be in separate rooms. Sully, I want you to go into the next room while Jenna makes her decision. Meemee will come with you and you will give her your decision. If you so choose to use the Club's resources you will sign the contract."

"What's in the contract?" she found herself whispering.

"If either of you break the contract by leaving the other," Meemee said, "then, Sully, your bar is forfeited to the Ménage Club and, Jenna, you will forfeit your antiques shop to the Club as well."

Her tummy twisted as Sully frowned. She could feel his doubts intermingle with hers. Could they stay together for one year without breaking it off?

"You cannot discuss it with each other. Do you trust one another enough to sign these contracts? If not, you will not be given a second chance to join. Sully and Meemee, leave the room now."

Before he let go of her hand, Sully squeezed her fingers. Was it a squeeze of reassurance?

Sweet heavens! Could either of them make such a huge decision based on impulse and instincts? It was insane, wasn't it?

She tried to read Sully's expression, but couldn't. His face remained blank, as if he were deep in thought. He stood slowly, grabbed his robe and slipped into it, concealing the gorgeous muscles in his ass from her.

The instant the door closed behind him, Tony asked her the dreaded question.

"What is your answer?"

"Yes," Jenna found herself whispering. Yes, she would risk her heart for another chance with Sully. But would he do the same?

"Sign on the dotted line then. If Sully decides not to join, both contracts are null and void. Is that understood?"

She nodded and the click of a pen quickly followed.

With an oddly steady hand, which surprised her, Jenna signed the contract. For some strange reason, she thought the contract would place a heavy weight on her. It didn't. Actually, it set her free. The Ménage Club would give her the hope and the trust she needed to be with Sully forever.

She had to trust he would want the same thing. She had to trust what he'd said earlier that the reason he had come back home was to be with her.

She found herself giggling as she handed back the paper to Tony.

"Welcome to the Ménage Club, Jenna. We'll work hard with you to keep our success rating."

She nodded as she watched him leave and held her breath as she waited to hear Sully's answer.

* * * * *

"And what is the prize when we make the year?" Sully asked Meemee as he quickly signed the contract. Instincts had told him Jenna would sign too. She loved him and he loved her. They just needed a little bit of time getting back on track.

"Do we get to own Ménage Club?" Sully asked jokingly as he handed the contract back to Meemee.

"Close. You will become part owners of the Club, yes. You will be allowed the privileges of ménages whenever you wish and know you are experiencing it in a safe environment. You may also, if you wish, participate in helping other couples in need such as yourselves, that is, if you don't break the contract."

"We won't break the contract," Jenna said as she entered the room where he'd been sequestered. She'd put that sexy white chemise on again and he couldn't wait to get her out of it.

"With the Ménage Club behind us we're going to make it," she said softly, her gorgeous blue eyes sparkled with happiness.

Yes, they would make it, of that he was sure.

"And on the odd chance you don't make it, we will take your businesses away from you and they will be sold – the money goes to a charity of your choice," Tony replied as he strolled into the room.

"Hmm, that's a noble cause. Maybe we should break up right now?" Sully teased as he reached out to Jenna, pulling her onto his lap.

She smiled warmly and melted against him like a cat. Her sweet scent swarmed all around him, making him hard again, making him want to cuddle her, be intimate with her and talk about their future.

"And give up a year of ménages...with you? No way, Sully Hero. You answered my ad for A Hero Needed and now that I have you I'm never letting you go."

"I do love the sound of that, Jenna MacLean. And I know it won't be easy regaining your trust but, I promise, you'll have a lot of fun practicing trusting me again."

In answer she nipped sharply at his chin and curled her arms around his neck, her eyes smiling mischievously. "Then let's get practicing."

Also by Jan Springer

∞

About the Author

❧

Jan Springer writes on four acres of paradise tucked away in the Haliburton Highlands of Ontario, Canada. Past careers include Accounting, Truck Driving, Farming and Factory work but her passion for writing won out in the end. Now Jan writes full time and is a part-time caretaker. She enjoys kayaking, hiking, photography and gardening. She is a member of the Romance Writers of America and Passionate Ink (RWA Erotic Romance chapter). She loves hearing from her readers.

Jan welcomes comments from readers. You can find her website and email address on her author bio page at www.ellorascave.com.

Tell Us What You Think

We appreciate hearing reader opinions about our books. You can email us at Comments@EllorasCave.com.

Why an electronic book?

We live in the Information Age—an exciting time in the history of human civilization, in which technology rules supreme and continues to progress in leaps and bounds every minute of every day. For a multitude of reasons, more and more avid literary fans are opting to purchase e-books instead of paper books. The question from those not yet initiated into the world of electronic reading is simply: *Why?*

1. *Price.* An electronic title at Ellora's Cave Publishing and Cerridwen Press runs anywhere from 40% to 75% less than the cover price of the exact same title in paperback format. Why? Basic mathematics and cost. It is less expensive to publish an e-book (no paper and printing, no warehousing and shipping) than it is to publish a paperback, so the savings are passed along to the consumer.

2. *Space.* Running out of room in your house for your books? That is one worry you will never have with electronic books. For a low one-time cost, you can purchase a handheld device specifically designed for e-reading. Many e-readers have large, convenient screens for viewing. Better yet, hundreds of titles can be stored within your new library—on a single microchip. There are a variety of e-readers from different manufacturers. You can also read e-books on your PC or laptop computer. (Please note that Ellora's Cave does not endorse any specific brands.

You can check our websites at www.ellorascave.com or www.cerridwenpress.com for information we make available to new consumers.)

3. *Mobility.* Because your new e-library consists of only a microchip within a small, easily transportable e-reader, your entire cache of books can be taken with you wherever you go.

4. ***Personal Viewing Preferences.*** Are the words you are currently reading too small? Too large? Too... ANNOYING? Paperback books cannot be modified according to personal preferences, but e-books can.

5. ***Instant Gratification.*** Is it the middle of the night and all the bookstores near you are closed? Are you tired of waiting days, sometimes weeks, for bookstores to ship the novels you bought? Ellora's Cave Publishing sells instantaneous downloads twenty-four hours a day, seven days a week, every day of the year. Our webstore is never closed. Our e-book delivery system is 100% automated, meaning your order is filled as soon as you pay for it.

Those are a few of the top reasons why electronic books are replacing paperbacks for many avid readers.

As always, Ellora's Cave and Cerridwen Press welcome your questions and comments. We invite you to email us at Comments@ellorascave.com or write to us directly at Ellora's Cave Publishing Inc., 1056 Home Avenue, Akron, OH 44310-3502.

COMING TO A BOOKSTORE NEAR YOU!

ELLORA'S CAVE

Bestselling Authors Tour

UPDATES AVAILABLE AT

WWW.ELLORASCAVE.COM

Discover for yourself why readers can't get enough
of the multiple award-winning publisher
Ellora's Cave.

Whether you prefer e-books or paperbacks,

be sure to visit EC on the web at
www.ellorascave.com

for an erotic reading experience that will leave you
breathless.